Bailey in the Corner

Black Jacket Publishing

Published by Black Jacket Publishing
Farmington, UT

Copyright © 2023 by Lindsay Hiller
Cover art created by Dustin Hansen
Cover art copyright © 2023 by Black Jacket Publishing

All rights reserved. No part of this book may be reproduced or used in any format or in any medium without the prior written permission of the author or publisher. To request permission, contact the author at Lindsay@Hiller.co

First Paperback Edition - December 2023

Paperback ISBN:978-1-962734-00-4
E-book ISBN:978-1-962734-01-1

www.LindsayHiller.com

This is a work of fiction. All names, characters, businesses, places, events and incidents in this book are the product of the author's imagination or are used fictitiously. Any resemblance to actual persons, living or dead, or actual events is purely coincidental.

The best kind of friends are writer friends.
You guys are my favorite.
This book's for you.

Amy:

← YOU..!!!

Your voice matters! Never let anyone tell you otherwise!

Bailey in the Corner

Liz H... (signature)

a novel by
Lindsay Hiller

Black Jacket Publishing

← YOU!!!
Your voice matters!
Never let anyone
tell you otherwise!

Chapter 1

Daisy Ann Rose, my best friend of twenty years, pushed a pair of fifteen-pound dumbbells over her head. She stood in the center of the brightly lit stage, surrounded by cameras and other hopeful auditioners, trying to earn a spot on MaxFit99, our boss's next exercise program and his first ever *live-streamed* show.

In our office I was a nobody, which was why I was filling water bottles offstage. But Daisy had been in three of Jared DiMaggio's prior shows, and he'd personally invited her to audition again—he needed top talent to broadcast live. And now that his company was searching for another on-staff fitness pro, Daisy needed to nail this audition. If she impressed him enough, he'd promote her from the marketing department and give Daisy her own exercise show.

On stage, Jared strolled between the auditioners, cueing their lifts and counting reps, occasionally adjusting their form. My heart pounded; I'd been in love with Jared for years. Daisy stood front and center as she pressed her weights into the air, smile glowing, hair in perfect red ringlets. Her technique was perfect—

—except her elbows.

They dipped too low between each press. Her shoulders were burning out. If Jared noticed, he might not pick her. Daisy needed to fix her form before it was too late. I tried to motion with my own arms, to mimic a proper shoulder press, but she couldn't see me through the bright stage lights. And I couldn't speak without disrupting the entire audition.

Jared moved closer and worry seized my lungs.

But then I found my answer on the sound crew's table in a little cardboard box: a dozen tiny earpieces and a microphone switched to *off*. I slipped one tiny ball of plastic and metal into my hand, and when Daisy paused before her last set, I rolled it onto the stage at her feet. She stared for a long moment, panting from exertion, then slipped it into her ear.

I switched the microphone to *on* as she started her final set, pushing the dumbbells above her shoulders. Time to save her career.

"Daisy?" I said into the mic.

Her eyes snapped to mine.

Jared looked too and I groaned. He had an earpiece as well. But it was too late to back out now. "You're dropping your arms too low between each rep. Keep them above shoulder-level."

After a pause, she nodded and corrected her form for the final ten reps, right as Jared returned to the front of the stage, his eyes still on me. I scooted deeper into the off-stage shadows as he called the audition to a close. When he didn't look again, I blew out every bit of air from my lungs, sagging with relief as Daisy dropped her dumbbells with a crash and a grin. A throng of other auditioners swarmed her before she could even put them back on the rack, squealing and begging to take selfies.

At thirty-five, Daisy was older and more experienced than most of them. Plus, she worked with Jared himself and had an enormous following on Instagram. When she landed a spot on this weightlifting program, then earned her own show, her social status would skyrocket. Considering the marathon-level of effort we'd put into her practice sessions, she deserved it all.

I shoved past the weight racks that reeked of sweat and rubber, then through the crowd, carrying an armful of Daisy's essentials. Best-friend privileges meant skipping to the front of the line. The college girls watched me with envious eyes.

Bailey in the Corner

"You were perfect!" I said, handing her a protein shake. "Drink this first, then the Blue Juice. And here's your phone. Marco called. I said you'd call him back." Marco was Daisy's latest fling, an Italian with a jewelry store. She never kept boyfriends long, but this one had lasted three whole weeks. She was holding out for a gift filled with diamonds.

Before Daisy could thank me, someone tapped my shoulder.

Jared DiMaggio himself peered down at me in all his muscular glory. As a YouTube Super-Trainer, he rarely noticed anyone who couldn't deadlift at least twice their body weight. He motioned for me to follow him away from the noisy crowd into the kitchenette at the edge of the gym. Away from Daisy.

"Hey," I squeaked. In my five years as his office manager, we'd rarely spoken. I'd never stood close enough to watch the sweat drip down his bare chest after a workout or see the streaks of gray in his jet-black hair. But I'd been in love with him since college. Not only was Jared devastatingly handsome, but he'd single-handedly founded one of the widest-reaching fitness companies in the country. His confidence had always drawn me to him, perhaps because he embodied everything I lacked.

"Was that you feeding cues to Daisy during her audition?"

"Yes," I said again. I wasn't very good at talking to people. Also, how did Jared not stink after an hour of lifting weights? In fact, he smelled like pine trees. I leaned in closer. Yup, pine trees. Pine trees from heaven.

"Great idea," he said, nodding slightly. "You improved her technique."

My eyes snapped to Daisy. Her eyes locked on mine. Had she heard him over all the noise in the gym?

She returned to her audience, and I exhaled sharply. She must not have heard. My shoulders relaxed as Jared walked away, and I swung my long hair behind me. I kept it braided, of course, because any hair too limp to hold curls should be kept out of sight. Daisy's thick red hair, on the other hand, curled so tightly it stuck out of its ponytail in perfect ringlets.

LINDSAY HILLER

Her mixed Irish and Hawaiian heritage gave her glowing olive skin and a smile that filled her whole face. Daisy Rose dazzled the world for the both of us.

I didn't mind being the plain one in our duo. After thirty-four years, I'd grown used to my pale skin and crooked smile. And since Daisy didn't care, I didn't either.

What's wrong with your eyes? she had asked the day we met, when I was a mousy fourteen-year-old, all alone at the annual fair. Daisy wore expensive sneakers and a Tommy Hilfiger jacket, but as the new girl in town, she was equally friendless.

I forgot my glasses, I said. *My eyes cross without them.*
Wanna go on this ride with me?
Sure. I'm Bailey.

Daisy choked on her laughter when she discovered I'd never ridden the Gravitron. I peed my pants when the floor dropped out, but she stuck around the rest of the night even though my eyes stayed crossed and my pants took an hour to dry. She stuck around when my mom yelled at me for smelling like urine, her voice so piercing the entire county heard. Daisy stuck around the rest of childhood too. I held my breath every day in high school as the last bell rang and I'd sprint out of AP Calculus, desperate to reach her before she drove off.

But Daisy always waited, her BMW full of jocks, the passenger seat empty. When a boy asked why she saved the front seat for a dork like Bailey Dupree, Daisy punched him in the nose.

Now, my turn had come to support her as she—fingers crossed!—landed the role that would finally launch her public fitness career.

"Are you auditioning tomorrow?" a soft voice asked.

A short, stocky woman stepped beside me. She appeared my age, with dyed black hair she'd tied into a low ponytail. An orange tiger tattoo covered her left shoulder, and a jewel-encrusted dagger stretched down her right thigh. In the gym that morning, she'd lifted heavier dumbbells than half the men.

Bailey in the Corner

"No," I said. "Are you?"

Her face turned red as a beet. "Live-streaming to fifty thousand people would give me a heart attack."

"Me too. I'm Bee."

The girl's blush deepened. Yes, apparently she could turn redder than a beet. "I'm Stella."

Then Daisy arrived, sliding herself between us. She stared at Stella until she took the hint and walked awkwardly away.

"I met her this morning," Daisy said, frowning at Stella's back. "She's new here. Trust me, she's not our type."

Stella had seemed nice, but Daisy was a great judge of character. Me, on the other hand . . . my high school boyfriend had performed spontaneous magic tricks and kept a baby alligator named Snoopy in his backpack. We only lasted six days. After him, Daisy chose our social circle. If she didn't want Stella around, I trusted her.

"How was my audition?" Daisy asked.

"Amazing! You've been in his casts before, so you're an easy pick for this new show, and a solid contender for the permanent position. You're the only one who kept your elbows pinned to your ribs during bicep curls."

She handed me her earpiece. "Only because *you* fed me cues." Her voice was too calm, too quiet, and my mouth dried out. She must have heard what Jared said.

"*You* did the hard work, Daisy." I tried to keep the mood light and cheerful.

She studied me, expressionless.

"Are we still going out tonight?" I asked, trying to assess the damage.

Daisy switched on her smile. "Of course! It's your birthday!"

If she heard my exhale, she didn't let on. "I splurged and bought myself a present. Want to see?" I led her through the heavy, metal door separating the JD Fitness gym from its business office. "I want to pretend to be young for one last night."

LINDSAY HILLER

Daisy leaned against the stale-smelling carpeted wall of my cubicle, sipping from her new MaxFit99 water bottle. Blue Juice was Jared's patented blend of post-workout nutrition. Nobody ever bought it. They bought his line of exercise clothes, though.

I opened my desk drawer and retrieved my gift: a brand-new, delicately folded, all-black dress, still with the tags. My twelve-year-old daughter had picked it out. I passed it carefully to Daisy and held my breath. She set down her juice and lifted it in the air. It hung low off the shoulders, hugged tight around the torso, and fanned out around the knees. It could really twirl. I loved dresses that twirled.

"Fearless Felicity reviewed it on her blog," I explained. "Mia found it on sale, and I couldn't turn it down."

"Fearless Felicity approved of it?" She caressed the edge, eyebrows raised in surprise. "Well done, you'll look gorgeous! Perfect timing that Mia's at her dance thing tonight. No one will suspect you have an almost-teenager. Want to see my dress?"

Daisy disappeared and I did a happy dance. I could count on one hand the times my style satisfied her high standards. Daisy, goddess of fashion, would die before wearing last season's styles. I did wonder about Mia, though. Right this moment she was auditioning for what could turn into the biggest ballroom performance of her life.

Daisy returned ten minutes later, freshly showered and holding a maroon cocktail dress against her body. It gathered between the breasts with a diamond brooch the size of a plum and consisted of so little fabric it couldn't possibly twirl childishly around her knees. It wouldn't even reach them, but it *would* be sexy.

"Wow," I whispered.

Daisy laid her dress across my desk, but her foot caught the leg of my swivel chair. She stumbled sideways and her elbow knocked over her water bottle. The lid popped off, and Blue Juice dumped everywhere. All over her dress.

Daisy gasped and jumped away from the dripping liquid.

Bailey in the Corner

No. No no no no no.

I yanked it away from the juice and assessed the damage. The dark stain covered the entire left side. "I can fix it!"

"In half an hour?" Daisy moaned.

I glanced at the clock, counting down the final minutes before our dinner reservation. We'd miss it if we didn't leave now.

I shoved my birthday dress toward her. "Wear this."

Daisy froze, staring at my offering. "But what about you?"

I assessed my current outfit: black leggings from three seasons ago and a pale green T-shirt with two stains. Not my best look. Daisy, on the other hand, wore shimmering pink leggings from Jared's newest line, and a white sports bra that revealed her perfectly flat belly—Daisy never ate a carb that didn't fit perfectly into her allotted macros.

True, the silky fabric of my birthday dress would hang off my hips like a salsa dancer, but my body paled in comparison to Daisy's hourglass shape. Why ruin a perfect dress with my oversized thighs?

"I don't care what I wear, as long as we're celebrating together." I tossed her the dress and she hugged it to her chest.

"You're the best! Where are we eating?"

"Frenchie's, my favorite."

"Will you add a person to our reservation?" She held my dress up against her body and swished the bottom back and forth. "I invited Marco."

My breath caught. "The diamond guy? To my birthday dinner?"

"He's totally in love with me." She dropped into my desk chair and spun in a circle. "Besides, it's about time you two finally met."

"I'll be the third wheel!"

"Not at all. Trust me, you'll love him."

This wasn't the first time she'd made me the third wheel. Sophomore year of high school, Daisy insisted we be each other's Homecoming dates. High school boys were lame, she'd said. We bought matching green gowns of stiff, beaded satin and spent every minute planning. But then I overheard her dad screaming at her in the parking lot before school. She avoided me for a week after that, and I assumed Homecoming was canceled.

Until she called, the morning of the dance. *Excited for tonight?*
Are we still going?
Of course! I'll pick you up at seven.

She acted as if that horrible morning never happened. When evening arrived, I donned my pale-green formal gown and twirled my hair onto my head. But when Daisy picked me up, she wore a flaming red miniskirt, thigh-high boots and a black leather corset that shined in the glare from my porch light. I looked like a tween compared to her ruby-red lipstick and push-up bra.

Worse, Daisy brought a date.
Isn't he cute? He goes to MSU.

Still, she made her sexy, leather-clad, college-aged date sit in the backseat. Riding shotgun belonged to me.

Now, after twenty years, it still did.

"I don't think I can change our dinner reservation," I said, as she slid my black dress up over her hips, right there in my cubicle. "The restaurant's totally booked."

"It's okay. I know a better one, trust me." Daisy grabbed my phone and pushed a few buttons. "Can I make a reservation for tonight, please? The manager already said he could fit us. Table for two, please."

"Two?" I asked.

Daisy laughed into the phone. "Sorry, reservation for three. Yes, we can pull an extra chair up to the side for her. Perfect. Thanks!"

She pulled off her shimmering pink leggings, smoothed out her dress and looked . . . flawless. She flipped open her phone's camera and checked her makeup until a text came through.

"Marco's waiting outside! Go make yourself presentable, then we'll walk out together."

Bailey in the Corner

I hurried to the locker room but groaned at the stains under my arms. Why did I always sweat so much? And did my shirt have to match the color of that pea-green Homecoming dress? The color of old soup? I longed for Daisy's pink leggings. But they wouldn't flatter my body the way they did hers—safer to stick with what I had. I re-braided my tangled mess of hair. This would have to be enough.

Besides, Daisy wouldn't care how I looked.

I put on my most cheerful birthday face and returned to my desk, but Daisy wasn't there. Her cubicle sat empty too, though it smelled like a recent spray of her favorite lavender perfume, so I sprinted to the lobby and pushed through the double front doors. Frigid, autumn wind pushed against me as an icy fear crept down my spine.

Daisy was there, in the driver's seat of her latest BMW, bright red with the engine running. Right as I waved, she turned her tires and pulled into traffic.

"Daisy, wait!" I yelled, but she picked up speed.

Certainly, she'd made a mistake, she hadn't seen me. But as she drove away, Daisy's eyes held mine long enough to say otherwise.

It sank in slowly, though I should have seen it coming. After her audition, in her moment of glory, Jared had given *me* a compliment, instead of her. Now, the balance of power between us had to be reset. So, she left me behind, wearing my new dress, on my birthday.

The Gravitron floor dropped out underneath me all over again.

The sidewalk swayed.

I grabbed a lamp pole to keep from falling. Daisy had crossed a line that could not be uncrossed. I saw it in their silhouettes as her car disappeared down the street.

Daisy let Marco sit in the passenger seat.

Chapter Two

Dark clouds filled the sky as I clung to the lamp pole—the only thing keeping my world in balance. The cold metal stung my fingers, but I didn't let go. It was solid, strong. It wouldn't drive away without me.

Daisy wouldn't either . . . Yet here I was, on a busy street, completely alone.

She probably assumed I'd lost her the spot on Jared's show. But Jared was *happy* with her performance. He wanted *more* behind-the-scenes help, not less. And considering she'd already been on three of Jared's shows, she was practically guaranteed a spot! If only she'd given me the chance to explain.

"DAISY!" I howled, sprinting down the sidewalk and waving my arms. "Daisy, stop!"

A low-hanging branch from the trees lining the street whipped my cheek, stinging my skin.

I stopped at the corner, panting, as the roar of her engine faded in the distance. I called her cell, but she didn't answer. I tried again, then stared at my phone, willing it to ring.

It didn't.

If she'd just listen, we'd be together right now, celebrating her audition. We could do my birthday another time, I wouldn't care.

Except that I did care. Not about my birthday, but about her punishing me for being helpful.

Bailey in the Corner

Thunder cracked and sleet poured from the sky, scratching at my skin as I ducked for cover under a quaking tree. I'd given her everything she'd ever needed. Even in high school, when she climbed the tree outside my second-story window with a bloody lip from her dad. I hadn't thought twice, I just cleared out half my drawers and let her move in. We'd vowed to never abandon each other, but it hadn't kept her from punishing me. That night, she read every word of my diary. She'd claimed that if I knew about her problems with her dad, she deserved to know my secrets too.

In fact, how many times had I rescued her from a tight spot, only to be punished for witnessing her weaknesses?

A fire inside my chest fought against the water on my skin, an anger building up I couldn't squash down. I'd trusted Daisy with *all* my secrets, even the dark ones. For twenty years, I'd followed her to college, to our first adult jobs, then to JD Fitness five years ago. I trusted her judgment in all our major life choices, especially in our shared love for Jared DiMaggio.

I trusted her.

Today, I *helped* her.

Then she punished me by driving away without me?

A group of women left the JD Fitness building, most in workout gear and sweatshirts. My body froze, rigid. Had they seen Daisy drive away? Seen me run after her, screaming her name? I wanted to vanish like an ant through the cracks in the sidewalk. One look and they would see everything in my face: Daisy left me, I was alone on my birthday. All I needed was a sign saying *LOSER*.

But they walked right past me, not stopping, not saying hi. My presence left zero impression. This was worse than a *loser* sign. After five years working together, they didn't know who I was.

But they knew Daisy.

The sleet turned to October rain and I stared at my dark phone, disgusted at my lingering hope that Daisy would call. The autumn wind blew, stinging the scratch on my cheek, but I wasn't cold. I wasn't warm,

I wasn't anything except uncomfortable in my skin as I second-guessed every decision I'd ever made.

On impulse, I scrolled through my "recent contacts" and dialed the restaurant she'd called from my phone.

"The Silver Salmon," a voice said. "How can I help you?"

I hung up.

The Silver Salmon? I hated that restaurant, how the salty smell of fish lingered in the air while I ate, clung to my skin like syrup that wouldn't wash off. Daisy knew it too. She'd always known it, since I worked there the summer before college. Why would she make a reservation, on my birthday, at my least favorite restaurant?

Because she never planned to take me.

"Bee?"

My jaw tensed as I whirled around. "Stella?" I couldn't hide the tremor in my voice.

"Your face is bleeding. And you're soaked. Are you okay?" She peered at me through the rain, her black hair sticking to her face where it had come free from its ponytail, her frown reaching all the way to her dark eyes.

My phone chimed.

Daisy!

I pushed past Stella, knocking her purse off her shoulder, and hurried back into the stuffy lobby of the JD Fitness building. It was rude, I knew, but I needed to read this in private.

The Latest news from Fearless Felicity!

An email.

But I barely had time to breathe before my phone rang in my hand.

It wasn't Daisy, though, it was Amelia. My Amelia. All the tension in my body released and I put the phone to my ear.

"Mia? How did it go?"

Bailey in the Corner

"Terrible!" my twelve-year-old daughter sobbed, her high voice even squeakier through her tears. "Bruno's hurt, you have to come. He's on his way to the hospital."

I tried to stay calm. "Slow down and tell me what happened."

"Our audition ended," Mia said, her voice shaking, "and Bruno stormed off the stage. He was yelling, and he tripped down the stairs. He broke his leg, Mom. I could see the bone."

"Was he yelling at you?"

"Who else does he yell at? Now we can't go to the final audition on Friday! His mom was freaking out, screaming at everyone in Romanian."

I slung my purse over my shoulder and jogged to my car, relieved that I wasn't at dinner right now after all. Nadia Pichler yelled in English all the time. She only yelled in Romanian when things were really, really bad. "I'm on my way," I said. "I'll be there in an hour."

Nine months ago, Mia had seen an ad for a breast cancer fundraiser, a performing arts banquet that would air live on national TV from New York City. She'd made it her mission to earn a spot on the show. She endured hundreds of hours of private dance lessons—from me and her studio instructors, hundreds of late nights rehearsing. She even endured Bruno and his mother. Now, a week before the final round of auditions, her dream had crumbled.

"Is it okay if we don't hang up?" Mia's voice sounded so small, so defeated.

"Of course."

Forty-five minutes later, I pulled into the St. Louis Performing Arts Center, an enormous theater with a mostly empty parking lot. Mia was sitting on the curb in her blue, feathery waltz dress, her head in her hands, feet bare despite the cold. When I reached her, she buried her face in my shoulder, sobs shaking her petite body.

"I'm so sorry," I whispered, supporting most of her weight. "We'll work this out."

"How? Bruno can't dance and the final audition is on Friday."

Mia peered up at me with the brown eyes she'd inherited from her half-Cuban father. Tears streaked down her cheeks, leaving trails of blue stage makeup, strands of her shoulder-length brown hair sticking to the salt water on her face.

"I don't know yet, but it will." My words sounded too hollow, and we slumped onto the curb as I trailed my fingers across her back.

"Sorry to ruin your birthday dinner with Daisy," Mia finally said, leaning against my shoulder. "You shouldn't have had to drive all the way out here."

"You didn't ruin anything." Daisy had beaten her to it. I rested my cheek on her head. "You're always most important."

She took a slow, heavy breath. "I guess this is the end for me. There's no one at my studio who could replace Bruno."

"No one?"

Mia shook her head, her shoulders sagging. "I really wanted this. I worked so hard."

My shoulders sagged as low as Mia's. Why did this happen to such a good kid? Why couldn't I take away her pain? Instead, I held her tight, held her pieces together, so she wouldn't fall apart.

It didn't work.

She fished a red dance shoe out of her dance bag and wound up as if to throw it.

I yanked it away. "Those are expensive."

"Fine." She grabbed a metal-spiked shoe brush and chucked it across the parking lot. It hit the cement with a crack, the spikes breaking off the wooden handle.

"I hope you won't need that."

"I won't," she grumbled. "Twelve years old and my dancing career's already crashed and burned." She popped a piece of candy into her mouth and glared at the cement as my phone rang. It was the dance studio.

"How's Bruno?" I asked.

Bailey in the Corner

"His shin bone snapped," Mia's instructor said. "He's having surgery tomorrow morning. How's Mia?"

"Disappointed."

"Is she open to trying another partner?" Mia raised her head, listening closely. "Our choreographer claims his nephew's pretty good."

Mia's cheeks turned ghostly white. Bruno's ballroom skills had far surpassed any other boy in the area—otherwise she would have ditched him years ago.

"What do you think?" I asked.

Skepticism dripped from her eyes, but after a long moment, she nodded.

"Let's do it," I said into the phone.

"Great. I'll have him call you in a few."

When I hung up, Mia's face remained guarded. "I'm not getting my hopes up," she said. But her voice already sounded lighter.

"Do you know this kid?"

"No, but the studio hires Mr. Esposito to choreograph the dances for the advanced team. They've won every competition since they found him."

"So, if he says his nephew is good . . . ?"

Tentative hope inched across Mia's face. "He probably is. Anyway, I'm starving."

Back in my car, Mia cranked up the 90's music. I knew she felt better when she rolled down the window and sang Matchbox Twenty at the top of her lungs. We were halfway through the drive-through line when Mr. Esposito finally called—and we realized we didn't have a place to practice. We couldn't use Bruno's basement where Mia usually rehearsed, and the studio classrooms were filled with evening lessons. I only knew of one empty gym.

"Maybe my work would let us use their stage, just for the week."

"Text me the address," he said. "We'll meet you there."

When I hung up, Mia beamed. "Want to know the best part of today?"

"Getting a new dance partner?"

"No. The fear in Bruno's face as he fell backward."

"Mia!"

"It's true," she laughed. "He's such an ass."

"Hey! You owe me a dollar."

She fished through her dance bag and handed me four quarters. "Worth it," she said, but then her smile faded. "What if Mr. Esposito's nephew isn't good enough?"

I squeezed her arm across the center console right as my phone chimed with a text message. It was Daisy.

Hey girl! Can I call you?

I stared at the message, those six words, my skin turning cold. *Now* she wanted to talk? Did she send that text as she ate my birthday dinner without me? Another one came through.

Did you see Fearless Felicity's new article? If not, READ IT!

"Mom?"

I tried to refocus on Mia. "If the nephew doesn't work out? Then you won't make the show, and it will be okay. You've done so much to be proud of."

My phone rang and Daisy's name appeared on the screen.

"Aren't you going to answer?" Mia asked.

An hour ago, I'd been desperate for her to call. Now, I couldn't bring myself to answer. Over the years I'd learned that Daisy always came back after she'd punished me. She needed me, needed my loyalty, needed me to still be here after she cooled off. The punishments always ended with a text declaring I'd been punished enough. We were even. I was forgiven.

Punished enough?

Forgiven?

Who was *she* to decide when I deserved punishment?

I dropped the phone inside my purse, focusing solely on my daughter. No distractions, no personal crises. No dwelling on my own problems.

Bailey in the Corner

"Was that Daisy?" Mia scrutinized my face as she awkwardly changed from her performance dress into leggings and a hot pink tank top.

"I'll call her later. You're more important."

"More important than Daisy?"

"Always." I zipped up my purse to hide my phone. In fact, my excitement for tonight's rehearsal surprised me. Dancing was infinitely more fun than sitting in The Silver Salmon smelling like fish.

Mia's phone beeped and she held it up. Daisy's name popped onto the screen, accompanied by a photo of a purse. "That's her fourth birthday gift idea today," Mia said.

"For me?"

"No, for me."

"Your birthday isn't until next month."

Mia texted Daisy back as the muscles in my neck stiffened. I never liked when Daisy texted her, but I couldn't exactly stop it.

"Here we are." I pulled into the JD Fitness parking lot, where a shiny black car had parked in the spot closest to the door. "That must be them."

Mia bounced with excitement as we bundled up in our jackets and crossed the dark parking lot. They stood by the door, waiting. The nephew's short, dark hair fanned across his forehead, and he had the lean build of a natural athlete. His uncle wore dark slacks and a black button-up and carried a shiny black cane. His jet-black hair matched his nephew's, though he stood a couple feet taller, and he walked with the confidence of someone who knew exactly where he was going.

"You must be Mia," Mr. Esposito said, his voice low and casual. "This is my nephew, Jackson."

Mia pointed up at me. "This is my mom, Bee."

A grin lit up one side of Mr. Esposito's face. "Nice to finally meet you."

"Finally?"

"Daisy and I were at dinner when the studio called. I'm Marco." He stuck out his hand.

I didn't shake it. I couldn't.

Daisy's new boyfriend was also Mia's choreographer? And he abandoned their dinner to help me teach Mia to dance? Did Daisy have any idea how much physical contact this would require?

If not, she'd find out soon.

And when she did, she'd kill me.

Chapter 3

"I thought you sold diamonds," I blurted.

When I still didn't shake Marco's hand, he brushed it through his loose black hair. "I do. Dancing's a side gig."

"Hope you haven't been waiting long," Mia said.

"Not at all. After the studio called, Daisy brought me back here to grab my car, then I went to pick up Jackson. But I'm an idiot and locked my keys in my car in his driveway." He punched his nephew lightly on the arm. "This guy had to climb in the sunroof to open the door."

Mia laughed, but I backed away from them both until I hit the glass door. "You're the choreographer?"

Images flashed through my mind: Marco and I dancing as we taught the kids, Daisy walking in, seeing my hand in his, Marco's arm around my waist. She would freak out. My hands trembled and my purse slipped through my fingers, crashing onto the ground and spilling its contents into a puddle.

"I got it." Marco knelt and smoothly slipped my phone and chapstick back into my purse. His black button-up stayed perfectly tucked into his slacks, and every hair stayed in place. Not one scuff marred his pointy black shoes. Even his cane, with a silver knob on top, shined with fresh polish. Daisy would have looked so classy on his arm, especially in my black dress. I glanced at my stained green shirt and winced.

Marco held out my purse, but I didn't take it. I studied his eyes instead, searching for any hint of the danger so typical in Daisy's favorite men. The worst was her older brother, Dominic.

"Mom?" Mia nudged me.

Her voice snapped me into the present. Mia chewed her nails, Jackson's shoulders tensed, and Marco leaned casually on his cane, watching as the cold rain started sprinkling again. He didn't *look* dangerous, not like Dominic had.

"Thanks for helping us out last minute," I finally said.

"No problem. It's a good excuse to hang out with Jackson." But Jackson glared at his uncle and scooted closer to Mia.

"I'm Bee Dupree," I said.

"Bee Dupree?" Marco laughed, like I was joking. "That's very . . . rhymey."

"It's really Bailey. Bee's a nickname from school."

Marco held the door and I led everyone inside, through the lobby, into the sea of cubicles. All the lights were off except the conference room, so I led the group that direction.

"I've heard about you," Marco said to Mia, "but you're not in any of my classes. Did you really level out of every advanced group?"

"Yeah, last year." I could hear the smile in Mia's voice. "I still take some classes for fun, but my mom and Bruno's mom coach me now, and Mom pays the teachers to give us extra private lessons."

I peeked inside the conference room and found Jared sitting with Lauren Cross, his second-in-command, at the long table covered with papers and taffy wrappers. With her pixie-cut blond hair, Lauren was as tiny as Jared was huge, and they were deep in discussion over the first round of candidates who auditioned for MaxFit99. Marco and Jackson waited in the hall, but Mia followed me through the door.

Lauren's eyes narrowed, as sharp as the points on the collar of her business suit. "Why are you still here?"

Bailey in the Corner

I almost ducked under the table to hide—Daisy always did the talking for me. "We need the gym," I squawked, so loud that Mia cringed. Lauren raised an eyebrow. "Ours is full and my daughter needs to rehearse a dance."

"Go ahead," Jared said, at the same time Lauren said, "No way."

"But we need it!" I begged. I could have said it more professionally. Or respectfully. Or any way less pathetic than begging. That dark space under the table beckoned.

"It's all set up for tomorrow's audition," Lauren said sourly.

I took a deep breath, willing my voice to stay steady. "We won't touch anything, we just need the open floor in the middle."

"No. Too much liability."

Jared put his hands behind his head. "Isn't that why we have insurance?"

"Sure," Lauren said, "but I'm the one who has to deal with the claims. Not you."

"You worry too much." Jared turned to me. "It's fine. You helped Daisy today, I owe you. How long do you need the gym?"

"Till ten or so, for the next four days."

"That should be okay."

After an awkward wave, I nudged Mia out of the room.

"Thanks again," I said to Jared.

"Sure thing, Bree."

I closed the door behind us, too quickly so it slammed.

"Did he call you Bree?" Mia asked.

Marco cocked his head. "He doesn't know your name?"

I groaned without answering and led them through the cubicles, then through the metal warehouse door to the gym on the other side—the same one Daisy had auditioned in hours before.

"Woah," Jackson said, taking it all in. The far half of the warehouse had been converted into an extensive gym, complete with several copies of every lifting and cardio machine ever invented. The closer half held a giant, ground-level stage, decked out with a giant backdrop to make it look like a studio gym. Dumbbells lined the left side, pull-up bars across the right, and the front had no wall at all, just a sea of cameras, stage lights, and chairs for the crew. The only downside was the lingering smell of sweaty bodies. It radiated from the walls.

And to our left stood a kitchenette. Small, but packed with nutrition supplements.

"This is where you work?" Jackson asked, looking around.

"It's pretty awesome," I said. "Do you think the stage is big enough?"

"Plenty," Marco replied, clicking his cane on the wood floor as he felt the stage with his shoe. "It's not too slick, and not too sticky."

When the boys wandered far enough away, Mia leaned toward me. "Why does he have the cane? How can he dance if he's injured?"

"I have no idea," I whispered back.

"Shall we get started?" Marco looked at his watch. "We're running low on time."

We all dropped our bags and Mia fished my ballroom shoes out of her dance bag: beige heels with suede bottoms and a thin ankle strap. She tossed them to me as the guys put on their black Latin shoes.

"Aw, hell," Mia said, glaring at the bottom of her dark blue heels. She chucked one of them back into her bag.

"Watch your language!" I said. "What's wrong?"

She held up her other shoe, displaying the gunk built up on the suede bottom. "I don't have a freaking shoe brush."

"That's what happens when you chuck it across a parking lot," I said.

"I've got one." Jackson sat cross-legged next to Mia and dropped a brand-new brush into her hand. He pulled out another with a worn handle and used the bent metal spikes to scrape the bottom of his shoes clean.

"Thanks," Mia said, cleaning her own shoes and then handing the new brush back.

"Keep it," Jackson said. "Uncle Marco gave it to me, but I like my old one better."

Bailey in the Corner

I flinched at Jackson's dig, but Marco didn't say anything. He turned to Mia instead. "How long have you been dancing?"

"My mom stuck me in all-day lessons in like, first grade."

"All day?"

"After school. I think she's living vicariously through me."

Marco turned to me. "What about you?"

I cringed, unsure how to answer. Daisy had begged me to take a ballroom class with her our freshman year of college. She quit two weeks in, but I was already hooked.

"Daisy convinced me to join the dance team at MSU," I told Marco.

"Daisy dances? She never mentioned it."

"She didn't stick with it."

"Do you still dance? I've never seen you at the studio."

"She stopped dancing after college," Mia said, "when she got pregnant with me. But now she gives me and Bruno private lessons."

Marco kept his eyes trained on Mia. "And your dad? He doesn't dance with you?"

"He's gone. He doesn't want to meet me."

"Oh, I'm sorry," Marco said.

"I'm not. He was a jerk."

"That's enough, Mia," I said, standing up to end their conversation and stop her from spilling even more of my personal life. I tested my shoes on the stage floor. Marco was right: not too slick, not too sticky.

"What about you?" Mia continued, ignoring me. "How did you learn to dance?"

"My mom was an instructor, back in Italy," Marco said. "When she moved to the States, her English wasn't strong enough to keep teaching professionally, but she taught me and my sister, Jackson's mom. We both danced in college."

"Have you always been a dance teacher?"

"His wife left him," Jackson said before Marco could answer. "He took up teaching instead of wallowing in self-pity." Marco opened his mouth to argue, but Jackson shrugged. "That's what my mom said."

"What about you?" Mia asked Jackson. "I've never seen you at the studio."

"My mom taught me a long time ago, but I don't dance much anymore."

Mia gave me a worried look. Why would Marco volunteer his nephew if the kid didn't dance? Did he have any idea what was at stake for Mia?

"Then why start up again now?" I asked.

"My mom made me. She wants me out of her hair."

Mia's eyes doubled in size.

"His parents just split up," Marco explained. "His dad moved to Tennessee and his mom's working two jobs to pay for legal bills. It's been a rough month."

"It's fine," Jackson grumbled. "Neither of them can stand me, anyway."

"That's not true," Marco said. "But it would be easier on your mom if you helped her out more."

"Like you're one to talk," Jackson snapped. "You're always traveling, so you're not here for her either!" He threw his old shoe brush against the wall and the metal spikes snapped off, scraping across the cement floor like Mia's had in the parking lot. "Whatever," he growled, and he stomped away, across the stage.

Marco watched Jackson go, then slid his back down the wall until he reached the ground, rubbing his face with his hands. "Jackson's been acting out since his dad left. My sister needed help."

"It doesn't sound like he wants to dance . . ." Mia said, her voice so timid I could barely hear her.

"Don't let him fool you, Jackson's medaled in eleven competitions. But we only learned about this show an hour ago. Give him time to get used to the idea. Shall the rest of us get started?"

Bailey in the Corner

Marco unscrewed the top of his cane and pulled out a long, cylinder tube nearly the length of the entire shaft. He shook its contents out into his hand: a pocket knife, a needle and black thread, a narrow tin of gum, packets of Gatorade powder, a vial of water, and a few other items I couldn't see.

"Woah," Mia said, as Marco popped the lid off a tiny box and dumped out three pills. "It's like a dude purse."

"Breath mints?" Marco dropped one in each of our hands. "If we're all dancing, we may as well have good breath."

His words sank into me like an anvil and my eyes darted toward the door to the office. Daisy wasn't in the building, of course. But what if she forgot something and swung by? Or came to watch? As Mia's coach, I'd obviously need to dance with the choreographer, but that was only okay *before* I knew he was Daisy's boyfriend. If she saw us, she would be angry. And jealous. She would punish me even more.

What if Mia's audition got caught in the crossfire? Daisy could ruin this for her.

"Do you carry the cane just to hold random stuff?" Mia was asking, eyes full of laughter.

"It's weird," Jackson grumbled, skulking at the back of the stage, fists deep in his pockets.

"No, it's awesome."

I'd have to keep Daisy away from these rehearsals. Far away. And hope Marco didn't talk about them.

He stowed everything back in the cane. "Selling diamonds, I spend time with wealthy guys who use canes. It was weird until I cracked my kneecap and needed my own for a couple of weeks. Turns out, it's impressively useful." Marco tossed his cane straight up so it flipped in the air, then caught it neatly by the handle. He poked the tip into our pile of bags and scooped them all up by the straps, then slid them smoothly into a row along the wall. "I've carried one ever since."

"Does everyone stow stuff inside them?" Mia asked.

"Nope," Marco said, winking at her. "Just me. Now, it's time to dance."

Marco held out his hand to lead me onto the floor. I glanced at the door again.

"Everything okay?" he asked.

No, everything wasn't okay. Daisy wouldn't show up, right? She couldn't. "Everything's great," I lied.

Then I placed my hand inside Marco's outstretched fingers.

Chapter 4

"What kind of dance would you like to perform?" Marco asked Mia as we moved to the center of the wide floor. The stage lights glared down, blinding my eyes as his warm fingers gripped mine like a practiced ballroom dancer's: tense but fluid.

"Bruno always wanted to do smooth dances," Mia said. "Foxtrot, or Viennese Waltz."

Marco's mouth turned down. "But what do you like?"

"Latin."

"Then we do Latin. Do you have a favorite dance?"

Mia grinned. "Samba."

Jackson hurried over. "I suck at Samba. Cha-Cha's better."

"Let's do both, then," Marco said. "And maybe Rhumba as well. What do you think of dancing a medley?"

He'd pointed the question at me, but his fingers distracted me too much to focus. They still held mine even though we weren't dancing. Long scars trailed from his fingers to his wrists. They felt too intimate to touch, but Marco didn't let go.

"Rhumba?" I finally asked. "Isn't that a little sexy? They're only twelve."

"Naw," Marco said. "It's intimate, sure, but doesn't have to be inappropriate. These kids could pull it off. And if their judges know anything about ballroom technique, they'll be blown away." Marco squeezed my fingers.

How could he be so calm? Every nerve in my body stood on edge, but he slid his free hand through his hair so casually.

"We'll start with Cha-Cha, then pick up the pace with Samba, then knock it out of the park with a Rhumba ending. I'll splice the music together once we've nailed down the steps."

Jackson rubbed the back of his neck, but Mia beamed.

"You can choreograph all that in a couple days?" I asked.

"I'll take the best parts of routines I wrote for the formation team, then modify them for a solo dance. I'll just need you to help me figure out the transitions."

"Want me to make costumes?" I asked. "I sewed for my college team, and I made all Mia's competition dresses."

Marco grinned, his first real smile since I'd met him. A dimple appeared in his left cheek.

I dropped his hand.

"Absolutely," he said. "I was going to borrow costumes from the advanced team, but these two are so small they probably wouldn't fit."

"Can we start dancing?" Mia glanced at her watch. "We only have an hour until ten."

I glanced at the closed door one more time, then looked at Jackson, whose fists were still shoved deep in his pockets.

"Are you ready?" I asked him.

"I guess."

Marco took a deep breath, and then a switch flipped. He became a completely different person. Gone was the casual guy with a cane full of secrets.

"We'll start with Cha-Cha," he said, turning on music. "I don't know anyone's skill level yet, so I'll teach one minute of an advanced routine, then we'll speed it up and modify from there."

Jackson chewed his lower lip, but Mia put on her serious face.

Bailey in the Corner

"You two will start in dance position," Marco said to the kids, "and Jackson will spin Mia away until you're separate, side-by-side. You'll both do a basic Cha-Cha step in place, then Mia will do a spot turn, then forward locks to catch up with Jackson. You'll both break into a time step with Guapucha timing, but when the music breaks, you'll *stop*, hold still for two beats, then dip Mia slowly over your right leg."

Marco took my hand to demonstrate the steps. He carried the faint scent of cologne, something expensive, tropical.

After one last glance at the door, I let him lead me through the opening sequence. He led with firm fingers, no pulling or yanking. He knew where he wanted me to be, and so I lengthened my steps to match his. When the music slowed, he dropped his hands to my hips and dipped me backward from the waist, my hip bone locking against his. It was more contact than I'd had with a man in a very, *very* long time.

When he pulled me from the dip, he took an extra second to make sure I landed flat on my feet. My cheeks burned hot, but Marco didn't seem to notice. He dropped my hands and walked to the kids, counting the beat as they attempted the same steps.

I blew out an enormous breath. There was nothing intimate about this dance. Nothing romantic or sexual. We were instructors, and ballroom dancing meant touching each other. Professional, technical, nothing else. I could do this.

"Ready for the next piece?" Marco asked, and I nodded, my confidence growing.

He pulled my body against his and pressed his hand against my shoulder blade. His torso felt solid and his bicep bulged under his shirt where my left hand rested. When he spun me into a backward lockstep, his pressure on my hand was so subtle, so delicate, like he was asking me to follow and I had the option to join him or walk away.

For years, I'd been coaching Mia side-by-side with Bruno's mom. I'd forgotten how much I loved dancing with a real partner—until I swiveled over Marco's foot and he crashed to the floor with a harrowing thump. I froze, holding my breath, bracing myself for him to blow up the way Daisy sometimes did. Instinctively, I stepped to the side, putting myself between Marco and the kids.

Marco brushed off his pants and climbed to his feet. "Come here," he said, voice steady, pulling me back into dance position. "Watch this." He repeated the step again, slowly, pausing at the point where I'd tripped him. "See how I'm stepping back right when you swivel past?"

"Yes."

"Do it again, but lift your foot higher, so you don't knock my foot out from under me."

I repeated the step, and this time I missed him by several inches.

"Perfect. Mia, did you see what your mom did? I don't want you to knock Jackson over when you're auditioning on Friday."

Mia practiced it with Jackson, then Marco moved on to the next section. His outburst never came. Instead, he stayed focused on Mia.

"I like the way you roll through the ball of your foot," Marco told her, his eyes glued to her feet. "It keeps your hips exactly where they need to be."

Mia beamed and doubled her efforts.

"But I need you to move double-time on the step right after."

"Like this?"

"Yes, but faster or Jackson will plow you over."

They rehearsed over and over until Mia's cheeks burned red and Jackson needed water.

The kids took a break while Marco showed me the beginning of the Samba sequence. It had been a long time, and Samba was tricky, but Marco held me with firm hands so I could pick up on his rhythm.

"Excellent," he said. "Does that feel comfortable? It doesn't need to be perfect; we just need to match."

"It's great," I said, relaxing into his hands and letting him mold my movements to match his. Marco wasn't dangerous. He hadn't lost his cool a single time tonight. Nothing could shake him.

Bailey in the Corner

Until the Samba.

After a quick water break, Marco had the kids practice a basic Samba step for five full minutes, insisting their rhythm needed to match before we could move on. He clapped his hands to create the unique beat, the kids moving their feet in time.

It became immediately clear why Jackson preferred Cha-Cha.

"It's good enough," Jackson groaned when Marco told them to try again.

"Your hips don't match," Marco said. "There's no point learning the routine until the two of you can move together. Now try again."

"I'm tired," Jackson said. "Can't we be done for today?"

"We only have three more nights."

"I don't care about the audition. I didn't sign up for this. I suck at Samba."

"You're just out of practice. You'll get it. Try again."

Marco knelt to watch their hips. Jackson took Mia's hands and they danced the basic step again, until Marco stopped them. "You're too stiff."

"I need a break."

"You need to focus."

"Don't tell me what to do." Jackson stormed off the stage into the sea of treadmills, leaving Mia by herself, close to tears.

Marco stomped after him, but I grabbed his arm. "Give him a few minutes to cool down."

He checked his wrist. "It's past ten."

"Trust me on this one."

He moved to the drinking fountain instead. If Marco was the earth, Jackson was an earthquake—the only thing strong enough to crack holes in the ground.

"Hey, Bee?" Marco called. "You have a phone call."

"On your phone?"

"It's Daisy."

I stepped back, my heart rate doubling. "Don't answer. I don't want to talk to her."

Marco's eyes darted to the phone, then back to me. "Sorry, Bee, I already answered. She's waiting on the line right now."

Chapter 5

Marco placed his phone in my hand, mouthing *Sorry.* I stared at it, Daisy's name in big letters across the screen. There she was, inches away, almost a voice in my ear. I knew exactly what she would say. *You've been punished enough, I forgive you.* But who was she to *forgive* me for doing nothing wrong?

Honestly, Daisy suffered so many of her own demons, she probably had no idea she'd hurt me.

I put the phone to my ear. "Hello?"

"Bee!" Daisy's voice rang with relief. "I need your advice, it's an emergency."

So, she wasn't calling to forgive me. The call was about *her*. She expected me to come to her aid? After she ditched me?

I hung up.

Marco cocked his head. Mia did too. Even Jackson emerged from his cloud of anger to listen.

Oh no.

Mia's phone rang from where she'd stuck it inside her sneaker against the wall.

"Don't answer it."

Mia scrunched her nose. "Did you guys get in a fight? At your birthday dinner?"

Marco's eyes snapped to mine. "It's your birthday?"

I sucked in a breath. The more Marco knew, the worse Daisy would look and the more backlash I'd face.

But Mia answered for me. "Yeah. Mom bought a new black dress and everything."

Marco rubbed his chin, piecing things together. "You mean, Daisy's new dress?"

Mia's jaw dropped. "No wonder you hung up on her."

I closed my eyes, willing Mia to stop talking, to stop painting an ugly picture of Daisy. But at the same time, Mia's shock gave me a twinge of validation.

Marco used the tip of his cane to scoop up our bags, then deposited them cleanly into each of our arms. "I don't know about Daisy, but I do know the ice cream place down the street is open late. My treat."

My stomach twisted tighter. What if Daisy caught us out together? But then I heard Mia's voice—a mixture of exhaustion and excitement. She deserved ice cream.

By the time we stepped outside, the rain had stopped, night had fallen, and the kids sprinted ahead. The air smelled like wet dirt and cooled my skin, even through my jacket. We started down the long sidewalk toward the ice cream shop at the end of the road, but every time a car passed, I tensed, bracing for Daisy's arrival. Every time Marco's arm brushed against mine on the narrow walk, I glanced back, expecting Daisy's accusing glare. Every click of his cane down the silent street screamed exactly who I'd spent my evening with. By the time we reached the restaurant, my exhausted nerves wanted to flee, to escape.

"Can I ask you a question?" Marco asked. It was the way his eyes settled softly on mine, not judging, not accusing, only curious. No one ever bothered to be curious about me.

"Sure."

"Why did Daisy invite *me* to dinner on her best friend's birthday? Where were you?"

I said nothing.

Bailey in the Corner

"Did she ditch you? If so, I swear I didn't know."

Again, I searched his face and found nothing but sincerity, and possibly regret. But it didn't change the fact that he was Daisy's boyfriend and would likely tell her everything I said.

"I don't want to talk about it."

"I don't blame you." He peered mischievously from the corner of his eye. "But we held hands dancing for the last two hours, so we're basically best friends. You have to give me something."

Against my better judgment, I laughed. But it didn't last long. How would Daisy feel about our hands touching while we danced, our legs pressing together, faces inches apart?

"There's nothing to tell. Daisy's the best." I took a page from her book and gave him my brightest smile, but Marco only cocked his head as we reached the brightly lit ice cream shop. He put one hand on the door, but held it shut.

"The best? Even though she ditched you on your birthday?"

Sirens blared in my head, so loud I barely registered his words. I couldn't turn him against Daisy. "I hurt her feelings. It was entirely my fault."

"What did you do, kill her cat?"

"Of course not! But it's complicated. She's complicated." I reached over his hand and pulled the door open. "And her boyfriend is the last person I'd discuss it with."

Marco stopped the door with his shiny black shoe, his voice instantly soft. "I'm not her boyfriend, we've only gone on three dates. And why would I keep dating someone who ditches her best friend?"

"Don't say that," I whispered. What would she do if he broke up with her for my sake? What if her punishment somehow spilled over into the evenings? Would it interrupt Mia's dance practices? "You can't make her mad. You can't even mention that you know she ditched me—at least until Mia's done with her audition."

"Until Friday?" Marco laughed, but it fell quickly from his face. "Wait, you're serious?"

I nodded. Could he see the desperation in my eyes?

"With our late-night dance practices, I won't see her anyway. But after we buy ice cream, you have to tell me why."

We followed the kids inside, to an empty restaurant filled with booths. The smells of waffle cones and soft-serve ice cream washed over us as we ordered. Marco made a point to pay for us all, and Jackson made a point not to thank him. We found a booth big enough for four with a table-top juke box, but Jackson stalked toward the far side of the room.

"You're not going to sit by your uncle?" Mia's eyes jumped between us all, but Jackson only scowled.

"It's fine," Marco said. But when she joined Jackson, Marco stabbed at his ice cream with his spoon, scrunching his forehead. "Did I seriously order bubblegum?"

"Here, trade me." I slid him my bowl of caramel and took a bite of his, savoring the sweet flavor as it melted on my tongue. My dad used to love bubblegum ice cream. We ate it every Friday Movie Night until he died. Then Daisy decided it was too juvenile for our grown-up, mature lifestyles. Caramel was the *only* way to go. I'd never eaten bubblegum ice cream since.

Marco dug into his new bowl. "Today is the most time I've spent with Jackson in years. I'm usually traveling for work, so I only see him at holidays."

"You didn't need to travel this week?"

"I was supposed to. I'd scheduled a convention for tomorrow morning, but when the studio called, I sent my business partner instead."

"Was that hard to rearrange?"

"Yeah, but it's worth it if I can help Jackson. I want to show him not all men are jerks."

Marco stared out the window, so I poked at my ice cream. "What do you do at conventions? You own a jewelry store, right?"

Bailey in the Corner

"Close. I'm a diamond supplier. I sell them *to* jewelry stores."

"Do you own a mine somewhere?"

"No." Marco pulled a business card from inside his cane and passed it to me. "I own a lab where we manufacture synthetic diamonds."

"Synthetic?"

Marco's eyes darkened. "I don't like the slave labor in diamond mines. My diamonds are perfect and beautiful. Unfortunately, they're also extremely hard to sell."

I rested my chin on my fist, studying the brown of his eyes and the shape of his lips. He spoke so easily, like he felt no need to censure his words, like he didn't fear the possibility that someone might overhear. How would that feel?

"How come?" I asked.

"People are traditional, they like diamonds pulled out of the ground. Aristocrats like the hunt of chasing down a giant one with fewer imperfections than their neighbor's. It's a status thing."

"You're saying stores won't sell your diamonds because customers don't want fake ones?"

"They're not fake, they're just not mined from the ground. But the days of the wealthy aristocrat are ending. The younger generation doesn't care. They're perfectly happy with a large, sparkling, less-expensive diamond."

"And at conventions, you explain this to jewelry store owners?"

Marco scraped the last of his ice cream from the bottom of his bowl, his spoon scratching against the cardboard. "Exactly. It's my job to convince jewelers there's a market for synthetics. They're coming around, but slowly."

"Seems like a good cause, and one you're passionate about."

"What I'm not passionate about is staying home to manage the lab all week. Administrative work is insanely boring."

I couldn't help but laugh. "I'm an office manager. All I do is administrate."

Marco winced. "Sorry."

"Don't be. I'm not great with people, like you seem to be. Daisy always does the people-ing for me." At least, she used to.

Marco perked up. "I almost forgot!" He unscrewed the top of his cane and dug through the canister until he found a match. He struck it on the table with a grin, then stuck it into my last bite of ice cream like a birthday candle. "Happy birthday, Bee. Make a wish."

Watching Mia, I knew exactly what to wish for, so I closed my eyes and blew out the candle. But when I opened them, Marco had grown serious.

"What happened tonight, between you and Daisy?"

I didn't answer.

"Bee? I'm kind of worried about you."

His words pierced me. I always did the worrying, nobody ever worried about me.

"She's my best friend . . ." But the words fell flat, my heart pounding in my ears, my tongue heavy. Where was Daisy's courage when I needed it? She kept it locked away, only sharing when she needed a wingman on her crazy adventures.

At that moment, Mia caught my eye and waved.

She had an endless well of courage. Maybe I could too. I had found the nerve to hang up on Daisy, after all.

"I'll tell you what happened if you promise not to break up with Daisy until after Mia's audition. I don't want any of Daisy's drama spilling over into her life this week."

I held out my hand so he knew how official this pact would be. Marco stared, then slowly shook it. Satisfied, I leaned toward him and began my story.

"Today is my birthday, so I made reservations for me and Daisy at Frenchie's, my favorite restaurant . . ."

Chapter 6

When I finished, Marco leaned back and folded his arms. "Let me get this straight. Jared complimented *you* for improving Daisy's audition? What did he say to Daisy?"

"Nothing."

"Did she do a bad job?"

"Not at all. She was the best one out there. She'd been prepping like crazy, hoping that Jared would be so impressed he'd give her her own exercise show." I rubbed the match between my hands, black soot staining my fingertips.

"Then she ruined her dress, so you gave her yours?"

"What else could I do? She'd been so stressed about her audition, I wanted her night to be perfect."

"What about *your* night? *Your* birthday?"

"I don't care what I wear."

Marco's eyes dropped briefly to my pea-green shirt, and I squeezed my arms to my sides to cover up the sweat stains. Maybe I cared a little.

"Is that when she called me?"

"I don't know. One minute we were going to Frenchie's, then you guys drove away without me."

"All because Jared gave you a compliment?" Marco's face scrunched in concentration, but his eyes frowned, like he couldn't connect all the pieces. He tapped his fingers against the table, the only sound in our brown vinyl booth.

"I should have handled it better. I should have deflected, pointed his attention to her so he could praise the proper person."

"You think you deserve to be punished for this?"

"She's not punishing me, exactly."

"She's punishing you."

I paused. "Fine. But I humiliated her, so she's humiliating me back, and now we're even. She does this all the time."

Marco's voice dropped so low, so quiet, I had to lean forward to hear him. "Did you go out of your way to embarrass her?"

"No."

"Did you make a conscious effort to outperform her?"

"Of course not."

"Jared said something kind to you, and Daisy felt threatened—as if *you* succeeding meant she must have failed. Like it's impossible for you to both do well at the same time. It's not your fault she felt threatened, Bee. In fact, none of the fault belongs to you."

His words swept through my head like a whirlwind. Part of me knew he was right, but he was also very wrong. Wasn't he? Sure, Daisy's punishments were sometimes harsh, but they were always fair. One humiliation for another. They came from a place of love; she needed me as much as I needed her.

But then why had it felt so freeing to hang up on her?

Was Marco right? Was none of the fault mine? Were my punishments undeserved? The ground shifted beneath me and I didn't know where to land my feet.

"Daisy's always been there for me," I said. "I was always a loser, but she stayed with me every day for twenty years."

Marco stewed over my words for a long, silent moment, then he spoke carefully. "Did she stick around because she cared about you? Or to take advantage of you?"

Bailey in the Corner

I already knew the answer: Daisy was *always* there for me, even beyond childhood. She helped me through my parents' accident, my surprise pregnancy, and years of depression. Daisy's loyalty shined bright through every moment of our history.

But Marco's question refused to fade.

The ground shifted again, but this time it didn't stop. Smoke from Daisy's fires filled my lungs, my stomach, my head. Everything burned, every memory rearranged. I loved her. I'd always loved her. Didn't she feel the same?

"Just breathe," Marco said, placing his steady fingers on my arm. I closed my eyes and focused on the warmth in his fingertips, the only thing in the room not burning. "Keep breathing, nice and slow."

"How do I fix this?"

Marco folded his arms, my skin turning cold where his hand had been. "You can't help Daisy. She has to choose to change, when she's ready. But you can help yourself. Spend time with other friends, focus on your own goals and hobbies, that sort of thing."

Friends? Hobbies? The room spun faster.

Marco must have seen my panic because he put his hand back on my arm. "Do you have family, or other friends?"

"No. Just Daisy." She liked when it was only us.

"Does Daisy?"

I paused. How many framed pictures filled her cubicle? She had dozens of friends, but she kept me separate. "Yes."

"Do you date?"

My throat tightened. "I think I'm invisible."

Marco laughed. "I highly doubt that."

"I'm serious. I've loved Jared DiMaggio for five long years, and today's the first time I've stood closer than five feet away from him."

Marco pulled his hand away. "Celebrities probably have to ignore most women."

"It's not just him." The women in the parking lot had walked right past me. "No one knows who I am. Every day, I feel like I'm standing in a crowded room, screaming at the top of my lungs, but no one can hear me. Seriously, I did that today when I chased Daisy's car down the street." My cheeks burned, so I buried them in my hands.

"Tell me honestly, how often do you talk to people at work? Do you ask them about their lives, and tell them about yours?"

"I'm so bad at making friends," I said. "I always screw up."

Ever since my failed social attempts in high school, I'd stuck by Daisy's side like a puppy. She made friends for both of us. But without Daisy . . . What would happen at work tomorrow? I really *would* be invisible.

"You're doing fine right now."

I paused. I hadn't said anything stupid tonight. Yet.

"Start with something small," he said. "Tomorrow, at work, I want you to talk to one new person."

"One person?" Daisy wouldn't like that.

"Strike up one conversation. Ask them about their life, learn things you can bring up again later. And talk about yourself."

I leaned away. "Myself? This sounds difficult."

"You're just out of practice." The corner of Marco's mouth turned up. "But maybe start with someone less... intimidating than Jared DiMaggio. Save him for day two. Or maybe day seven."

"What's funny," I said, rubbing my forehead with both hands, "is that Daisy thinks she's perfect for him because they're both fitness-famous. He's a YouTube star, and she has ten thousand Instagram followers. But she can't see past his muscles to the brain that earned his fame. I'm the one who keeps her marketing department afloat, I cue her lifts to make her look better on stage, and I was a kick-ass trainer before my last job fired me. If I wasn't completely invisible, Jared and I would be perfect for each other!"

"You just need to stand closer than five feet away."

Bailey in the Corner

"Exactly! Why does romance have to be so hard?" I slumped back on my bench and glared at the ceiling.

"Does anyone at the office know you do all those things for Daisy?"

"Definitely not." I couldn't risk receiving credit for Daisy's work again.

"Maybe you should tell them. Make yourself less invisible."

I shook my head. He didn't understand. I couldn't be good at "fitness things" at the same time as Daisy. Only one person could fit on her first-place podium. In fact, I couldn't do anything to outshine her, not without facing her backlash.

"Fearless Felicity wrote an article about this a few hours ago," Marco said. "She's a world-famous fitness blogger. Do you ever read her?"

"Everyone reads her."

Marco nodded. "Go read this one again. Seriously, Bee, it was amazing."

"My name is Bailey, not Bee." The nickname suddenly sounded like sandpaper against my eardrums. "Our first week of college, our sexy doorman mixed up our names on accident."

One of Marco's eyebrows quirked upward. "You had a sexy doorman?"

"You'd agree if you saw him. Daisy realized our names sounded too similar, but she liked that hers was two flowers in a row—Daisy Rose. It only made sense that I changed mine."

"To Bee?"

"She picked it."

"And you were okay with that?"

He asked it like I had a choice.

Marco leaned forward, looking directly into my face. "A name is part of your identity. By changing yours, Daisy said your identity didn't matter, while hers did."

An employee's voice rang through the building announcing closing time. The kids made their way to our table, but Marco kept his attention on me. I squirmed. Daisy's attention never stayed in one place longer than a few seconds, I hardly ever squeezed a word in.

"In your head," Marco said, "what do you call yourself?"

The answer came instantly. "Bailey."

"Well, Bailey, can I call you by your real name?"

The second it rolled off his tongue, I was transported back to high school, snuggling next to my dad on the couch, watching a Friday night movie and eating bubblegum ice cream. When he called me *Bailey*, all my fears melted away.

"You okay, Bailey?" Marco asked, and I nodded as I stood, more okay than he'd ever know. Hearing my own name felt like finding a lost piece of myself. Marco had returned it, with a bowl of bubblegum ice cream.

"Thank you." I hoped he could hear the depth of my appreciation.

Marco held the door open. The aroma of recent rain danced in the wind, the frosty air prickling my arms through my coat. The kids jogged ahead as we made our way back to the JD Fitness building.

"What will you do tomorrow, when you see Daisy at work?" Marco asked, his cane clicking as we crossed the office parking lot.

Tomorrow? Tomorrow was Jared's second round of auditions—he'd asked Daisy to be his on-stage assistant. That meant hair and makeup and hours poring over outfit options.

"She needs my help."

"But what do *you* need? Will you forgive her?"

"I always forgive her." But the words tasted like a lie. I'd been her doormat for so long, apologizing when I'd done nothing wrong. "I think I'll keep my distance." Daisy wouldn't like it, but the idea sparked excitement inside me. "What do you think?"

Marco shook his head. "It doesn't matter what I think. Or what Daisy thinks. It's *your* life. You just have to make a choice and stick to your guns."

Bailey in the Corner

My excitement doubled. "I'll do my best, if you keep your end of the deal. Don't shake things up with Daisy. Not yet." I glanced at Mia and Jackson, chatting by my car. Daisy had never gone as far as lashing out on Mia, but that didn't mean her drama couldn't boil over into Mia's world. We needed to protect Friday's audition.

Marco watched them too. "It's good to see Jackson smiling. Tomorrow then, at seven? I'll bring both kids straight from the dance studio. We'll bring dinner too."

"Thanks, Marco."

"Happy birthday, Bailey."

Mia and I waved to the boys as I pulled out of the parking lot, my heart light enough to fly away. Even the old-car musk from my dingy carpet couldn't break my smile. But the farther we drove, the harder it became to cling to that feeling. Daisy had given me the tiny disco ball hanging from my rearview mirror. She'd given Mia that pink tank top last Christmas. She'd even picked out this car from the used car lot. Daisy had helped weave together so many threads in my life.

If I pulled too hard, everything could come unraveled.

Chapter 7

I drove to work the next morning repeating Marco's challenge in my head. *Put yourself out there. Make one new friend.* I could do this. Really, I could. My palms weren't even clammy, though my left leg wouldn't stop bouncing as I drove.

Daisy's shiny red BMW was already in the office lot, but I strode into the JD Fitness office confident I could avoid her. But one step in, I stopped in my tracks, bracing myself by leaning against the scratchy carpeted wall of the nearest cubicle. Daisy's voice carried through the room. My resolution faltered.

I texted Marco, but my finger hovered over the *send* button. He'd probably forgotten me entirely by now. But when Daisy's shrill laugh grated down my spine, I hit send.

Are you sure about this?

His answer came immediately.

Absolutely, Bailey! I've been wondering about you all morning, keep me updated!

My racing heart slowed and my tense fingers relaxed, especially as I read my real name. I could do this. And if I kept to the building's edges, I could avoid seeing Daisy altogether, at least until the company-wide morning workout in twenty minutes.

But when I reached my cubicle, I froze. Daisy was sitting in my chair holding a bundle of "Happy Birthday" balloons, grinning like a child at a

Bailey in the Corner

surprise party. Not one, but five bouquets of flowers covered the shelf above my desk, and a large purple gift box bearing a frilly green bow filled the floor. Three smaller gifts filled the open space on my desk. Daisy pounced, wrapping me into a hug.

"Happy belated birthday!"

"Thanks," I stammered, too shocked to do anything else.

"I hope you don't mind your gifts are a day late."

"Gifts?"

"And let's do your birthday dinner Friday night at this new bar downtown, I'm dying to go. My treat!"

Daisy's words flew at me so fast I couldn't follow. "Birthday dinner?"

"We could go sooner, but I know you're busy with Mia's auditions. Marco's coaching, right? I'd love to come watch. And did you read Fearless Felicity's article yesterday? It was weird—worst thing she's ever posted."

I kept my eyes trained on her mouth, her bright-white teeth sparkling as she flashed me her dazzling smile. She sounded so genuine, so excited to celebrate.

"Workout's in fifteen minutes." Daisy held out a rectangular packet of Green Fizz, Jared's pre-workout energy supplement. All employees had unlimited access to his powders, but I stared at it like she'd offered me poison. She shook the little packet, urging me to take it, to affirm our friendship by accepting her peace offering.

But did I want peace?

Make one new friend. Marco's words echoed through my head.

If I made peace, Daisy wouldn't let me talk to anyone. My quest to make a new friend would end before it started. I took a step back, focusing every ounce of my attention on that little packet of Green Fizz. If I accepted it, everything would return to normal. But if I refused, I could never go back.

Was it worth the risk? My freedom?

"Dominic's back," Daisy whispered.

My eyes snapped to hers. "When?" The room spun, like the walls couldn't remember where they belonged. Only one person in the world scared me this way.

Daisy's brother, Dominic.

"I called you last night—I said it was urgent."

And I'd hung up on her. All the air sucked out of the room.

"He came back yesterday; he's here for a couple of weeks." Daisy's eyes swam with a plea for my help. Dominic was three years older than Daisy and he'd gained custody of her—and their small fortune—when their father died our senior year of high school. At first it had been a party, Daisy and Dominic spending money like royalty.

Then something changed.

Daisy would regularly show up to school with a black eye or split lip. She never admitted it was Dominic's doing. She loved him, worshipped him. But I saw the way she tensed when his temper flared, heard the strain in her laughter when he surprised her with cocaine for her birthday our freshman year of college. He was wild, irrational, unpredictable.

Daisy's world changed when he moved to Georgia after college. Both of ours did.

But now he was back.

"Have you seen him?" I asked.

"He's sleeping on my couch. He's different this time, Bee. He's not the same guy as before."

She sounded sincere. Like she'd forgotten all the ways he'd hurt her—all the ways he still could. Nausea rolled through my stomach and my feet took another step back.

I bumped into the wall of my cubicle, knocking my favorite picture onto the floor. Nine-year-old Mia had just won her first dance competition and her huge gold medal eclipsed her petite body. I bent down to pick up the frame, but froze, my fingers inches away. In the picture, Mia and I stood in front of a podium with Daisy between us, one arm wrapped tightly

Bailey in the Corner

around my daughter, hugging her close. Daisy's other arm was around me, but she held me a foot away, like I was an interloper in their family photo.

I sucked in a breath, the mixture of roses and Daisy's lavender perfume burning my nose. How had I never noticed our positions in this picture? She held Mia so close, so possessively, like my daughter was more hers than mine.

"You'll help me avoid Dom, right?" Daisy asked. "You did ruin my dinner with Marco last night, so now you owe me."

I'd ruined *her* dinner?

My eyes darted back to hers and I could see her studying my expression, watching to see if she'd pulled me back in. Instead, I slipped the photo out of the frame and tore it down the middle, separating Daisy from Mia. Daisy gasped, but I tucked Mia's portion into my pocket and threw the rest in the garbage. Daisy was toxic enough on her own. If her brother was back, she'd leap to new levels of unpredictability.

The choice was simple.

I stood, feet planted firmly, and looked Daisy square in the eye. "From now on, I'll get my own Green Fizz." Then I walked away with my head held high.

With every step I stood taller, even as her fiery eyes burned into my back. But then she hurled the powder packet at me, hitting me square between the shoulder blades.

I whirled around. "Are you kidding me?"

"You think you're too good for me now? Did you find someone better? Someone else to hold your hand each time you screw up your life?"

I flinched—her words sliced too close to the truth. We both knew my high school friendships had ended in disaster, but none of them topped that one night in college. The most reckless, terrifying night of my life.

But I couldn't back down now.

Without responding, I strode away, through the maze of cubicles, barely holding myself together until I collided with something enormous. My phone skidded across the carpet and I landed hard on my knees.

I peered up, dazed, at the man who'd crashed into me. His deep blue eyes smoldered down, and I sucked in a breath as I stared into the face of Jared DiMaggio.

All thoughts of Daisy fled.

"Let me help." Jared reached out a hand and I stared at it, my brain growing fuzzy. "Are you hurt?"

I took his hand. Callouses covered his warm fingers.

"No. And thanks." I stood slowly, to lengthen the time our hands touched. He never broke eye contact, even after I found steady footing.

Jared tugged the hem of his forest-green athletic shirt. "You look familiar. Do I know you?"

Jared DiMaggio, my boss of five years, *still* didn't know me? How far had Daisy crammed me under her rock? Jared stuffed his phone into a polished leather holster on his hip.

"Wait, you're Daisy's friend—you helped with her audition. Remind me your name?"

"Bee. I'm the office manager."

"Sorry Bee, tons of people work here. I won't forget again."

Only thirty-six people worked here, and I did my job well. On days I didn't come in, the office fell apart. How did no one notice? Well, Lunatic Lauren noticed me, every single day, but she was the one person I wanted to avoid. I'd rather be invisible than suffer the wrath of Jared's second-in-command.

Jared strolled toward the gym, typing into his phone like he'd already forgotten me. "Oh, hey," he said, "if you're the office manager, have you seen the contract with ZBC TV? No one can find the latest version."

JD Fitness had been trying to land a network TV deal for ages. So far, the parties couldn't come to an agreement.

"It's on Cinnamon's desk."

Jared stopped walking, surprised, maybe even impressed. "Whose desk? I don't know where the new people sit."

I almost laughed. Cinnamon wasn't new.

Bailey in the Corner

Jared followed me as I wound through the cubicles. Three executive offices lined the right wall, occupied by Jared, Lunatic Lauren, and a ridiculous amount of storage. Across the building sat the gym and the stage where we streamed Jared's workouts, and the giant room to my left held the fabrication department, where the seamstresses sewed the JD Fitness clothing line. Cubicles filled the middle, with Cinnamon's desk near the center.

Right beside Daisy's.

Jared followed me to their shared, oversized cubicle, where lavender perfume still lingered in the air. I ignored the framed picture on Daisy's desk. She'd taken it herself, of the two of us, high up on a cliff, the night before we moved to college. A dozen other photos filled her desk as well, even one with Amelia. My own cubicle had only two lonely pictures tacked to the wall. Daisy starred in both.

I grabbed the contract, then jumped when I found Jared behind me. *Right* behind me. The heat from his skin radiated onto my face.

"Here it is," I squeaked.

He scanned the papers, relief filling his expression. "How did you know where this was?"

"I keep all the contracts. If they're gone, I always know who took them."

"That's useful. You just saved my lunch meeting."

Jared stepped closer. His eyes lingered on my hair, my face, the dip in my collar bone. His pine tree aroma blocked out Daisy's lavender. For the first time in who knew how long, I felt the opposite of invisible.

Daisy would have told me to back away. But a tiny voice, deep inside, wanted me to forget about her. For years, I'd ignored that voice, shoved it down and buried it. But today, it sounded so familiar, it sounded like *me,* and my relief in hearing it overpowered any rational thought. I didn't want to shut it up, I wanted to listen.

I wanted to reach out and touch Jared DiMaggio.

Apparently, Jared had the same idea. He tucked a stray hair behind my ear. Adrenaline shot through my limbs, and I shifted my weight, back and forth. I wanted to make a choice for myself, to do something brave, even if it was crazy.

Is this crazy? Daisy had asked me those exact words from the top of that cliff in the middle of the night, the summer her dad died. She'd laughed when she heard about his motorcycle accident. Then became horrified. A neurotic combination of relief and guilt that drove her beyond rational decisions. We'd both peered over the ledge into the black water below.

Will I die? she'd asked.

No.

Let's go higher.

No. Not higher.

Daisy had studied my face. This was our typical routine. She'd push the limits until I stopped her from going too far. I kept her grounded, she kept me from sinking too deep.

Jump with me.

She took my hand and her courage flowed into my veins. I had none of my own, but Daisy loved to share. I craved it, needed it like air to breathe, like water in a desert. She snapped a selfie, then tucked our phones into a safe place in the rock.

Ready?

Then we jumped into the lake, together.

Jared DiMaggio still stood inches away, but the photo on Daisy's desk taunted me—I'd been so desperate for her courage that I lived on the fringes of her life.

I still did.

I knocked the picture face-down on her desk, the frame splitting with a *crunch* at one corner. I hated that I only felt brave with Daisy. Hated that I only did crazy things that were *her* idea, had *her* stamp of approval. Hated

Bailey in the Corner

standing here alone, with Jared's undivided attention, but *she* still consumed my thoughts.

Time to listen to the voice I'd locked away.

Jared's fingers brushed against my arm, sending goosebumps across my skin. His green shirt clung tightly to his body, emphasizing the ridges of his abs. *This is crazy.* But courage coursed through me like it did every time Daisy convinced me to do something stupid. But this time, the stupid idea belonged to me. So did the courage.

I reached out to touch Jared's arm, but he adjusted at the last second and my fingers pressed against his firm stomach. The muscles beneath his shirt were hard as rock. When Jared didn't object, I pushed harder, running my hand along each bump, moving slowly toward his chest, then I risked a glance at his face. Jared watched my fingers with curiosity, but he didn't stop me.

"What the hell are you doing?" someone screeched.

I jumped back, crashing against Daisy's chair as Lunatic Lauren stormed toward us and jabbed her finger into Jared's chest. The sharply pointed collar of her gray pantsuit matched the pointed toes of her navy heels.

"You're ten minutes late to the gym, and you have a meeting in an hour! If you cost us this deal, I'll kill you myself."

Lauren was short enough that I could peer over the top of her pixie-cut blond hair, but she still seemed to tower over Jared.

"And you!" Lauren spun sharply in place and jabbed her finger into my shoulder. "Stop flirting with the boss. You're embarrassing yourself."

"I wasn't flirting," I whispered.

"You talk to people now?" She raised an eyebrow, but turned back to Jared before I could respond. "Seriously, Jared, get to the gym, and stay away from the groupies."

My pride ruffled and I stood taller. Normally I'd stay quiet, but today felt different. "I'm not a groupie."

"That groupie found the missing contract." Jared held it up.

Lauren glanced at me and paused. "She's still a distraction. Now leave."

"Yes ma'am." Jared swung his gym bag over his shoulder and strolled toward the warehouse.

"I meant what I said," Lauren hissed. "Don't flirt with Jared."

"I wasn't flirting."

But the farther away Jared walked, the clearer my mind became. *Did I grope the abs of superstar Jared DiMaggio? And Lunatic Lauren witnessed the whole thing?* I wanted to crawl in a hole and die.

"Oh, hey," Jared called, pausing at the far end of the row. "Did you say you're the office manager?"

"Yeah."

"Could you order more paper? The printer in my office is empty."

I nodded, not bothering to mention the supply room had five full crates. I'd ordered them last week.

"Thanks, Dee," he said as he slipped out the door.

"It's Bee," I muttered, then I followed him into the gym, my feet scuffing the ground.

Chapter 8

I pushed through the cold, metal door into the warehouse. The gym was full, the air chilly from the propped-open exterior door. I grabbed a packet of Green Fizz from the kitchenette and dumped it into my water bottle, chugging it down to wash away the bitter taste Daisy had left. I could do this.

The final staff members trickled in, grabbing dumbbells and claiming spots on the giant, open stage. Every employee would likely turn out, hoping for a leg-up in this afternoon's audition to earn a spot on Friday's live-streamed show. The room buzzed, everyone debating which weights to grab. You didn't want to lift too light, or you wouldn't impress Jared; but if you picked too heavy, you'd struggle on camera. Without knowing the lifts in advance, we all had to guess. I grabbed five- and eight-pound weights, then took a nervous breath.

Time to prove Daisy wrong. Time to make a new friend.

"Hello," I said to the woman beside me at the rack. She didn't notice, deep in discussion with someone else.

I brushed it off as a man approached, about my height and equally alone. "Nervous for today?"

He gawked at me, then waved at other friends. I folded my arms around my stomach as the stage filled, everyone clambering for a spot near the front. Then Daisy entered and her eyes instantly caught mine. We always worked out together, and our usual spot was still empty. But then

Cinnamon, her marketing partner and cubicle mate, trailed in, glued to her heels like a puppy. Cinnamon sneered the second she saw me, and swung her thick, straight hair over her shoulder. It hung to her butt, never in a ponytail, and she kept it dyed an unnatural shade of firetruck-red that suited her assortment of animal-print workout clothes. I suspected she kept it that color so she and Daisy could match, though Daisy's red hair was natural, and she'd never donned anything close to animal print. But their athletic bodies and exuberant confidence made them a formidable pair.

Taking my weights, I found an empty corner near the back, while Cinnamon claimed my spot two rows ahead. I tried not to watch them, tried not to hate Cinnamon for replacing me, or Daisy for letting her. I hadn't made a new friend yet, but I'd keep trying. It was only nine—the day had barely started.

Then Jared joined us on the stage and everyone erupted into applause. Someone even stomped their feet, making the stage vibrate. I couldn't resist joining in, gazing at his green skin-tight athletic shirt—and the sculpted muscles underneath. He shook hands with everyone he passed. My fingers still felt warm where I'd touched his abs minutes before. He'd stood so close . . . If only Lunatic Lauren hadn't interrupted.

On cue, she pushed through the metal door and followed behind her boss. No one shook her hand though—no one even looked at her. But they did clear a path as she stomped through, scribbling frantically on a clipboard.

Jared raised his hands and the crowd instantly settled. Despite working in his office every day, we all shared the same awe.

"As you know," he said, "the promo workout for MaxFit99 airs Friday afternoon. In a stunt never before seen in large-scale fitness, we're airing it to the public *live!*" Everyone cheered again, whistling and applauding. "We expect at least twenty thousand live viewers, plus twenty thousand more by the end of the day. I'll need to be on my A-game. But I'll need a top-notch cast who's just as incredible." Someone whistled, making everyone laugh. Jared took his clear water bottle, unmistakably

Bailey in the Corner

filled with Green Fizz, and raised it for a toast. "Here's to all of you who make this possible!"

The crowd roared as Jared bowed, then jogged off to grab weights. Excitement resonated in the air, everyone chatting about the workout to come—everyone but me. I stood alone, pulling on the lifeless braid hanging over my shoulder.

Daisy's voice carried over the crowd. "Please tell me you read it."

"Ugh. Yes." Cinnamon's shrill tone grated as she smacked her pink bubblegum. "It was horrifying."

"I miss the days when Fearless Felicity blogged about fitness clothes and workout supplements. Now she has opinions? Annoying."

Marco had said he loved yesterday's Fearless Felicity article. Did Daisy disagree? I stepped the tiniest bit closer. Daisy pulled her phone out of the pocket of her shimmering violet high-rise biker shorts. They matched her strappy sports bra, white with violet accents, and her sparkling new Nikes.

"Listen to this section," she said. "It's disgusting. 'Can we all agree, real success takes a village? Every time you succeed, give a shout-out to the people who got you there. I'll even take it one step further—the biggest compliment you can give is to shout their praise to everyone you know. If they share the credit, does it mean you failed? Of course not. In our world of personal YouTube channels and social media accounts, everyone can be an Influencer. Everyone can win. Don't step on people's heads to get to that finish line. Let them push you up there, then reach down and pull them up too. There's room on that first-place podium for everyone.'"

"It's kind of nice," Cinnamon said, running her hands through her hair. "She wants us to help our friends."

"Sure, if you know how to pick good ones." Daisy pointed her eyes straight at me. Even across the stage, I could read her message: the last time I'd picked someone for myself, I'd royally screwed up. Turning back to Cinnamon, she folded her arms, popping her hip as she spoke. "Fearless

Felicity is saying that if I do a stellar job, I should give someone else the credit."

"Oh." Cinnamon blew a bubble, then popped it loudly between her teeth. "Yuck."

Daisy stuffed her phone under her bra strap. "Exactly."

My shoulders tensed, prickling at every word.

"What I don't understand," Daisy continued, "is why Fearless Felicity wastes her time telling everyone to be *nice*. She hit a million followers two months ago, and people like Jared constantly beg her to blog about them. Then she writes garbage like *this*? If I had her level of influence, I'd make sure every person on the planet knew about JD Fitness. Jared and I would be world-famous."

I'd read every inch of that article, every word, and I'd hoped Daisy would see herself in there, see me, see how much I'd sacrificed to lift her up. She knew most of her success came from *my* hard work; I was her secret weapon. Or, had she hidden me so well that even *she* forgot about me?

My hands clenched, my nails digging painfully into my palms.

Daisy would never give anyone credit for her success—except herself. And when Jared awarded her with her own show and she finally became rich and famous, she would carefully select who to pull up behind her. *They* would be giving *her* thanks, never the other way around.

Daisy would never thank me.

"We're doing a Total Body workout today," Jared said, fumbling with his cordless mic, sending an obnoxious wave of static through the speaker. He pointed at Daisy. "Since you're assisting this afternoon, will you assist right now too?"

Daisy strode gracefully to the front, beaming at Jared. My phone beeped from the pocket of my black calf-length leggings. I paused when I noticed the snagged fibers along the front of my thighs. My shirt, too, had faded to a pale pink. It hadn't appeared so worn in my closet this morning.

Bailey in the Corner

In fact, Daisy never mentioned my worn-out clothes. Did she like knowing she was always better dressed?

I flipped over my phone and read a text from Marco.

How did it go this morning? Are you still alive?

No one except Mia and Daisy ever texted me, but Marco already messaged twice today—I'd never had so much phone activity.

I survived the first encounter, but I'm heading back into battle. Might not make it out.

A picture popped up of Marco spilling a handful of gumballs out the end of his cane.

I bought these for you. Stay alive long enough to put them on ice cream tonight.

I laughed out loud. Very loud. It echoed all the way to the high, metal ceiling. All eyes swiveled to me.

But Daisy batted her eyelashes straight at Jared. "Ignore her, she does stupid stuff when she's nervous."

Ugh, now no one would want to be friends. I was Daisy's cast-off, her pathetic ex-friend.

Fortunately, my Green Fizz finally kicked in. The heavy shot of caffeine exploded through my nervous system, putting my body on high alert. The beta-alanine settled into my muscles, pinpricks spreading across my cheeks and the backs of my hands.

You know what? I was *not* Daisy's pathetic best friend. I wasn't pathetic at all, and I could prove it. I grabbed my five- and eight-pound dumbbells and carried them back to the rack. Today was Total Body Day, and I could curl more weight than Daisy. I could squat more than her too, but not even Daisy knew it. Did I seriously grab lighter weights just to let her feel stronger than me? The same way I wore ugly clothes so she felt prettier? I swapped them out for fifteens and twenty-fives.

No one made eye contact, but I didn't care—I was tired of hiding myself away. My body was strong. I didn't need to act pathetic to be worthy of approval.

LINDSAY HILLER

Green Fizz raced through my blood, and I stretched my legs, ready to get going. Daisy narrowed her eyes, and Cinnamon whispered something that made others turn and laugh. But the girl next to me smiled, her tiger tattoo spreading down her arm from under the wide strap of her tank top.

Stella.

Jared flipped on his microphone. "All right, everyone, let's see what you've got."

He started the workout with a series of squats—my favorite. With a twenty-five-pound dumbbell in each hand, I powered through the first set until my quads burned and my glutes screamed. But I didn't stop. We moved to lunges and I zeroed in all my focus. Lunatic Lauren kept her appraising eyes on me; even Jared occasionally glanced my way, and once he double-checked the number stamped into my weights. When we moved on to sumo squats, I ran to the weight rack and bumped up to thirties.

The last time I'd lifted with this much intensity was the evening my parents died, senior year of college. I'd gotten the call from a neighbor. A freeway accident. I didn't hear much else. I just laced up my blue Nikes and sprinted out of our neighborhood, fleeing all the feelings waiting for me back in my apartment. I ran all night, sweating in the summer heat, gasping for breath in the scorching air. Long after dark, I found the campus gym, where I lifted the heaviest weights available until the morning sun peeked through the window. Class started in forty-five minutes.

I didn't go.

I didn't do anything but lift until Daisy found me, numb, empty. She pried my dumbbells from my cramped fingers, coaxed me back home, helped me shuffle through my parents' debts, sell off all their valuables except the house. Survive. I couldn't have done it without her.

And every time it became too much, she'd drive me back to the gym where we'd pummel my body until I couldn't feel anymore. It always felt good to push myself like that, to work the edge off of my emotions. It felt good today too, knowing I didn't have to hide behind eight-pound weights

Bailey in the Corner

I could carry with one finger. Jared's eyes lingered on me an extra second and I tightened my core, exactly how he'd instruct.

Stella caught my eye and grinned the second Jared moved away, and I couldn't help but return it. In fact, Stella held forties and made it look easy. Even as we moved into our third round, she kept her core solid, she breathed properly, grunting with every rep. She even kept her weight back in her heels. Her form was perfect, except for the lowest point of her squat. I set down my dumbbells.

"You have a butt wink," I whispered, as Daisy moved the class into their third round of lunges.

"A what?"

"It's where your hips curve under at the bottom of the squat." I demonstrated without weights. "Spread your feet wider, then make sure your knees aren't rolling in. And don't drop so low, even one less inch will make it go away."

"Like this?" Stella performed a perfect squat, without the wink.

"Exactly. And I can't believe you're holding eighty pounds. You're badass."

"Thanks, Bee." Stella wiped her sweat away with the edge of her shirt. "It's weird to lift on a stage, instead of a gym full of mirrors. I can't check my form."

"Call me Bailey," I said. "I'm going back to my real name."

"Bailey?" Stella paused. "I like it. Hey look, he's got a butt wink too." She pointed to a guy on our right.

"You should show him how to fix it."

"Me?" Stella's eyes widened.

"It's your first week, right? He's new too."

"Only if you come with me."

We scooted carefully sideways, earning a frown from Daisy. I pretended not to notice as Stella showed him what I'd shown her. Soon he could squat with perfect form, prompting four other back-row lifters to join us. Stella sent half of them to me, and we formed a small cluster to demonstrate how to keep your weight back in your heels and your chest lifted.

"Quiet down in the back," Daisy said into her mic, though I'd barely whispered. Her eyes darted through me and my group, assessing.

Yes, Daisy, I really am trying to make friends outside of you.

Her eyes narrowed. "Back row, return to your places."

But they only spread out a little and continued asking me questions. What did it matter if I helped eight people, when she was leading the other twenty? Apparently, it mattered to Daisy. We couldn't both succeed; it had to be one or the other. Jared, though, caught my eye with a nod, which sent butterflies through my stomach. The better I made them all squat, the better they'd look on his show. He even briefly joined our circle to compliment my arm alignment during shoulder raises.

By the time the hour ended, Daisy's mood had deflated, and Cinnamon was openly glaring at the back of the room. I guess making new friends also meant making enemies. But for once, I didn't care. I felt strong, I felt brave, I felt confident. And I didn't want it to end.

We finished with chest presses and I grabbed my heaviest weights yet—thirty five pounds in each hand. I'd never lifted so heavy, especially with exhausted muscles, but Stella grinned and I pushed them above my chest.

Nope.

Not a chance.

My arms gave out and the weights crashed to the floor. Instantly my eyes met Daisy's and she laughed into the mic for everyone to hear. Stella helped me put away my dumbbells, but it didn't take away the sting.

We took a few minutes to stretch, then the gym emptied into the locker rooms for pre-workday showers. Lockers slammed and the air filled with the loud, hot air from blow-dryers as women bustled to get ready. I slid into a fresh set of worn-out clothes, then re-braided my hair as Stella lingered near the door.

Bailey in the Corner

"I know you said you don't want to audition," I told her, "but you should reconsider." Women filed out of the locker room as the noise dimmed.

"Will you join me?"

"Not in a million years." We both laughed and my heart lightened. I didn't need to watch my words, make sure I wasn't too funny, or too witty. Stella accepted me—even when I lifted too heavy. It almost felt like friendship. Marco would be proud, so I snapped a selfie of the two of us and sent it to him for proof.

Then Daisy slipped between us, smelling like lavender despite just finishing a workout. Cinnamon leaned against the row of blue lockers behind her. She popped her bubblegum, then held one edge of it between her teeth while she grabbed the other side to twirl it around her finger.

Stella cringed. "Gross."

But Daisy stared down at Stella, arms folded, no emotion in her voice. "Get away from us," she said.

Stella's jaw dropped as Daisy angled her body to block Stella from my sight, then stuck both fists on her hips.

"What's going on today, Bee? You're acting weird. First, you refused my Green Fizz, then you stole the show during my workout." Her voice grew soft. "Were you jealous that my career's about to take off?" She glanced at Stella, who scooted into my sight, eyes darting worriedly between us. Daisy leaned in close but whispered loud enough for everyone to hear. "And now you're picking your own friends? You really want a repeat of last time? You're hanging out with the fat girl from the mailroom, for crying out loud. Have you lost your mind?"

"Daisy!" I said, but Stella gasped and sprinted out of the locker room.

"Nice one," Cinnamon cackled, but when I met Daisy's eyes, I found jealousy, not laughter, shining back. The old me would have reached out to reassure her, but I squashed that instinct in a second. Only one person deserved comfort right now, and it wasn't Daisy. Without another word, I sprinted out after Stella.

Chapter 9

I jogged a lap around the office, poking my head into all three executive offices, then zigzagging through the center cubicles. I even checked the conference room and the cafeteria. People gave me weird looks, but I searched everywhere except the fabrication room, which was strictly off-limits until Jared's new clothing line launched on Friday in coordination with his new show.

But Stella was gone.

Probably hiding from Daisy. And me.

She wouldn't want to be friends after what Daisy had said. And maybe Daisy had a point—when I went on that date, the night of my parents' funeral, I could have gotten hurt. I could have died. I'd never been so wrong about someone.

But Stella stayed on my mind as I did my morning work. I filled slow cookers with soup and prepped salads for lunch in the cafeteria. I restocked the staff supply of Green Fizz, Purple Protein, and Blue Juice packets. And when Jared left for a meeting, I tiptoed into his wide, silent office and filled his printer with paper, then left a few extra reams on the narrow table beside it.

"That was fast," Jared said.

I jumped, heart racing, and whirled around to find him leaning casually against his door frame. "Where did you come from?"

Bailey in the Corner

He strolled past me and swiped his car keys off his desk, leaving the scent of pine in his wake. "Can't get far without these. Thanks for the paper." He winked as he left, my heart still pounding.

But Stella still didn't return.

Walking through the building felt off too. No one spoke to me, like usual, but today their silence dug under my skin and grated my nerves. I'd always had Daisy to talk to, and who needed other friends when you had her? But after a taste of true friendship with Stella, I knew what I was missing.

Part of me longed for Daisy, or at least the idea of her. I missed the comfort of assuming we'd spend time together, without needing to ask. I missed knowing we'd get lunch every day, knowing she'd pass my desk to chat every time she got bored, which happened twenty times a day. I missed familiarity. Predictability.

She ditched you on your birthday.

But I didn't miss her deciding where we'd hang out, who we'd spend time with, or when I needed another punishment. I hated being swept into the corner anytime I got in her way.

By eleven, I was so preoccupied with Stella's absence, I struggled to keep working. I ran payroll, puzzling only a moment when I read Lauren's note to skip the executives' monthly bonuses. I opened Jared's file of bills that he'd approved for each department head and paid them on the company card. Then I did the same for Lauren.

Did anyone know it was me who paid their bills?

Next, I opened the company bank accounts and ran a report of the month's pay-per-click ad bills, then spent twenty minutes analyzing the fees against Daisy and Cinnamon's ads for MaxFit99 and our new clothing line. As usual, the ones I'd doctored received five times more clicks. I also tallied which platforms got the most traction (Instagram) and which clicks ended in the most actual purchases (Amazon.) When I'd typed out my findings, I forwarded my full report to the marketing department, which meant Daisy and Cinnamon. Daisy would present my numbers at the next department head meeting, and everyone would be impressed with her analytical skills. She might even get a bonus.

Until today, this had never bothered me.

Next, I pulled up their folder of Friday's ads. Each one featured Daisy or Cinnamon, holding dumbbells or sipping from MaxFit99 water bottles. The real star, though, was the clothes. Jared's new autumn line would launch on Friday, right as the MaxFit99 promo went live. He called it the Waterfall Collection. In every picture, the ladies wore shimmering leggings or shorts made of a fabric so sheer I could almost feel it slip through my fingers. No one but the seamstresses and the marketing department had ever seen it in person. The ad formatting, though, clashed horribly with the photographs.

"Bee!" Daisy's shriek carried all the way across the building.

On instinct, or maybe habit, I sprinted to her desk. "What's wrong?"

She grabbed my hand, pulling me to her computer where she and Cinnamon pored over those very same mediocre ads. "We desperately need you."

"Seriously," Cinnamon chimed in. "You always make them look so much better."

Normally, I would painstakingly explain graphics techniques they could never quite grasp. Today though, I hesitated. Daisy noticed.

She ditched you on your birthday.

"Please, Bee? You're brilliant at this stuff, and Jared needs them to look perfect for Friday."

I paused, lingering on the way he'd winked at me after he'd caught me in his office refilling paper. She wasn't wrong about Jared; he needed quality ads.

Daisy squealed as I slid into her chair, but today I didn't teach her anything as I fixed the mistakes in her ads. In each one, I blew up the JD Fitness logo, changed the frilly font to something legible, and dulled the background to draw immediate attention to the bright clothes.

Bailey in the Corner

Last, I eyed Cinnamon. "The bright red hair clashes with the green leggings. Makes you look like a Christmas mermaid."

Daisy snickered as I dulled Cinnamon's hair to a dark brown, making Cinnamon scowl. At last, I leaned back in Daisy's chair, grinning as the two of them dazzled from the screen in their shimmering gear. What I wouldn't give to look a fraction as beautiful.

Daisy nudged me with her shoulder. "What would I do without you?"

I stared back, unmoving. Last night, Fearless Felicity had proclaimed people should give credit when it's due, and here Daisy was, giving me credit. So why did it make me uneasy? Maybe because this "credit" would never go beyond this cubicle. Did Jared know I made all their ads? Of course not.

"I don't know what happened this morning, Bee," Daisy continued, "but can we put it behind us? Get lunch?"

She ditched you on your birthday. She ditched you . . .

"I go by Bailey now," I blurted.

Daisy paused. "No, you don't. You've hated your name since you were a kid."

I sat taller in her chair. "I'm serious, it's Bailey."

Cinnamon laughed. "What kind of crazy person randomly changes their name? What's next, inviting Lunatic Lauren to get tacos with us? That's worse than Stella!"

"Maybe I will," I fired back, my indignation rising.

"No, you won't," Daisy said, brushing me off and turning her full attention to Cinnamon. "Have you seen Lauren today? She's pissed at Jared. She's been raving mad all day."

Steam bubbled up inside me like a kettle about to explode. Could I not pick my own name? Like I couldn't pick my own friends? And what if I *did* want to invite Lunatic Lauren to lunch, who were they to stop me? Daisy's ads still glowed from her computer screen, so I highlighted all the files and hit *delete*. Every last one of them, erased in an instant. They could figure it out on their own from now on.

"Hey!" Daisy cried, but I slammed back Daisy's chair and marched straight to Lauren's office, Daisy and Cinnamon scurrying behind me.

Lauren was screaming "YOU IDIOT!" into her desk phone. As soon as she saw me, she slammed it onto the receiver with a *crack*, wadded up a piece of paper, and threw it at my forehead. I froze when it hit me, then Daisy and Cinnamon exploded into cackles.

I spun on my heel and fled, their giggles chasing me into the bathroom where I hid in a pale pink stall. My breaths came short and fast as I buried my face in my arms. Why had I been so stupid? Lunatic Lauren? Of all the people to invite to lunch . . . Maybe Daisy was right. I did always pick the worst friends, the worst people.

The worst dates.

The last time I'd tried was the night of my parents' funeral.

Daisy and I had just returned to our apartment. My eyes burned from crying and my body drooped, too heavy to lift. Daisy practically carried me to my bed, but the second my head touched my cozy pink pillow, the emotions rose inside me like a hurricane, wailing through the air and beating against my body. I had to go, had to get out, had to escape the pain, or numb it, or . . .

Avoid this pain by embracing another one.

I sent a flurry of texts to the one person wild enough to distract me from my agony—who just happened to be in town for the weekend.

Half an hour later, my date arrived: Daisy's brother, Dominic. He leaned against the doorframe smelling of cigarettes and liquor. His eyes roamed over my long, bare legs, then lingered an extra second on my barely covered breasts. Then they locked on mine, and I knew I'd made the right choice. All I wanted was the wildfire burning inside him. I wanted it to burn me alive, destroy my feelings, free me from this plague of pain.

Daisy's eyes had filled with terror, then her entire body trembled violently. She squeezed my hand and refused to let me go. When I shoved her away, she slid me a can of pepper spray and a condom. I dropped them in the trash on my way out, letting the black night envelope me as I climbed

Bailey in the Corner

onto his motorcycle and wrapped my arms around the waist of the worst person on the planet.

Two weeks later, I discovered I was pregnant with his child.

But I never told him.

Daisy didn't either.

Nothing would be worse than Dominic laying a finger on Mia.

Chapter 10

Okay, Lunatic Lauren was a bad choice for a lunch date. But Stella?

Stella's eyes didn't burn like Daisy's or Dominic's. In fact, Stella welcomed me, boosted my self-confidence. And she didn't make me feel foolish or stupid.

When I tiptoed out of the bathroom for lunch, Daisy and Cinnamon were digging through the supplement packets on the cafeteria counter. I hid outside the door, pressing my back against the white wall, listening through the crack under the hinge.

"I still can't believe she went into Lauren's office," Daisy said. "Bee has zero ability to stand up for herself."

"She's so weird," Cinnamon muttered. Their voices moved to the other side of the cafeteria, so I pressed my ear to the crack, straining to hear. "But she's a genius at marketing. Can you believe she deleted our ads? Let's hope she keeps helping us—our bonuses get bigger every quarter."

"Yeah," Daisy snorted, "until she screws up and gets herself fired again."

Multiple thumps interrupted the conversation, followed by a crash, then Cinnamon's shrill voice jumped two octaves. "She got *fired*? Tell. Me. Everything."

Bailey in the Corner

I hurried away before she shared my shame with the entire cafeteria, beelining for the privacy of my car. Maybe I'd go to Frenchie's, ask if they could fit a table for one pathetic loner into their lunch schedule. But I stopped in my tracks at the entrance to the mailroom.

Sitting on the floor, with her back to the wall, drowning her sorrows in a box of Hot Tamales, was Stella.

"There you are!"

I inched inside the mailroom, noting the faint aroma of cinnamon in the air. The room had been converted from a small conference room, and the rectangular table in the center was littered with unopened mail. Crates of envelopes and plastic-wrapped fabric skeins lined the walls, the material shielded from view by layers of brown paper.

Stella raised her candy box in greeting.

"I'm so sorry about Daisy," I said. "She was out of line."

"Isn't she your friend?"

"No." I spoke too loud, too quick. "I don't know. I'm taking a break from her."

"Smart. Hot Tamale?"

I joined her on the ground as she dumped candies into my hand. "I love these. I ate them every single day when I was pregnant."

"You have a kid?"

"Mia. She's twelve."

I'd started craving hot tamales a couple of weeks after my reckless night with Dominic. Five boxes a day hadn't stopped the cravings, even when I threw them back up every hour. Daisy figured it out first, then raced to the store to buy me a pregnancy test. I peed on the stick then stared at the blue line.

It stared back at me.

Pregnant?

I was still a kid myself; how could I raise one? With college to survive, an entry-level part time job, no family, and no help? I only had water rushing in, gushing over my head, drowning me. My baby deserved better. It deserved parents equipped to love and care and protect. Not me. Not Dominic.

Shit. Not him. My hands trembled until the test clattered to the floor. Anyone but him.

But Daisy took my fingers, squeezed them in her lap, and promised to help hold my head above the water.

I'm here. You're not alone. We'll figure it out together.

Stella must have seen the emotions on my face because she dug into her purse and pulled out a full, unopened box. "You look like you need these more than me."

I opened the candies and dropped a handful of spicy sugar into my mouth.

"You know," Stella said, "there are better friends out there than Daisy."

"I know." I popped another handful into my mouth before I'd swallowed the first. "But maybe she's not all bad. I couldn't have survived my pregnancy without her." And she'd been right to try to stop me from going on that date. Maybe I'd gone too far when I deleted her ads for Jared.

"Then where is she right now, as you drown yourself in candy?"

"It's complicated." Silence followed and I leaned my head back against the wall. "I'm sorry about what she said to you, it was horrible."

"Yeah, it was. Joke's on her though, because I like my size. Girls like her think larger women are gross, like we aren't all born with different body sizes. Sure, I wear plus size clothes, but I'm healthy and full of energy, and I can out-lift Daisy any day. If being skinny means giving up my strength, I'm not interested."

"Here, here." I raised my candy box in a toast. "I'd love to hear you say that to Daisy." What I didn't say was that I'd give anything for a fraction of her self-image. My outfit was cringe-worthy while Stella looked stunning in her navy-blue shorts and baby-blue tank. They accented the hints of blue in the dagger tattoo slicing down her thigh.

Bailey in the Corner

"I'll never understand," Stella said, "why women try so hard to tear each other down. There's room on the first-place podium for all of us."

My eyes snapped to hers. "You read Fearless Felicity?"

Stella grinned. "I love her."

"Me too. So why are you sitting on the floor?"

Stella's eyes scrunched around the edges. "Two reasons. First, I forgot my lunch and I'm starving, but all I have are Hot Tamales. Second, Lauren was supposed to teach me to run the mailroom, but I think she forgot. When I asked for help, she threw a wadded-up paper at my shoulder."

"She got me in the forehead ten minutes ago."

Stella chuckled and stood, scanning the piles of mail and fabric. "I'm too scared to try again, so I'm hanging out until someone notices my job isn't getting done."

I stood too, about to pop another handful of candy in my mouth, but I paused. In the comfort of Stella's company, I no longer craved comfort food.

Then Daisy arrived in the doorway and my peaceful moment vanished. She scrutinized Stella until Stella shrank in on herself, then turned her brightest smile at me. "Ready for lunch, Bee?"

The invitation clearly didn't include Stella.

I glanced between them, torn. Perhaps I'd been too hard on Daisy. Perhaps I should recreate their ads after we returned from lunch. But a bitter tang filled my mouth. Go to lunch with the person who just told Cinnamon why I was fired from my last job?

"It's fine, Bailey," Stella said. "Go ahead."

But the choice between them was easy. Manic laughter bubbled up from my chest. Reckless probably, but I didn't care.

Only one of them was willing to use my real name.

"Sorry, Daisy," I said. "Stella and I already have plans."

Daisy smiled brighter, as if it could cover the rage dripping from her eyes, then walked away without a word. I tried not to tally how many times

I'd rejected her this morning, and how many punishments I had coming. The second she left, we both let out a *woosh* of breath.

"You didn't have to stay," Stella said.

"Of course I did, you're better company. Plus, if someone doesn't train you, this whole place will fall apart." I meant it too.

Over the next thirty minutes I showed her how to open and sort the mail, deposit checks through the bank scanner, and deliver paperwork to Accounts Receivable. All that remained were the giant rolls of fabric leaning against the walls.

"These go to the fabrication room," I said, "but I'm too tired to carry them."

"Me too. I'm starving."

She followed me to the cafeteria, where the aroma of soup rose from the crockpots and saturated the air. Stella's hands dropped to her growling stomach. We stuffed our faces, but I checked over my shoulder every few minutes, like Daisy would pounce and spoil my peace. Every time she wasn't there, I relaxed a tiny bit more.

"I feel so much better," Stella said when her spoon clanged against the bottom of her empty bowl.

I led her to the counter at the far end of the room. "These are Jared's nutrition supplements. We sell them online, but employees can use all they want, free."

Stella grabbed a packet of Blue Juice. "I know this one."

"That's our best option. It's all the essential amino acids that help with muscle soreness. There's also the Green Fizz pre-workout drink, Purple Protein powder, Red Recovery—which is a casein protein to take before bed—and the Neon Nutrition Shake. Next time you're starving after a workout, drink any of these."

Stella tucked a couple Purples into her pocket before we returned to the mailroom. "Thanks for showing me all this," she said. "The mail's been piling up, and the FedEx guy keeps dropping off bins of fabric. Do we need to do anything with it before we take it to the fabrication room?"

Bailey in the Corner

"Just check it into inventory."

After marking them "delivered" in the computer, we loaded our shoulders with as many skeins as we could carry. I felt so cheerful, I didn't even check for Daisy before we crossed the building.

Someone had taped a giant KEEP OUT sign to the fabrication room door, and Stella paused. "Are we allowed in here?"

I hoisted the fabric higher up, my anticipation growing. I'd wanted to go into this room for months. "Nope. But if they want their Waterfall fabric, they'll get over it."

The fabrication room was a madhouse, and ten degrees warmer than the rest of the building. Four women and one man sweated over whirring, thumping sewing machines, each on its own six-foot table. Three additional people scurried about, cutting, sorting, and pinning, like bees swarming their hive. Or tailors with a deadline.

But the fabric instantly drew my eye—yards and yards of shimmering, iridescent cloth in various states of cutting and sewing. It hung from large rollers attached to the ceiling, cascading down like a dozen waterfalls, giving the tailors easy access and keeping it off the dirty floor.

"The Waterfall Collection," Stella whispered. "I see where it gets its name."

I brushed my hand across the closest stream of fabric. It seeped through my fingers like silk, like water. I took a picture and texted it to Mia. She responded immediately, three rows of starry-eyed smiley faces.

"What are you doing in here?" a screechy voice yelled.

A large, Black woman came charging toward us. Lyneeka Hansley was the head of the fabrication department, and the entire staff knew she was tasked with keeping the fabric a secret.

"We have today's delivery."

"And yesterday's," Stella added sheepishly. "I didn't know what to do with it. Bailey's showing me."

"Bailey?" Lyneeka blinked three times as she sized me up.

"It's my real name."

"I'll call you whatever you want," she said, "but you aren't allowed in here. Drop off the fabric, then out you go."

We followed Lyneeka through the roar of sewing machines, then deposited the plastic-wrapped skeins on a back table. The tailor there was sewing cuts of fabric into a full pair of leggings right before our eyes. Stella leaned in closer to watch.

Lyneeka eyed her suspiciously. "Who are you, again?"

"This is Stella," I explained. "She's new in the mailroom, but Lauren's too busy to train her."

"So you volunteered?"

I nodded.

"Without Daisy?"

I nodded again.

"And you've changed your name to Bailey?" She rubbed her forehead like I was giving her a headache.

"I'm branching out."

Lyneeka dropped her hands, the corner of her mouth turning up. "Good for you." Then she stuck out her hand to Stella. "I'm Lyneeka, I run this chaotic mess. Normally we're more organized, but we're pulling twelve-hour shifts to prep for Friday morning's online orders."

"It's amazing," Stella said, eyes wide as she peered around the shimmering room. "I've worn Jared's clothes for years. I can't believe they're made right here."

"If you need anything, let me know. Our staff is like family, we're happy to have you."

Family? I'd never been part of that family.

"I can help sew," Stella said. "I have experience."

"Our machines are full . . ." Lyneeka stepped back, looking Stella up and down with an appraising eye. "You know what we need, though? A size-large model for Friday's ads."

"Wait, what?" Stella turned red up to her ears, making Lyneeka laugh.

Bailey in the Corner

"Do you know how to lift? You'd need to pose with weights."

Stella's eyes shot to mine, blinking rapidly.

"I've seen you lift," I said. "You're crazy strong."

"I'm not a model," Stella objected. "I'm too big."

"You're perfect. Plus, you'd get to wear Waterfall pants."

Stella's eyes darted to the silver cloth hanging from the ceiling.

"At least try them on." Lyneeka held out a pair of glittering turquoise shorts and a white tank top. "You can dress in the bathroom."

Stella chewed her lip until I nudged her. "You've got this."

She grinned, then hurried off to change. When she returned, her countenance sparkled as much as her shorts. "I don't even feel . . . fat. I hate how people gawk when I wear tight-fitting clothes, like it's not allowed. But these pants? I feel so sexy."

"You look sexy too," Lyneeka said. "You've got nothing to be ashamed of."

"But will Daisy want me as her model?" She asked it so quietly, I barely heard over the sewing machines.

"You're exactly what this company needs," Lyneeka said. "You aren't stick thin, you're healthy, and you're confident in your size."

"I used to teach fitness classes," Stella said. It made sense, after seeing how patiently she had taught our little cluster in the gym this morning. "I was a personal trainer first, but my boss refused to give me a full class. He said I needed to slim down, like the yoga girls."

Lyneeka snorted. "What a pig."

"Then the high fitness teacher quit, so I covered her class for a week. People loved it so much they demanded I keep the job permanently. He couldn't say no after that."

"Damn straight," Lyneeka said, hugging Stella from the side.

"Then why do you work in the mailroom?" I asked. "Why not apply at a gym? Keep teaching?"

Stella's cheeks flared pink again. "It took years to gain their respect. When my dad got sick and I moved here, starting over felt too daunting."

"I get that," I said, but I took her by the shoulders and guided her to a full-length mirror against the back wall. "But look at yourself. You have *nothing* to be ashamed of, and nothing to prove."

But we still had to convince the marketing department.

We had to convince Daisy.

In the time it took Lyneeka to call her, my heart rate doubled. Maybe she'd still be at lunch. But Daisy poked in her head ten seconds later. Her jaw dropped at Stella's shorts.

She crossed the room, eyes burning. "What's this?"

My mouth parched as the battle brewed in Daisy's face.

Lyneeka's eyes hardened. "Remember we talked about finding a size-large model? I found one." She pulled a hairbrush from a box, untied Stella's hair, and began styling it. "I'm also in charge of hair and makeup," she explained.

"Stop," Daisy said. "She's not modeling the Waterfall Collection."

"Yes, she is. She's gorgeous, and you need a model who looks good in the new pants."

"She's off-brand."

"What does that mean?" Lyneeka paused with the brush.

"It means I'm too big," Stella said.

"Sorry," Daisy said, not looking sorry at all, "but I know what Jared wants in his ads. It's not you."

Stella nodded, swallowing hard as she left to change clothes, but Daisy winked at me with laughter in her eyes. *Laughter?* As if I'd laugh *with* her?

"Stella, keep the pants on," I said, never taking my eyes off Daisy. Stella paused. They all did. "We sell pants of *all* sizes." I took a step closer, facing Daisy straight-on. "Stella's in great shape. You have no right to insult her."

This was much worse than ignoring Daisy all day, worse than needing space. I'd never called her out before, especially not with an audience, but I didn't back down, even when her eyes narrowed into angry slits.

Bailey in the Corner

"I have no right? I'm the marketing department, and I say no."

"Fine. Then I'll go over your head. I'll ask Lauren."

Knives shot from Daisy's eyes like I was nothing. Dirt. The enemy. But then she smirked. "Twice in one day? Go ahead, she's still in the conference room. She'll rip you apart and eat you alive."

When she motioned for me to lead the way, I marched right past, toward the enemy, straight into the jaws of death.

Chapter 11

The thirty steps to the conference room passed much too quickly. Daisy and I had always faced these job-threatening situations together. But now her footsteps behind me ticked like a clock, counting away the final seconds of my life—or at least my career.

I paused, hand on the metal doorknob.

Stella and Lyneeka were watching from the end of the hall with solemn eyes. But then Stella waved, sending the warm glow of friendship straight into my chest. I hadn't felt that in years and I didn't want to lose it now. So, I pushed open Lauren's door and stepped inside.

Daisy followed me in and spoke before I could. "Bailey wants to make the new girl a model."

"The mail girl?" She turned her eyes back to her heaps of paper as if we weren't worth her time. "What do you think?"

Daisy picked at her nails. "She's totally off brand."

"Then why interrupt me about it?"

I stepped away from Daisy. "Because Stella's stunning in the pants, and Lyneeka said you need a plus-sized model."

Lauren frowned, eyes darting between us. "You two don't agree?"

"No," we said at once, our voices too loud.

"We know nothing about her," Daisy said. "Do we want to turn a stranger into one of the faces of JD Fitness?"

Bailey in the Corner

"She's one of *us*," I protested. "She's exactly who *should* represent the company."

Lauren tapped her pencil against her lips, pensive. "What does Lyneeka think?"

"It was her idea," I said.

"Good enough for me. Daisy, send her to the stage. I'll text the photographer to meet her there. I want her ads in my inbox by the end of the day, then I'll make the final decision."

Lauren shoved aside a rustling stack of papers and zoned in on her laptop, like we'd already left. I snaked around Daisy, anxious to take the good news back to Stella, but Daisy grabbed my arm before I could pass.

"You've only known Stella one day," she hissed. "She's nothing to us. Is she worth ruining our friendship over?"

Daisy peered into my eyes with a glimmer of shock. Or perhaps betrayal.

But I thought of how Lyneeka had described the office as a family—and how I longed to be included. I remembered eating lunch with Stella today, unjudged, not shoved in a corner. Daisy would rather I ate alone. She'd keep me alone forever.

But I really liked Stella.

Daisy tapped her foot on the ugly blue-and-red carpet.

"Yes," I said. "Stella *is* worth ruining our friendship for, because if this was a real friendship, you wouldn't make me choose between you."

Lauren's eyes snapped up, but Daisy's narrowed. All signs of the woman I'd called my sister disappeared. Her fingers twitched as she tensed her jaw. I'd seen this version of Daisy before too, but never from the opposite side of an argument. A volcano stood between us now, blazing with fire, waiting to erupt.

"Not a real friendship?" Daisy sneered. "Then I'll stop rescuing you from your screw-ups. We'll see how long you survive without me."

"I don't need you to save me."

"Yes, you do. You always have."

"Well not anymore," I said. "And never again!"

Daisy pulled open the door, but paused, a wicked smile creeping across her face. "You know what? Fine. You want to go to war? Let's fight this out and see who wins." She leaned closer. "Spoiler alert, it won't be you." Then she walked away, never looking back.

War? With Daisy?

The door closed behind her with a sense of finality. Whatever I'd just done, couldn't be undone. I wasn't passive-aggressively avoiding her anymore—we'd declared war. And Daisy would fight to the death.

"That was . . . underwhelming."

I jumped, forgetting Lauren worked at a table ten feet away. "What was?"

"That pathetically boring fight. At least yell or hiss next time. Someone needs to knock Daisy off her high horse."

Despite Lauren's sarcastic words, a hint of something flashed across her face. Approval? Solidarity, maybe?

But Lauren was dead wrong. She'd only heard our spoken words. The real threat snaked beneath them. How far would Daisy go to win this war?

The ground swayed and I sank into a chair.

"Don't get comfortable," Lauren said. "Go back to work. Wait, print this contract for me. I can study it better on paper." She tossed me a flash drive, then shooed me out of the room.

I walked slowly toward the copier, trying to fathom the consequences of what I'd done. Only time could tell how much collateral damage there'd be. I rubbed the small, torn photo of Mia between my fingers.

Don't let her lash out at Mia.

The copier screeched as it printed, clearly on its last leg, and I opened Fearless Felicity's blog on my phone. I skimmed the comments. Every single one was positive.

I love everything about this article. Thanks, Felicity!

We need more of this in the world. Why do women always tear each other down? Come on girls, let's pull each other up!

Bailey in the Corner

Perfect article to start my day. I'm taping this on my daughter's wall.

My phone dinged, and when Marco's name appeared on the screen the tension in my shoulders released.

Are you surviving? I don't want to eat this bubblegum alone.

My fingers itched to type out every detail of my morning, but the contract finished printing. All I said was:

I'm going to need those.

Is that good? Or bad?

Both? I'll tell you tonight. It's been a long day.

Hang in there, you've got this.

I grabbed the warm papers off the printer and headed back to the conference room, but my steps slowed. It was an agreement between JD Fitness and ZBC Television Network to broadcast MaxFit99—and there was a signature scrawled across the bottom. My eyes nearly popped at Jared's per-episode payment.

"Are we finally going on TV?" I handed Lauren the contract.

"Maybe." She brushed one hand through her pixie-cut blond hair until it stuck out in a frazzled puff. Her eyes moved rapidly through the pages while she fervently scratched her cheek with her free hand. Red streaks formed on her skin, but she didn't stop until she slammed the papers on the desk.

"That asshole! *He* approached us about streaming our show, *he* made the terms of the original contract, but now he's changing it. A week before we go live!"

"Who?"

"Christian, a ZBC exec. He's decided we're competing for our spot against that idiot Michael Kay."

"The French guy with the sword?" Michael Kay was another YouTube Super-Trainer with a massive following. His episodes had cheesy themes like "Bring Your Baby to the Gym Day" or "Halloween Costume Day." He started every show by swinging around his fancy French sword. "That guy's weird."

"Yup." Lauren's eyes darkened. "But he's popular."

"So is Jared."

"I know! But Christian's at Michael Kay's studio today, watching them film, then he'll fly here Friday to watch us before he makes a final decision."

"Is that bad?"

"Yes," she moaned. "We've never live-streamed a show before. We usually film in advance and then edit. Plus, Jared just hired a new stage crew, a bunch of his old college friends with nowhere near enough experience. He didn't even warn me first." Her eyes glossed over as she spoke, like she'd forgotten I was there. Like she was talking out loud to herself. "Jared will die when we lose the show to Michael Kay. Anyone would be better than that guy."

"What's the solution?" I asked. "Can we do a few dress rehearsals before Friday?"

"Yes, except Jared isn't picking the final cast until Thursday afternoon. And Christian keeps changing what he wants in the show." She held up the new contract and dropped it back on the counter. "He wants to double the size of our on-stage cast, but he's cut our budget in half." Her eyes zipped back and forth across the paper. "And costume specifications, backdrop requirements . . ."

She scratched more welts onto her cheek. Then her eyes sprang open like she suddenly registered my presence.

"Go away, Bee, I don't even like you."

Her words knocked the air from my lungs. For a couple of minutes, Lunatic Lauren had behaved like a real human. But now, her fingers twitched like she was suppressing the urge to wrinkle the top page of her contract and throw it at me.

I walked out the door, but paused before closing it, tired of people talking to me like I didn't matter.

"Hey, Lauren?" I leaned against the door frame, ignoring her glare. "I'll stay out of your way, but don't speak to me like that. It's awful."

Bailey in the Corner

Surprisingly, her scowl dropped, and she took a slow, heavy breath. "You're right," she said. "Sorry, Bee, I'm overwhelmed and need it quiet."

"I can respect that. And I go by Bailey, now. It's my real name."

For a brief second, her eyes may have softened, and the corner of her mouth may have twitched upward.

"Sure thing, Bailey. Will you close the door on your way out? Auditions start in twenty minutes, and I need to finish reading this contract."

"Of course."

I left the conference room feeling a tiny bit guilty for calling her Lunatic Lauren all these years.

Chapter 12

By the time I headed toward the gym, a steady buzz of excitement filled the office. Auditions for MaxFit99 would go "live" at three o'clock, and it was almost time. It wouldn't actually air on YouTube, but we would pretend it would. We'd treat it like a dress rehearsal: camera recording, ads running during breaks, no retakes. Jared wanted to see how everyone performed under pressure—especially Daisy, in case she earned her own show after this ended. Plus, we only had today and tomorrow to perfect the process before Christian decided the fate of JD Fitness's television career.

A dozen staff members milled around in their best workout gear, planning to audition. A handful of walk-ins came too, hoping to claim a spot. The brightly lit stage bustled with noisy crew members, and up on the far wall, above the row of treadmills, the giant TV displayed a countdown dropping toward zero. 18:24, 18:23, 18:22. It was almost three o'clock.

But no one was ready. The warehouse roared with chaos, like a zoo with no cages. Anxiety crept down my back as Jared's new stage crew scurried past, yelling to one another over the noisy room. Cables trailed the ground with no attempt at organization, people constantly stumbling over them. Lyneeka had taken over the kitchenette and auditioners crowded in for hair and makeup touchups. They had dropped their gym

Bailey in the Corner

bags wherever they found space, and now milled around waiting for instruction, getting in the way of everyone else.

Stella found me as soon as I arrived. "Is it always like this?"

"We've never done this before."

The room's volume increased another notch as the giant countdown reached fifteen minutes. I almost didn't hear my phone chime. I pulled it out and laughed. Marco had sent a selfie of his afternoon meeting in a fancy restaurant with two men and a woman. All four smiled for the camera, but Marco had angled the phone to capture three canes leaning against the table.

Proof that I'm not the only weirdo who carries a cane.

A fraction of my anxiety evaporated, at least until Daisy strutted in. Everyone hushed, staring. She wore yellow, shimmering pants. *The* pants. Waterfall pants, with a matching yellow sports bra. Most staff had never seen the new fabric in person. People crowded around her, running their hands up her leg to touch the material. Daisy basked in the attention.

My phone beeped again. Marco had sent another picture, this one taken discreetly under the table. He'd unscrewed the cap of his cane and dumped out a small bag of stick pretzels.

Reason #427 to carry a cane: when clients order gross appetizers, I always have a back-up plan.

I laughed again, and Stella craned her neck to see what I was looking at. "Who's that?"

"My friend, Marco." He had found a creative way to solve his problem. Perhaps I could too. "Cameras roll in eleven minutes. Want to help me organize this chaos?"

Stella nodded, and with one last glance at Marco's picture, I told Stella what to do. We started with Green Fizz, dumping powder packets from a giant basket in the kitchen into cold water bottles from the fridge, then handing one to each auditioner. "For energy on stage," I told the newcomers.

Next, I sent Stella out for zip ties and we wrapped the stray cables into bundles. The old stage crew would have known better than to leave these strewn across the floor.

"What if we rolled up the carpets from the lobby and brought them in here to cover the cables?" Stella asked. "Then people could walk over them without tripping."

"Brilliant."

While she grabbed the mats, I gathered everyone's smelly gym bags and stashed them on the treadmills, far away from the production crew. We couldn't have a cameraman tripping while filming. Then I encouraged everyone to warm up on stage, ignoring Daisy, who kept her blank eyes on me as Lyneeka styled her hair. I knew that look—she wasn't happy.

Finally, I pulled another thirty water bottles from the fridge, for a second round of Green Fizz halfway through the workout. But when I reached into the basket, the packets were gone. I pulled out the box in the cupboard, but it was empty too. There had been hundreds only minutes ago.

My lungs seized as I frantically searched the rest of the cupboards. Only one minute remained on the countdown clock, and I didn't have time to hunt down more. Where did it all go?

The big metal door clanged open, and Jared jogged in, waving as everyone cheered, their whistles piercing my ears. The sound guy clipped his mic pack to his waistband. He tucked the microphone headset into his ear, then raised his hands to quiet the room.

"Are we ready?" The whole room cheered again. "Come find your spots on stage, we go live in thirty seconds." He used his fingers to make quotes around the word *live*, reminding us that today's audition was a practice round for Friday's live-streamed show.

My nerves buzzed, and I longed for my own bottle of Green Fizz to get me through the next hour backstage. Someone dimmed the warehouse lights, and the white stage lights turned on instead. Twenty-four people crammed onto the stage, far too many for the space, but they did their best

Bailey in the Corner

to spread out. Jared bounced from one foot to the other, warming up his muscles, and Daisy took the spot beside him. Lauren stalked into the room, glasses on her nose, clipboard in her arm, already scribbling notes.

"Quiet on the set!" someone yelled, and a hush descended. No one moved, no one spoke, and the TV counted down the final five seconds. Four. Three. Two. One.

Showtime.

"Hello!" Jared said, smiling into the camera, pretending it was live. "Welcome to my newest exercise program, MaxFit99. Today, we're doing a total-body workout. Let's start with a warmup."

He bounced side to side, swinging his arms in slow circles, and everyone on the stage copied him exactly. Lauren scribbled more notes, circling the auditioners in a slow, wide arc.

"Today, we have something special to announce," he continued. "As you all know, we've kept the Waterfall Collection a closely guarded secret since we first announced it. But today's your lucky day—it's finally available! In fact, my assistant is wearing one outfit right now. Daisy, how does it feel?"

"Amazing. Like cool water against my skin." She'd memorized that line in advance, and would use it in the real show on Friday. It was written across most of her ads.

When they finished warming up, Jared sent everyone to collect their dumbbells while Daisy demonstrated the first lift for the camera. I tiptoed into the kitchen and added Blue Juice to each water bottle. Fortunately, it hadn't gone missing with the Green Fizz. I brought one bottle back to the edge of the stage.

Stella eyed it and whispered, "What's that for?"

"In case Jared's thirsty."

"Genius."

Neither of us took our eyes off him as he moved the group into their next lift. He walked with infinite confidence in his perfectly white Nikes and spoke to the camera with larger-than-life authority. He didn't even look nervous.

The rest of the auditioners, however, weren't doing as well. Fifteen minutes in, six had stopped for water, three took long breaks, and ten couldn't stay on rhythm with Daisy and Jared. The final five, though, were competing fiercely for Lauren's attention.

"Cut!" the cameraman bellowed, and everyone stopped for the first commercial break. Cinnamon broadcasted the first Waterfall Collection ad to the giant television, with a tiny countdown ticking away in the bottom corner.

Daisy hadn't added Stella to the commercials.

"Two minutes, starting now."

Everyone hurried off-stage and guzzled the Blue Juice I'd laid out for them. Someone spilled theirs on the stage, someone else spilled on the kitchen floor. But Daisy, who had her own bottle of imported spring water, tripped over a camera stand and spilled it all over her legs.

All over her yellow pants.

She shrieked, staring at her ruined outfit. Ninety seconds until showtime.

"Change into these," Lyneeka said, tossing her some black leggings off a rack of spare clothes.

Daisy didn't try to catch them. She let them bounce off her stomach and drop to the floor, like Lyneeka had offered her poison instead of a solution. Most of the crowded warehouse drew quiet as Daisy fumed. Even Jared's eyes widened as he took in her pants.

The funny thing was, I knew exactly how to help her.

She ditched you on your birthday. She declared war.

Would she help me if our roles were reversed?

Today? Probably not. But when I'd truly needed her? When I'd sunk into postpartum depression after Mia's birth? She'd been there. Daisy had found me on the floor of my closet, nipples cracked and bleeding, crying

Bailey in the Corner

helplessly, hiding from the screaming baby I didn't know how to care for. She'd scooped Mia into her arms and made her a bottle of formula.

Don't, I'd said. *Breastfeeding is better.*

Not if it kills you. I'll feed her, you sleep.

For the first time in days, Mia had stopped crying and my aching body relaxed. *Thank you, Daisy.*

"I can dry Daisy's pants," I whispered to Stella, the warehouse now silent.

"In ninety seconds? How?"

I kept my eyes fixed on Daisy, debating. Part of me wanted her to struggle. She had declared war, after all—we both had—which meant she'd attack anytime. And after the last twenty-four hours, she didn't deserve my help. Worse, how would she feel about *me* being the one to save the day? Again.

But my eyes darted to Stella, then Lyneeka. What would they think if I intentionally let the show fall apart? Then I settled on Lauren, her perfectly angled suitcoat skewed. Marco's words echoed in my ears. *Make one new friend.* Lauren needed today to go well. She needed to know we could succeed in front of Christian on Friday.

I raced to Daisy's side and pulled her into the kitchen. Stella blocked her from view using an oversized gym towel.

"Take off the pants," I told her.

"Here?" Her eyes widened, horrified.

"No one can see you behind the towel."

Glaring at Stella, she pried off the wet pants and threw them at me, but I laid them out on Lyneeka's ironing board, turned off the steam function, and ironed out the water. In less than a minute, the pants were dry.

Twenty seconds left.

Daisy slid them back on and yanked the towel out of Stella's hands, bumping into her as she sprinted back on the stage. Jared shot me a thumbs-up and my stomach flipped like a pancake. He held my eyes until

I gestured back. With ten seconds left, the sound guy clipped a microphone onto Daisy's ear.

Everyone breathed a collective sigh of relief, right as the ad on the TV ended. "Round two!" Jared smiled into the camera.

That's when things fell apart.

A man hit a woman's head with a dumbbell. Not too hard, but the woman shrieked, and Lauren pulled her off the stage, muttering about liability and concussions. Five minutes later, two guys in the back row tapped out. They'd been showing off, lifting way too heavy, until one pulled a muscle and they stomped away, cursing. Three minutes later someone kicked over their Blue Juice and the right side of the stage had to pause while the crew cleaned it up.

Then Daisy's sports bra split at the seam.

At first, no one noticed except Stella, who nudged me. When Daisy lifted her arm in a shoulder press, I saw the fabric pulling apart around her ribs. Any second, it would rupture completely.

"Cut!" The camera guy cued the second commercial break, and most of the girls swarmed Lyneeka for touch-ups on their makeup.

"I can fix this one," Stella said, her voice so quiet it barely floated to my ears.

"Me too."

Neither of us moved.

"She really is a bitch," Stella added.

Daisy flirted with Jared, completely unaware her bra would burst any second. Part of me squirmed. She'd saved me so many times over the past twenty years. Did she deserve to have it rip on-stage?

Still, my feet didn't move, stuck to the cold floor like super glue.

I'd already saved her once today, only fifteen minutes ago. And instead of saying thanks, she'd knocked Stella over. Did it make me a terrible friend that I couldn't ignore that? Would a better friend rescue her? A good friend would move her feet and sew the damn bra back together.

But we were at war, and I was winning.

Bailey in the Corner

"Aw hell," Stella said. "I can't just leave her there."

The glue unstuck from my shoes.

"Come here, Daisy." I lifted her arm and showed her the single thread holding her bra together. The clock ticked quickly toward zero.

"I'll hold the fabric," I said. "Stella will stitch it."

Daisy lifted her chin. "I don't want her chubby fingers touching my clothes. You do it."

Stella scowled, then strolled away to help Lyneeka. I watched her go, tempted to let Daisy fend for herself. But when her clothes split on stage, would she pin the blame on me?

"I can sew it," I said, "but I need a second set of hands."

Daisy narrowed her eyes. "Then you should have picked a better new friend. Do it alone and do it quick."

When Daisy raised her arm, I pulled the fabric together with one hand, awkwardly stitching beneath her armpit with the other. It wasn't pretty, or neat, and it needed twice as many stitches as I had time for.

I only pricked her once.

"Watch it," she growled, as the cast regathered on stage. Fifteen seconds remaining. "And hurry."

I tried to be understanding about her mood. Her career hung on the line, after all. Her spot on MaxFit99 and her future with her own show on the JD Fitness channel. She'd saved my career once too, after I'd lost my dream job writing for the *Arts!* section of the newspaper. Thanks to my lingering depression and the challenge of raising a toddler alone, the bank was foreclosing on my parents' house. I'd lost nearly everything they'd left me. Then Daisy offered me her old receptionist job at Lucky 7 Gym.

Free childcare for employees. Mia will be twenty feet away.

I'd never been offered a brighter lifeline.

"Done," I said, and I carefully released my grip on her bra. The stitches would hold, hopefully. Daisy twisted back and forth, and when her bra didn't pop open, she took another step back, tripping over her gym bag and spilling its contents. Hundreds of little green powder packets dumped onto the floor.

"The Green Fizz?" I asked. "You stole them?"

Daisy said nothing.

"Were you trying to sabotage everyone else?"

Or trying to get back at me?

Her eyes turned sharp and cold, then she jogged straight to the stage without a backward glance, without an explanation, without a thank-you for sewing her bra. She moved differently too. A cloud of frustration altered her posture, her mannerisms, her motions.

"You're welcome!" Stella shouted at her back, and Daisy stopped, mid-step, spinning slowly around under the bright stage lights. Storm clouds gathered in her eyes. At least she wasn't fake smiling—things always turned nasty when she pretended to smile.

As if she read my mind, Daisy turned on her brightest grin and strolled to Jared's side.

Dread oozed through me, like tar seeping over my limbs.

"And . . . we're live!"

Jared let Daisy lead round three. To everyone else, it began smoothly, but I knew better. The way she darted glances at Stella, a sneer barely hidden . . . Something sinister was coming.

Daisy walked around the stage, calling out lifts as she weaved between auditioners, occasionally whispering cues in their ears to correct their form. But no one's lifting technique improved. When she passed nearby, I discovered why. She looked directly at Stella as she said to a woman, "Suck in your stomach. Fit people don't look round."

The woman paused, jaw open, but Daisy had already moved on to the next person, speaking too quietly for us to hear. The auditioners fell apart. Even the best five fumbled over lifts, lost their good form, or visibly tensed whenever Daisy wandered nearby.

Jared and Lauren frowned, puzzled.

Bailey in the Corner

Daisy grew bolder. As the third segment neared its end, she tapped a man's shoulder who had picked overly heavy dumbbells. "You can put your weights away and go."

"Seriously?" He dropped his dumbbells with a *thump* and sat up from his chest presses. "I'll grab lighter weights, I just didn't want to interrupt."

Daisy's eyes dropped to his round belly, and she gave an exaggerated eye roll. "Don't bother, you're not what we're looking for."

An eerie silence stretched out as he left, then the final minute fell into chaos. Every auditioner's eyes followed Daisy, their hands shaking or form slipping as she neared. When the stage manager called for the third and final break, they set down their weights without any of their previous enthusiasm. Tension strangled the quiet air.

"This is a disaster," Stella whispered.

I barely heard her. Daisy draped a silk robe over her shoulders and glided through the room like a diva. Even this morning she hadn't been so recklessly overconfident. My stomach churned. This was my fault. She was punishing me by humiliating all these people.

I had to fix it.

Weaving through cameras and giant lights, I found the sound guy in his booth. "Do you have more earpieces?"

"Dozens, why?"

"Can you give one to everyone on stage? And give me a mic?"

He glanced at Jared and Lauren, who were whispering in a dark corner of the warehouse.

"Trust me," I urged. "I'm going to salvage this disaster of an audition."

With a nod, he pulled out a large box of earpieces and rushed to distribute them. With ten seconds left, Jared resumed his spot leading the workout. Only one part of my crazy plan remained, and I steeled my nerves.

"Can I share your clipboard?" I stood next to Lauren. She looked equal parts shocked and annoyed that I would speak to her, but her paper was exactly what I needed—a page of small photos with names. Before she could answer, the warehouse lights dimmed, the stage lights turned up, and the final segment began.

"Welcome back," Jared said into the camera. "We have one final round before we move into our cooldown; let's give it everything we've got!"

The crowd on stage did not share his excitement, and Lauren grunted as Jared demonstrated a curtsy lunge. I glanced at her red clipboard for a name.

"Mark," I said, speaking low into my microphone, "don't let your front knee cave inward when you lunge."

Every face on the stage swiveled my direction, but five of them made the adjustment I'd recommended to Mark.

I gave him a thumbs-up. "Much better. You're doing perfect." I scanned Lauren's clipboard again. "Alena, try not to bend forward when you lunge, your chest is caving in. Much better, you look great."

Within minutes, the mood of the room shifted. The on-stage enthusiasm returned. I coached each auditioner, emphasizing what they did well in addition to correcting their form. When Jared started the cooldown, I switched to only calling out compliments, grinning into the mic. In fact, the only person not smiling was Daisy, and I made a point not to look at her. When the workout ended, Jared marched straight to me, eyes shining. "Brilliant. You saved the whole thing."

I couldn't form words, so I held out the bottle of Blue Juice I'd made for him at the start of the workout.

"Thanks, Bee," he said, and I melted that he'd finally remembered my name. It wasn't my real name, but anything was better than nothing—it meant I'd made enough of an impression to earn a spot in his memory.

"It's Bailey, actually."

"Thanks, Bailey. Will you do it again tomorrow, for the entire audition? And come to our weekly management meetings. We need more problem solvers like you."

Bailey in the Corner

On the inside, I shrieked like a schoolgirl. But to his face, I tried to stay cool. "Sure. That sounds great."

Then the stitches on Daisy's bra ripped.

She screamed like someone had doused her in ice water, then hunched over to cover her exposed chest. Everyone froze, gaping at the flash of breast under her arm as she clung to the torn fabric.

"Didn't you just sew that?" Lauren hissed.

Cinnamon bolted off the stage for Daisy's robe, then flung it over her body. Daisy pulled it tight and stood tall, glaring straight at me.

"You did that on purpose," she snarled, her voice sharp and cutting. The entire room stilled. "You're so desperate for attention, it's pathetic."

"Attention? Seriously?" My voice rose, shrill. "I stitched your bra one-handed because *you* refused to let Stella help."

Her expression said everything—I'd done it again. I'd ruined her moment to shine. Stella pushed toward me, but Lyneeka cut her off, whispering in her ear and giving me a fierce nod of approval. Or thanks. Or maybe encouragement. Whatever it was, it bolstered my confidence as I stared Daisy down.

The auditioners' eyes locked on Daisy too, but their hands were clenched. Wait, were they on my side? Had helping through the earpieces earned their loyalty?

Daisy realized it the same second I did.

"You know what? Screw you, Bee. After everything I've done for you, you'll regret betraying me."

She stomped out of the room, but not before someone yelled, "Her name is Bailey!" Daisy froze, then kept walking as the room burst into applause. "Thanks for helping with the mic," someone said, while others patted my back and shook my hand. "You saved the day."

I wanted to smile, I wanted to bask in their attention and enjoy their appreciation, but my eyes stayed glued to the metal door where Daisy had disappeared. Exhaustion bubbled up inside me. A lifetime of playing this endless waiting game. When would Daisy punish me next? Would today be a happy one, or had I crept too far out of my corner? Was it time for her to shove me back in?

My heartbeat pounded in my ears.

Daisy was no longer the girl from my youth. She wasn't the friend who'd fed my starving daughter, who'd saved my house from foreclosure, or found me a job with a built-in daycare. She wasn't the girl I'd loved like a sister. My only family.

I slipped away from the crowd and pushed through the door to the office side of the building. With everyone still in the gym, the sea of cubicles was empty, quiet. I took the long way to my desk, letting the silence soothe my nerves.

But I froze, halfway to my desk, when I passed the floor-to-ceiling windows near the lobby. In the parking lot, under the brown light of the setting sun, Daisy stood beside her shiny red BMW. And next to her stood a man I hadn't seen in years. The man I'd sworn to keep away from Mia, from myself, and from Daisy.

She'd brought him *here?*

Ice filled my lungs, spreading down my arms and legs.

Dominic leaned casually against her car, his black hair pulled into a ponytail, tribal tattoos lacing his sleeveless arms. He said something I couldn't hear, then walked around the car with his usual swagger. The ice in my lungs turned to frantic electricity.

The old Daisy would have never dared bringing him to the office, but then I'd never dared stand up to her.

Then Daisy looked straight at me, holding my gaze through the window. Her raised eyebrow told me everything: I'd brought this upon myself by humiliating her.

And if she'd bring him here, what would keep her from bringing him to Mia?

But she would never.

Fight or not, she'd never hurt my child that way. She'd never hurt her niece.

Bailey in the Corner

But she'd hurt me.

I bolted to my desk and buried my face in my trembling hands, trying to slow my racing heart. Daisy had said he was staying with her, but until I saw his face, her words hadn't sunk in. But they did now. *He* was where Daisy learned it. *He* showed her how to punish me. *He* taught Daisy to keep me in the dark, hidden in my corner, far from anyone's notice. Everything I hated about Daisy she'd learned from her brother. From his darkness, the shadow he cast.

But maybe I didn't want to be trapped in my corner anymore.

If this was a war, it was my turn to attack.

Chapter 13

Half an hour later, most employees had cleared out after the audition, but I still scanned the cubicles to ensure I was alone. Then I dimmed my laptop screen and logged into Fearless Felicity's blog. I knew exactly what I wanted her to write.

If Daisy hadn't liked her last post, she would hate this one.

Today, I typed, *I want to bring awareness to a parasite plaguing the fitness community: a gross lack of inclusivity. Or, put bluntly, fat-shaming.*

My heart poured through my fingertips, a drumbeat on my keyboard. I wrote about Stella, anonymously of course, and the difference between healthy body sizes and those with the genes to be size zero. I wrote about my time as a new mom and my unexpected difficulties with diastasis recti—a condition where your abs stretch apart and you lose your core strength and flat belly. I wrote about age and hormones and menopause, and how "healthy" looks different on everyone.

But mostly, I wrote about the hurtful judgments of women who should be motivating each other instead of tearing one another down. There was enough of that garbage in the world already.

What's with all these fitness shows with impossibly skinny casts? I wrote. *How does this empower regular people in their bodies? It only shames them for their size when they should feel powerful in their strength.*

My fingers flew faster the deeper I dove. I wrote to those nervously starting their fitness journey with goals that felt too daunting. I wrote to

Bailey in the Corner

those walking the difficult path alone, letting them know they weren't invisible. *We see you. I see you. You're so strong, don't give up.* And I wrote to those who'd made fitness a lifestyle and were crushing their goals, encouraging them to share their stories and empower their friends.

It's in each one of us, I wrote, *but none of us can do it alone. So, which type are you? The kind that sneers down your nose at anyone who doesn't "look the part"? Or the permanent cheerleader, shouting to the crowd a reminder that, once again, there's room on this first-place podium for everyone.*

My pulse raced as I hit "post," delivering it to over a million inboxes. I'd never written so much of my heart into an article, and despite my anonymity, I'd never felt so visible.

Comments popped up immediately.

PREACH, girl!

Thank you for this, it's needed to be said for so long.

Thank you, Fearless Felicity, for speaking on behalf of all women.

I had to laugh. The entire blog had been an accident, something I'd made for work a decade ago. But when Mia had registered for dance, the monthly fees instantly bankrupted me. Monetizing the blog saved us. Mia needed that money, which meant Daisy could *never* discover Felicity's identity. My level of influence would tear her apart with envy. She would steal the blog, ruin it, endlessly punish me—which would destroy Mia's dancing career.

Worse, though, was the simple fact that in my tiny, invisible life, this blog was the one place I felt *seen*. The one place I had influence, where I wasn't pushed aside or ignored. As Felicity, I could secretly be myself without fear of punishment or retribution.

My computer dinged with two incoming messages to Fearless Felicity. The first was a job offer which I deleted without reading. Requests for syndicated articles came in after almost every post. But I'd never said yes, never answered a single email. It wasn't worth the risk of someone tracing my identity.

I paused, though, at the second email, my curser hovering over the *delete* button. This one I opened, curious.

Hello, this is Christian from ZBC TV. I know you keep your identity a closely guarded secret, but I'd love you to appear on our network. We're starting a new health and fitness channel and would consider giving you your own show. Call me if you want to discuss options.
Sincerely, Christian Kohler

I leaned back in my chair, stunned. This was the same Christian coming to observe JD Fitness on Friday. It would mean worldwide exposure for Fearless Felicity, instant fame for me—for Bailey. My mind reeled and I bit my knuckle to hold back a giggle. For the first time, my fingers itched to respond, to at least gather details. But would he still want me when he found out I was a low-paid office manager in a tiny cubicle? And how long would it take for Daisy to weasel her way into our meetings and convince him she was the real genius behind Fearless Felicity?

I clicked *delete* before I could reconsider.

But I slammed my laptop shut and jogged to the conference room, where Lauren still hunched over her mounds of paperwork, fingers raking through her hair. Taffy wrappers littered the table and floor.

"Tell Christian he doesn't get to call the shots," I said, not bothering to knock. She leaned back in her chair, her third jacket button popping out of its hole.

"What?"

"When you give in to peoples' demands, they respect you less. If he wants to force more people on the stage, respond with a demand of your own. You need *more* money, not less. Stick to your guns so he'll think of you as an equal."

Lauren chewed the end of her pen, mulling over my words. "You think so?"

"I know so."

Bailey in the Corner

"Okay, I will." Lauren opened her laptop and furiously typed, the click of keys filling the silence as if I'd already gone. I nodded, satisfied, and walked out.

"Hey, Bailey?"

I paused and she tossed me a red taffy. When I caught it, she gave the tiniest nod and returned to her work. Red taffy? Anyone who liked cinnamon candy couldn't be too awful.

Less frustrated, I grabbed a box of fabric from my car and headed to the fabrication department. Now that I'd seen the Waterfall fabric, I hoped Lyneeka would let me use one of the six-foot tables in her off-limits room. Mia needed a mock-up of her costume, and I had two hours to sew it. But I stepped one foot inside the door and froze.

I'd expected some of the employees to have gone home, but the overly warm room howled with the sound of sewing machines, sergers, and busy employees. Even the warehouse team hustled by, noisily packing Waterfall clothes into boxes and slapping on shipping labels. These boxes were on their way to Influencers and bloggers who would receive them—and promote them—on Friday, perfectly timed to drum up sales. A carefully placed pair of pants could bring in a whole new customer base.

A box near the bottom drew my attention. It was addressed to a PO Box in Florida, but I knew it would then be forwarded to upstate New York, then to Ohio, and then finally land in a PO Box a few cities from mine. That's where I would retrieve it, so Fearless Felicity could wear them during her next workout and leave a public review.

Stella lit up when she saw me, sitting at the nearest machine as Lyneeka instructed her how to sew the Waterfall leggings.

"It's busy in here," I said, dropping my box on the table and sniffing the air. "And stuffy."

"Three days until we launch the Waterfall Collection," Lyneeka said. "We're working double shifts." She fingered my stretchy black fabric. "What on earth are you making? A black swimsuit?"

"Ballroom dance outfits for my daughter and her dance partner. This is a mock-up, before I make permanent cuts in the real fabric."

"I'm glad you aren't using *that*." She grimaced at the cheap fabric. "What will you use for the real thing?"

I had no idea. My eyes jumped from spool to spool of Waterfall fabric, where they cascaded down from the ceiling, each one a different color. "I'd kill for some of that. Even just scraps for the ruffles."

"That's the one thing you can't have." Lyneeka laughed. "But we have plenty of table space, and a couple spare machines if you're here after hours. Use whatever you need."

I should have thanked her, but my brain had already jumped four thoughts ahead, whirring through options I'd only just remembered. I couldn't use Waterfall fabric, but I had the next best thing.

"I'll be right back." I stashed my box in a corner and sped the three minutes to my parents' house. After their accident, I couldn't bring myself to sell it, so I'd raised Mia between the same walls I'd grown up in.

I burst inside, then paused to listen for any indication of Mia or Daisy's presence. Then I ducked into the master bedroom, closed myself into the small walk-in closet, and removed a false square of drywall near the floor. The open space held a box as big as a laundry basket, which I heaved out by the handle. Dust puffed into the air, and I coughed. But inside sat a treasure trove of silky soft, elegantly smooth, only-worn-once exercise gear. JD Fitness wasn't the only company that sent me free clothes in exchange for reviews—they hit my PO Box on a regular basis. I'd wear them once for an early-morning workout, wash them, then hide them in this secret box where Daisy would never find them. Many were special editions and she'd ask too many questions if she saw them.

I dug until I found last year's JD Fitness leggings and sports bra/tank combo. I had the set in red, orange, and yellow. They didn't shimmer like the Waterfall Collection, but they still sparkled enough to flatter the kids on stage.

Bailey in the Corner

"Perfect," I whispered, tucking all three outfits deep into the bottom of an oversized purse, then I grabbed a few extra items, just in case. I'd show them to Marco for approval, then cut them up before Daisy ever laid eyes on them. As far as she knew, Bailey Dupree could never afford JD Fitness clothes.

As I resealed the box behind my wall, a text came through from Mia.

I'm nervous for tonight. What if we can't learn the dance in time?

I paused, considering my answer.

You'll do your best and can feel good about it, either way. I'm working on your costumes right now. If nothing else, you two will look amazing.

I can't wait to see them! Thanks Mom!

Back at JD Fitness, I started on my all-black mock-up. When I finally basted the panels together, I glanced at the clock and grinned. Marco and the kids would arrive any second. I couldn't wait to show Mia her dress and teach Jackson more Samba. A shiver of anticipation zipped down my spine over another night with Marco. I wanted to tell him every detail about my day, especially the two, maybe three, new friends I'd made. He would be impressed.

At last, Marco texted and I ran outside to meet them. Mia squeezed me into a hug, and Marco waved hello with his cane—shiny black with a matching knob. But Jackson stormed straight past, into the building, shouting a curse word over his shoulder.

Chapter 14

"Is Jackson okay?" I asked, rubbing my arms as the cold wind picked up. Marco scratched his forehead. "I'll go talk to him." He handed me the bag of takeout and followed his nephew inside. Mia and I waited a few long minutes before following, but Jackson didn't sound any happier. He leaned against the wall in the little lobby, hands deep in his pockets, scowling. Marco stood close by, his shoulders hunched, at the end of a long, slow sigh.

When Jackson saw us, he scooted away from his uncle. "Whatever, let's go eat."

Mia gave me a worried, sideways glance before I led them to the warehouse kitchenette. It was a safer location than the main cafeteria. Daisy rarely stayed until seven, but better safe than sorry—especially with Dominic nearby.

"Mia took control of my radio on the drive here," Marco said. Everyone was digging into their burritos, sitting on the cement floor. The lingering smell of sweaty bodies competed with the delicious aroma of Mexican food. "That girl loves 90's music."

"All I did was turn up the volume," Mia argued. "It was a good song!"

"It was weird," Jackson grumbled.

"Crash Test Dummies aren't weird, they're obscure. There's a difference."

"I'll take your word on it," Jackson said.

Bailey in the Corner

I finished the last of my food and pulled out the mockup dress.

"You made this today?" Marco put down his burrito to examine the short, delicate sleeve of Mia's dress. Its tight-fitting bodice fanned out into a ruffly skirt. It would twirl in a full, wide circle. "It's perfect."

While Mia ducked into the locker room to try it on, I checked for any signs of Daisy, then laid out my secret gym clothes on the table.

"I think I'll use these for the ruffles." I pulled the fabric between my hands. "It's brand new and it sparkles when it's stretched."

Marco picked up one of the shirts, rubbing it between his fingers. "It sparkles?"

"They'll shine like stars under the bright stage lights."

His mouth turned up as he placed the shirt back on the table. "Where did you get these?" His eyes darted to the dingy clothes on my body, then back to the ones on the table. Heat rose up my neck, but Mia saved me by returning from the locker room. The all-black dress hung limply off her body, the skirt dragging on the floor. I grabbed my pins and tightened and shortened so I'd know exactly what size to cut the real fabric.

"I feel like Marco," Mia grumbled, when I accidentally poked her with a pin.

"Me?" Marco watched the process with interest.

"Yeah, colorless. Do you always wear all black?"

"Mostly, though sometimes I branch out to dark gray. It makes it easy to pick out my clothes in the morning."

Mia scrunched up her nose like he was crazy, but then rolled her eyes back at me. "Better than my mom. She only dresses like . . . a mom."

"Hey!" But I knew what she meant.

"I've watched you ogle nice clothes in the thrift store," Mia said, "but you buy the ones with stains. I don't get it—especially if you own stuff like this." She motioned to the clothes on the table. "Where did these come from?"

"I don't remember," I lied.

Marco's eyebrow twitched. "Which one do you like best?"

"Red."

"You should try it on."

I glanced at the door, where Daisy could walk in and catch me with the clothes. "No."

"Come on, Mom," Mia begged. "These are so cool."

"I just want to see how the fabric sparkles when it's stretched." Marco sounded too earnest, like he was trying not to spook me. "I'd have Mia try it on, but it won't fit her."

I stared them down for five full seconds. "Only if someone locks the big metal door. No one can see me."

Marco jumped to his feet, spinning his cane as he fulfilled my request. Mia shoved me toward the locker room. My feet grew heavier with every step, but when I stripped off my black pants and slid my legs into the red ones, I sighed. They felt like butter, conforming to every bend and divot on my legs.

I put on the red sports bra, and the new fabric clung softly to me, not abrasive like my old black one. And as I pulled the white tank top over my head, it felt like diving seamlessly into a pool, weightless and smooth. They even smelled new. Could clothes be more perfect?

I kicked my gross ones into a heap on the floor, then returned to the warehouse. Mia's jaw dropped wide enough to fit six burritos, and Marco stiffened, sitting taller.

"Holy shit, Mom, you look hot!"

"Dollar." I held out my hand.

"Worth it, again," she said, as she dug through her dance bag for money. "But have you seen yourself?"

"Am I sparkling?" I joked, spinning in a slow circle.

Marco nodded, rising to his feet. "How do you feel?"

"Honestly?" Why had I stopped wearing clothes like this? I had a very good reason, but right now, I didn't want to remember. "Amazing. Can I go change back now?"

Bailey in the Corner

"No," Mia said, at the exact moment Marco said, "Definitely not." He rubbed his palms on his shirt like they were sweating. "Should we dance?"

I needed to change back. I couldn't get used to these clothes—but they felt so perfect.

"Do I look okay?"

"Yes, you do. But what do *you* think? Do you like the outfit?"

Daisy would hate it. "A little too much."

"Then you should wear it. No shame, no fear."

Maybe he was right. "A few more minutes won't hurt anything."

Marco grinned, one side of his smile reaching higher than the other, then he held out his hand—an invitation to dance. For the first time in years, I didn't hide my legs under a desk or fold my arms to cover my shirt. I felt the opposite of embarrassed. Great, even. So, I placed my hand in Marco's and let him lead me onto the dance floor.

Marco switched instantly into serious mode. No more joking, no casual chitchat. He turned on the music and we dove into reviewing what we'd learned last night. As the kids improved, he increased the pace until they could dance the Cha-Cha segment at full speed.

"Ready for Samba?" Marco eyed Jackson, who was tugging the bottom of his shirt. "There's a lot to learn so I'll throw it at you fast, then we'll still have two days to nail it down."

Mia nodded enthusiastically, her hair bobbing against her shoulders, but Jackson stuffed his hands into his pockets.

"It starts like this." Marco walked me through the opening steps. Like yesterday, it felt clinical, professional, like solving physics equations with your body. Footwork first. Roll through your feet so your hips naturally follow, then add upper-body technique with a flash of flare.

Samba rolls came next, my back pressed against Marco's chest, his right arm pulling me tight against him while his left hand engulfed mine out wide. Our bodies spun, suctioned together inside a whirlpool.

"I like how you hook your foot around mine," Jackson said, as he and Mia attempted Samba rolls for the fourth time. "It keeps me grounded in place while I spin."

"Yes, good," Marco said. "Practice again."

Clinical. Like math.

Except this time, I wore ridiculously wonderful pants. Each time my body pressed against Marco's, I felt *aware*—of everything. Confident. Engaged. Instead of standing to the side and watching Marco teach, I jumped in and helped. The second Jackson started to shut down, I pulled him aside to walk through the steps. It turned out, he wasn't easily frustrated. He was easily frustrated *with Marco*. The fourth time I pulled Jackson away, Marco mouthed a thank-you and I had to laugh. It wasn't me, it was the pants. I was a different person, delirious from the fact that I had no reason to be embarrassed. A weight had lifted from my shoulders, like toilet paper no longer trailing from my shoe, and I kept laughing. And laughing.

"Are we done for the day?" Marco directed the question anywhere but at Jackson. "Or should we start the last dance? After Rhumba, all that's left are the transitions and the lifts."

"Rhumba!" Mia cheered, and Jackson lifted one shoulder. I knew him well enough now to know that meant yes. I nodded to Marco, and we dove back in.

But Rhumba was a whole different adventure. Where Samba was bouncy and quick, Rhumba was deliberate and sensual, a tease between the dancers. You drew close together, then pulled away. Almost lovers, then torn apart.

Marco kept his game-face on, ever the dance professional. Even the kids never once giggled. I, on the other hand, couldn't stay serious. I hadn't felt this sexy since my college days, and the first time Marco's hand trailed down my arm, my stomach tingled. I glanced at his eyes when I should have faced away.

He was looking at me too.

Bailey in the Corner

"I need a break," Jackson finally said. He slumped against the wall, but Marco urged him back up.

"We're nearly done."

"I'm tired." Jackson picked at a scab near his wrist, his shirt wet from exertion.

"Fifteen more minutes," Marco said, but Jackson removed his shoes. I showed Marco my watch and the tension in his shoulders relaxed. "Sorry, guys, I didn't realize the time." It was ten thirty—we'd danced for three full hours. Mia collapsed into a chair, but Jackson stuffed his feet into his sneakers and stormed into the kitchenette, pointedly ignoring his uncle.

"How about Blue Juice," I said, digging through a drawer. "It'll replace all those electrolytes we just lost." I pulled out four little packets and tossed one to each person.

Jackson caught his and froze, fingers wrapped around the packet. "Blue Juice?" He held it reverently as he peered at the words across the top. "My dad used to give me these after soccer games. Then last year, he got mad at my mom and threw my water bottle against the fridge. It burst open and dyed everything blue for a few days." His voice sounded far away, his head tilted so his hair draped to the left.

"I've never heard that story," Marco said softly.

"It doesn't matter." Jackson ripped open his Blue Juice and dumped the powder into his water bottle. "It was a long time ago."

"Hey, Jackson," I said, "want to see something cool?"

Everyone gathered their bags, and I led them to the fabrication room, hoping Lyneeka wouldn't freak out when I brought strangers inside. Only she and Stella remained, bent over their noisy sewing machines. They didn't look up as both kids stopped, gaping at the waterfalls of fabric hanging from the ceiling.

"You sent me a picture of this," Mia said. "But what is this place?"

"It's where they sew the clothes. But come here." I led Jackson to an entire wall of JD Fitness supplements, half of which were Blue Juice.

"Holy shit," he said, eyes trailing over the endless supply of his favorite drink.

"That's a dollar," I said, holding out my hand.

"Are you serious?"

"She's serious," Mia grumbled.

He dug into his bag and tossed a dollar in my general direction. It fluttered onto the floor, but as I scooped it up, the corner of his mouth lifted. I snuck him a couple spare packets of Blue Juice right as Lyneeka and Stella stopped sewing and shoved back their chairs, hard enough that they crashed to the ground.

"I'm sorry," I squeaked. "I know I shouldn't have brought them in here!"

But Lyneeka's eyes scanned every inch of my body. "Where the hell have you been hiding those clothes? Girl, you look damn good!"

Before I could answer, before I even started to scramble for an explanation, Jackson stepped between us and held out his hand to Lyneeka.

"That's a dollar."

Chapter 15

"Where did these clothes come from?" Lyneeka said after absently handing Jackson a dollar. He snickered and stuffed the crinkled-up bill into his pocket.

"They're old." I chewed on my lip, looking anywhere but at her face. "They've been in my closet for years."

"No, they're from last fall's collection. I sewed them myself."

Marco and Mia's eyes bounced between us, following our argument like bobbleheads.

"I'll go change."

"Don't," Stella butted in, her voice soft. "You look . . ."

"Better than usual?"

Stella grinned, sheepishly. "Really pretty."

"And who is this?" Lyneeka leaned back to assess every inch of Marco. Finally, her eyes lit up. "He's pretty cute."

"Marco," I said, and so there'd be no confusion, I added, "He's dating Daisy."

Lyneeka frowned, eyes guarded as Marco objected, "Only sort of—"

"Yes, you are. And this is my daughter Mia and her dance partner, Jackson. Jared's letting us use the stage to teach them a ballroom routine."

Stella's face lit up when I mentioned Jared, her long, black ponytail dangling over her shoulder. "You should wear that to work tomorrow—Jared won't be able to take his eyes off you."

I shook my head. "I'm never wearing it again."

"But you look so confident!" Stella insisted.

Marco unscrewed the knob on his cane and flipped up a straw, then raised it to his mouth to drink.

Lyneeka peered at him. "What are you doing?"

"I'm thirsty."

"But what is *that?*"

He held up the straw poking out of his cane. "It's my water bottle. Sometimes I get stuck in meetings and need a drink, so I engineered this cane into a self-cooling tube. With a straw."

"You made that?" Stella asked.

"It holds quite a bit. The exterior is lined with an anti-condensation film, so it doesn't sweat, and a tiny battery pack in the bottom powers the miniature cooling system."

Mia peered closer. "You turned your cane into a fridge?"

Marco laughed. "Basically, but it wasn't easy. My first attempt leaked coolant all over the floor at a black-tie fundraiser." He cringed. "It oozed all over the bottom of a lady's gown. Completely ruined it."

Stella gasped. "How did you fix it?"

"I threw it away and started over." He shook his cane, the water sloshing faintly inside. "This is my ninth attempt. It's come a long way." He winked at Mia. "The first eight ended in horrifying disasters, with coolant in places it didn't belong, and me feeling like an idiot."

What would it be like to have a wild idea, and just . . . try it? Without fear that I'd embarrass Daisy and start a war?

"Is that what happened to your hands?" Mia eyed the long scars trailing from his fingertips to under his sleeves. "Did you spill acid on them?"

Marco's smile faltered. "No, I got those in Africa." His voice shifted. "In a diamond mine."

"I thought you didn't get your diamonds from mines?" I said.

Bailey in the Corner

"I don't, but my dad does. My whole life, he groomed me to take over his import business." He unclipped the cuffs on his shirt and rolled up his sleeves. The scars traveled all the way to his elbows. "But he didn't think I'd be so rebellious. In high school he wanted me to work with him, so I signed up for every after-school sport on the planet. In college he wanted me to learn business, so I studied engineering instead. After I graduated, he took me to Africa to meet his diamond suppliers. They treated us like royalty, put us up in the fanciest hotels and restaurants, but I snuck down to the mine to see where the diamonds came from."

I'd seen enough documentaries to know about the African diamond trade, with kids in the mines instead of in school, and overseers with machine guns. Perhaps I was wrong, but Marco's hands said otherwise.

"The mine was awful," Marco continued. "Hundreds of people dug into the side of a mountain with only their hands, not even tools, to feel for the diamonds. Half of them were kids, fingers gnarled with calluses, hoping to find a big one and get double pay for the day. I walked right up to the cliff wall and joined them, copying the way they prodded their fingers into the hard dirt, inspecting every rock in case it wasn't really a rock. It took my dad six hours to find me. By then, my fingers had split and bloody dirt covered my arms. He had to take me to a hospital to clean me up."

Stella put her hand over her mouth, and Mia's eyes darkened. Not even Jackson twitched, leaning toward his uncle as he listened.

"That day I decided to create diamonds in a lab instead of mining them. When I told my dad, he flew into a rage, chucking his paperweights at me. But my grandpa gave me start-up money and I bought equipment the next week, then I brought on my roommate to run my lab while I traveled the country, convincing people to buy synthetic diamonds instead of imported. So far, it's going well."

I pressed my palm against my chest. "How did you find the courage to stand up to him?"

Marco held up his hands, permanently marked by that day in the mine. "I'll never forget what I saw, or the relief I felt when I walked away forever. It was time to forge my own path and stop following someone else's."

My hand slipped into my pocket, to the picture of Mia and Daisy I'd torn in half. I'd walked away from Daisy too, but I didn't share Marco's confidence. I wasn't anywhere near free of her. Not as long as she continued inflicting punishments on me.

But Lyneeka kept her eyes on Marco, studying him. "Did you say you're dating Daisy? You're not married?"

Marco stuffed his hands in his pockets and leaned back against a table. "Divorced, two years ago."

"She cheated on him," Jackson said, and Marco cleared his throat. But Jackson tilted his head, looking at his uncle. "What happened next with you and Grandpa? Are things better now?"

"Not really. I've tried, but I'm not sure we'll ever get there."

Jackson nodded, staring hard at the ground, but then he pushed through the middle of our circle and fled the room.

"Shit," Marco muttered, running his hand through his hair. "He's probably thinking about his own dad."

He followed Jackson but I grabbed his arm. "He won't want us to see him cry. Give him a minute."

"I'll find him," Mia said, "but first, you owe me a dollar." A hint of a smile reached Marco's face as he handed her a bill from his wallet. "Also, it's pretty cool how you stood up to your asshole dad." He snatched back the dollar and Mia ran out laughing.

We said goodbye to Lyneeka and Stella, then Marco followed me back to the gym to collect our things. The only light came from the small conference room where Lauren likely still pored over documents on her laptop.

Bailey in the Corner

Marco walked straight back out onto the stage, his shoes clicking in the cavernous room. "While we wait, can we run through the Rhumba again? I haven't figured out the ending."

I paused, aware of exactly how alone we were in the big empty room.

"You can tell me about your day while we dance. You made a new friend?"

I took Marco's hand in the center of the stage. "I did." He led me through the first steps. "In fact, I talked to three new people today. One was Lauren, who threw a ball of paper at my head. But also, Stella and Lyneeka. Well, I've known Lyneeka for years, but never really talked to her."

"Lauren threw paper at your head?"

"She's complicated."

"Clearly. But well done." Marco squeezed my hand while we danced, and my skin warmed. He always acted so comfortable—the way he'd opened up about his dad to a room full of strangers? It took all my nerve just to start a simple conversation with Stella. Why couldn't I be more like him? Walk away from Daisy like he walked away from his dad, without shaking in fear? I must look like such a coward.

Marco turned the music lower with the remote in his pocket. "How did Daisy take the new, outgoing version of you?"

"She's pretty mad. To start, she brought me a bunch of birthday gifts, but I blew her off and left."

"Gutsy," Marco said. He pulled me close to his right side, then spun me across to his left. "Maybe she'll realize the gifts should have come on your birthday, not after."

"It was terrifying. And then I made things worse in the gym this morning. She's furious. She literally declared war."

"She used those words?"

"Yeah, like we were back on an elementary school playground."

Sweat glistened on Marco's forehead as he angled his hand across my back to turn my body to the right. Each of his fingers slid across the bare skin on my shoulder.

"Then, during today's auditions, Daisy insulted the auditioners and the whole show fell apart, so I gave them pointers through their headsets."

"Did it help?"

I grinned. "Everyone cheered for me after the show. Jared even remembered my name."

"You must have made an impression." Marco twisted my body in three full turns. "What do you think about this final spin, for the end of our dance?"

I paused—I'd hardly paid attention to the steps. No one ever asked my opinion. "What about this?" I took his hands and led him through the final two measures, changing Mia's steps so she faced the audience, adding flare to the end of the routine.

"You're right," he said. "Much better. So how did Daisy take it?"

"She stormed out. I guess I don't blame her. I've let her call the shots for so long, I'm sure she's confused why I would suddenly change things up."

Marco paused mid-step, his eyebrows furrowing. "She's confused that you'd help people, instead of letting her hurt them? It sounds like you succeeded where she'd failed, and she's jealous."

"Honestly, in twenty years, I've never stood up to her." It had felt good to hold my ground, and I didn't regret helping any of those people. I chewed on my lower lip. "But part of me wonders if all this is worth upsetting the balance between us. I really hurt her feelings."

Marco dropped my hands and took a step back. "So, you're allowed to boost her career, but if you boost yours, *you're* the jerk?"

"That's not it." But the words tasted like sandpaper, dry and flat.

"She's manipulating you, Bailey."

Bailey in the Corner

"If you met her brother, you'd understand. He treats her like a bug he can flick around. Sometimes she treats me the same way. She doesn't know better."

"And that makes it okay?"

"No, but things are worse now because he's back in town. I know she loves me like a sister. Maybe she doesn't see what she's doing."

"She sees." Marco stepped closer. "She laughed at you, Bailey, on your birthday. We sat at the restaurant, and they brought cake and sang happy birthday, and she couldn't stop laughing. I didn't know why at the time, but it was because she stole *your* birthday cake. She ruined *your* special day. Two days in a row, you've saved the company from her screw-ups, but she's made you feel so awful that it's easier to defend her than to face her. Do you see that?"

Marco's words bounced inside my head like a spiked ball, trying painfully to fit among my memories of Daisy. She joined my family when I needed a shield from my mom, she gave me courage to go on adventures when I otherwise wouldn't have dared, she pulled me out of depression when I couldn't stand on my own two feet. Except every one of those memories came with their own spikes. Did she move in because we were sisters, or because I was her only option? Did she take me on her adventures to teach me courage, or because she needed my voice of warning? Did she hire me at Lucky 7 Gym because I needed a job, or so she could feel superior? I closed my eyes and took slow, steadying breaths as Marco's spiked ball settled in, right at home amongst the other spindly memories.

"Why do I keep doing this?" I whispered. "Why do I keep defending her?"

Marco inched closer as he rested his second hand on my other shoulder. "She's become a bad habit, and habits are hard to break."

"How did you find the courage to walk away from your dad?"

Marco's face sagged. "I hit rock bottom. I'd had enough." His eyes lingered on the white lines tracing his arms. "The scars inside me were much worse." He dropped both hands to his sides but didn't step away. "Is that where you're at with Daisy? Have you had enough?"

I wanted to say yes, to declare my freedom to the world, but I couldn't say the words. A deeper truth lay buried inside me.

She'll never let you walk away.

"Want to hear something stupid? I use tiny dumbbells in the gym to make sure she feels stronger than me." The words solidified how pathetic this bad habit had become. Marco looped a finger around one of mine, a gesture of solidarity. He knew what it felt like to be stuck in this hole and his touch grounded me. I wasn't alone.

"You're worth so much more than you think." These words carried no spikes. And as they entered my chest, they rose from my heart like they'd always been there, buried deep, forgotten until Marco stirred them awake.

I kept my eyes glued to our fingers, nervous to look at Marco's face. "You're right. She's a bad habit I don't know how to break."

"You should keep trying, though." Marco motioned to my clothes. "I like this version of you."

I cracked a smile. "The version that dresses above my pay range?"

Marco laughed and stepped back, leaving my finger cold as he dropped it. "No, the version with enough confidence to wear them."

My eyes met Marco's as his words sank in. Everything I'd done today built people's self-confidence—in the gym this morning with Stella, during auditions this afternoon with the microphone, even encouraging Lauren to stand up to Christian. I'd told them to find their best selves and put that version out into the world.

Where was that version of me?

Any time she peeked her head out, Daisy squashed her. But Marco didn't. Marco kept digging and digging, showing me new ways to find her, and I didn't want him to stop. I didn't want to hide anymore, I wanted to be *me,* whoever that was.

Bailey in the Corner

Marco grinned, as if he could read my thoughts. "You should dress like this for work tomorrow."

"Daisy would hate it." My answer came instantly, out of habit. A bad habit.

"So what?"

Daisy had to be the better dressed between us, just like she had to be the stronger lifter.

"I thought you wanted to break this bad habit?"

I did, desperately, with every ounce of my yearning. But would it be worth continuing this war? A hidden piece of me clawed her way out, while the rest searched for excuses to back down.

"I'm not fancy, Marco. I'm not cute or trendy or interesting. I'm a plain, boring mom."

The corner of his mouth quirked up. "I know first-hand there's nothing plain or boring about you. Daisy knows it too; that's why she keeps you hidden away."

"Okay, so then what do I do?"

Excitement danced in his eyes, filling the space between us. I wanted to be excited too, about whatever came next in my life. Whatever came *after* Daisy.

"You dress like this without caring if Daisy feels threatened. Fearless Felicity just wrote about how we should pull each other up, instead of knocking each other down. You should read it before tomorrow. You're *both* allowed to look good."

I laughed, suddenly weightless. Why had I sent that advice into the world, but never applied it to myself?

"I'm nervous," I admitted. "What will people say?" More importantly, what would Daisy say? She knew I couldn't afford these clothes, but she'd never piece together the clues and peg me as Fearless Felicity. Not if I stuck with common outfits.

"Who cares? You're not dressing up for them, you're dressing up for *you*. You deserve to feel confident—there's nothing sexier." He nudged me with his elbow. "Stella was right, Jared won't be able to take his eyes off you."

The kids burst in, their laughter piercing the bubble around us. As Marco left the stage, his words washed over me like a cold shower. I was in love with Jared DiMaggio, world's greatest super trainer—I'd almost forgotten.

Chapter 16

It took twenty minutes to pick out my outfit, but I finally slid into an endlessly soft turquoise sports bra with black accents, matching leggings, and a tank top. I finished with mascara and pink lip gloss, then curled the ends of my long hair for the first time in five years. I hardly recognized myself without a braid.

"Holy shit, Mom," Mia said, when I walked into the kitchen. She put a dollar on the table without being asked, then circled me like a vulture. "It's like I don't even know you."

"Do I look okay?"

"Better than okay." She squeezed me into a hug. "You're going to have the best day of your life."

I hugged her back. How much unhealthy behavior had I modeled for her by allowing Daisy to tear down my confidence? I hoped she could feel my apology through my arms. She deserved a mother who was an example of strength and courage. I would be that for her, from now on.

When Mia released me, I tucked her ripped photo into my pocket and dropped her off at school. Maybe the pants had tampered with my reasoning, but my fears over Daisy fizzled to a dull whisper.

Marco texted as I pulled into work.

How do you feel this morning?

Good! And nervous . . .

You've got this.

He was right, I could do this. My fingers fidgeted excitedly as I jogged inside, two minutes before the morning workout. I couldn't wait for Stella and Lyneeka to see me. And Jared. Maybe he'd ask me to assist during the workout. Last week, I would have turned him down. But today? No way.

The office was silent when I entered, so I dumped Green Fizz into my water bottle and chugged it while I hurried to the gym. But I stopped, two feet in. The workout hadn't started. Jared wasn't even in the room. Or Lauren, or Daisy. Thirty-ish employees milled around, waiting, bouncing in their shoes as their Green Fizz kicked in.

Stella's eyes doubled in size when she saw me. "You look amazing."

"You too." Black and white triangles decorated her tank top, the black perfectly matching her strikingly dark hair, and the tattooed dagger that poked out beneath her shorts. "Where's Jared?"

"No one's seen him yet. Lauren, either." She twisted her fingers, eyes darting around as she shifted her weight.

"Are you okay?"

"I think I'm going to audition today." She hid her face with her jet-black ponytail.

"YES!" I pumped my fist in the air. "What made you change your mind?"

She dropped her hair, her spine straightening. "Fearless Felicity published a new article. She said fitness should be about real people with real body sizes, and it made me think, why not? Why shouldn't I try? I got so excited I could hardly sleep all night."

"You'll nail it."

"Where's Jared?" Stella's eyes roamed the gym as the clock switched to nine-fifteen.

My Green Fizz was kicking in and my hands tingled, the buzz spreading up my arms. I bounced from foot to foot, unable to hold still. "I don't know, but a room full of people filled with energy from a bottle isn't a good thing."

Bailey in the Corner

My phone beeped with a message from Mia.

You looked amazing today, Mom. Just wanted you to know!

I grinned, adrenaline bursting through my body. "Why don't we teach? Just until Jared gets here."

Stella's eyes widened. "Are we qualified?"

I knew Stella was, she'd already told me about her high fitness class. I'd taught too, until Lucky 7 Gym fired me. My Ballroom Cardio classes didn't include weightlifting, but I'd gotten my Personal Trainer license right after I'd earned my journalism degree, to qualify me to write the gym's newsletter. My boss, Doug, had been thrilled—especially after he read my first few articles.

But Daisy wasn't.

Just don't take on too much, she'd said. *You'll spiral into another depression.* It had taken her six months to get licensed, but it only took me two.

Jared's employees were getting antsy, so I pulled Stella to the front of the stage and called for everyone's attention. "I don't know where Jared is, but I'll get us started until he gets here." When no one objected, I said, "Stella, want to warm us up?"

She got our blood pumping, then I opened up with squats, interspersed with intervals of cardio. We took turns leading, then walking around to correct form, high-fiving each time we switched places and making everyone laugh. It turned out that Stella was a natural entertainer, with a dry sarcasm that kept the mood light. I'd forgotten how fun teaching a class could be.

But then Daisy walked in, Cinnamon right behind her.

"What the hell are you doing? And what are you wearing?" She pounded over to the stereo system and shut off our background music with one loud thump.

I froze, mid-lunge, and everyone swiveled to face Daisy. Her burgundy ringlets stuck up from her ponytail like a crown, and her perfectly muscular body was swathed in silver Waterfall clothes. Cinnamon's outfit was identical in every way except hers was pastel green.

Daisy's eyes raked slowly down my body, taking in my flowing hair, my shirt, my pants, my shoes. Then her eyes snapped back to my face with a mixture of disgust and pity.

"I can't believe you're stealing clothes again." She shook her head as the entire room absorbed her words. "I thought you'd stopped."

The room spun. Murmurs bounced from lips to ears, too quiet to make out, though I knew exactly what they'd said. Why would anyone believe my word over Daisy's? At JD Fitness, she was royalty.

"And you?" Daisy strutted straight up to Stella. "I'm impressed someone your size had the nerve to get up here." Daisy rested her hand gently on Stella's arm, a show of sarcastic pity. "You poor thing, you must have read Fearless Felicity's article. Did you really sign up to audition? JD Fitness does not put fat girls on stage. You'll never be cast."

Stella's skin paled, so I stepped right next to her, linking my arm in hers.

"Don't worry," Daisy continued, strolling toward the exit, "I erased your name from the audition list. Saves you the trouble of having to walk all the way over there."

Cinnamon stayed in her shadow, smirking all the way. "I don't know why people read Fearless Felicity anymore."

As if they hadn't gushed over every Felicity article published in the past five years.

"I should start my own blog," Daisy said. "My first article will be 'Why Fearless Felicity is Wildly Overrated.'" Daisy paused at the door, then called back over her shoulder. "By the way, Jared called an emergency department head meeting half an hour ago. You're both late. Stellar first impression."

Then she pushed through the door and disappeared.

Chapter 17

The six other department heads were already seated at the large conference room table, Jared and Lauren at the top, and Daisy in the seat of honor at Jared's right. Behind them, a white board displayed pictures of every auditioner for MaxFit99, with scribbled notes that had filled the air with the sharp aroma of dry-erase ink. Stella and I dropped into the last two chairs.

"Is this everyone?" Jared, sporting a JD Fitness hoodie, seemed as focused as ever. Lauren, though, had dark circles under her eyes and water dripping from her hair like she'd dunked it in a sink. In fact, she still wore yesterday's pointy-collared gray jacket. Had she slept here last night?

"We have a serious problem," Lauren said. "Fearless Felicity posted a new article yesterday. Jared, will you read a piece of it?"

He cleared his throat, then paced as he read off his phone.

"'When did the word 'fit' become synonymous with 'skinny'? What about the moms whose bodies changed when they grew a new human? What about those whose genetic makeup lands them larger than a size two? Did you know, the average pants size for American women is sixteen? Yet they're bombarded with ads pressuring them to shrink dangerously small. What about people just beginning their fitness journey, or those who are working hard but haven't yet reached their goals? Why do we only celebrate when someone reaches that impossible size zero? We should celebrate the new mom trying to strengthen her body, and the dad who wants to be a healthier example for his kids, even if they aren't stressing about calorie counts.

"Being 'fit' isn't a final destination, it's a lifestyle. Where's the representation for people at every stage? When I pick a workout to stream, I don't want to see a stage filled with Influencers I can't possibly emulate. I want to see a diverse cast full of people who power through their good days, but also show up when they're feeling off. I want to see people who love their bodies no matter their size, shape, or age. And I want to see people pushing through their struggles, inspiring me to do the same.

"So, I ask again, why did we allow 'fit' to become defined as 'skinny'? They aren't the same, and they never will be. From now on, when I pick my workouts, I'll be choosing programs representing real people with healthy casts, who love their bodies no matter their size. And to those of you feeling discouraged, keep going. Keep growing those muscles, keep lifting those weights, keep putting in the work. But don't do it because someone said you need to be skinnier. Do it because you're strong, you're beautiful, and you're courageous. Never let the fitness industry define what 'beauty' should look like for you. You're beautiful exactly the way you are.'"

Jared returned to his chair and Daisy snorted a laugh. "She has no clue. No one would exercise with a cast full of fat people."

"You're wrong," Lauren said, scrolling through her phone. "Felicity didn't call us out by name, but every other fitness blog has. They've rallied around her, reposting her article on every platform. She's gone beyond viral—over ten million hits."

I opened the blog on my phone. For months I'd hovered barely above one million subscribers. Now I had six, and Lauren was right, over ten million views. I bit my lip to keep from smiling.

But Lauren rubbed the dark circles under her eyes. "People are calling for a boycott."

"Would they do that?" Lyneeka asked, her eyebrows drawing together.

Bailey in the Corner

"I think so. I've watched it unfold on my computer all night. By next week, the world will have moved on, but for now the hate mail's flooding in. A boycott right now would destroy MaxFit99."

Her words grew inside me like a gnarled tree. I'd written that article thinking only about Daisy and Stella. I hadn't considered how it could affect the company, or the entire industry. The last thing I wanted was to hurt JD Fitness.

"There's more."

More?

Lauren closed the conference room door before focusing back on the rest of us. "We dropped every penny we had into MaxFit99, plus took out hefty loans now long overdue. We offered huge payments for the cast, bought all new cameras and sound systems. We even pre-fabricated the Waterfall Collection assuming we'd make huge sales on Friday."

"What does that mean?" Cinnamon asked.

"It means we need record-breaking sales this weekend, or JD Fitness goes bankrupt. Everyone will be out of a job before Monday."

A heavy silence fell over the room. It crept into my bones, into my joints, into my knuckles. I hadn't meant to cause so much damage, I'd just wanted to put Daisy in her place. My stomach flipped, threatening to lose its contents right there on the table.

"What about the TV deal?" I asked. "Could that save us?"

"It's unlikely at this point," Jared said. "No one's pointing any fingers at Michael Kay right now. After this, I'd be surprised if Christian comes at all on Friday."

Lauren tapped the end of her pen against her teeth. "This got out of control so fast, I don't know how to fix it."

Maybe I could. I had an idea . . .

"Marketing?" Lauren asked, grabbing Daisy's attention. "Any ideas?"

Cinnamon opened her mouth, then closed it, while Daisy's face twisted into a sneer. "We publicly denounce Fearless Felicity?"

"Denounce?" Lauren motioned to the wall behind her. "Felicity pegged us perfectly. Every single candidate fits in the same demographic: overly fit and extremely skinny. The real fitness community spans every shape, size, and age." Lauren slumped back in her chair. "I just wish she'd waited until next week to call us out."

The silence smothered the room like a blanket.

Still, though, I had an idea. Daisy would hate it, just like the last time I voiced a big idea. I had run the Lucky 7 Gym newsletter for a year, and our following had jumped from three hundred people to twenty thousand. Everyone kept asking when I'd teach my own class, so I finally brought it up with Doug.

Ballroom Cardio classes? Let's give it a shot.

But when I told Daisy the news, she turned on her blindingly bright smile.

Just don't embarrass yourself. If they discover their beloved journalist is an inexperienced receptionist, you'll lose all your followers.

Embarrass myself? After all these years, her words still made me seethe. I looked at Stella, whose hands trembled in her lap, then at Lauren, who was a puddle of anxiety. Even Lyneeka picked the callouses on her fingers as her leg bounced under the table.

But I knew exactly how to fix this. I'd spent enough years as a public figure to understand what the masses would receive as authentic, and what would seem contrived. I couldn't let the company fall apart, but speaking up would begin a new round of Daisy's wrath.

My eyes darted to my turquoise pants, my bright white shirt, my hair flowing over my left shoulder. I'd forgotten how sexy I looked, how sexy I felt. I could do this. Whether or not anyone knew it, I was perfectly qualified to save us all.

"Confidence is sexy," I said. Every face turned directly to me. "We need to rebrand MaxFit99, but we need it to look like this was our intention all along, not a reaction to Felicity's article."

Bailey in the Corner

Lauren's forehead scrunched in confusion. "And our new slogan is 'Confidence Is Sexy'?"

"No, because not everyone cares about feeling sexy. But every one of our customers cares about feeling fit and confident. I'm thinking 'Fitness for Everyone.' Hear me out." I pointed to the wall of photographs behind her. "You're right that they're all equally slender, but you know what we *do* have? Age variety. We have college athletes, moms, and a young grandpa. I bet we have people who need to modify certain exercises due to long-term injuries. Those are authentic disadvantages that make them relatable role models for people at home."

"Keep going," Lauren said, perking up.

"Do you know what they all have in common?"

"They're unattractive," Daisy muttered.

I completely ignored her. "They're all confident. Nothing's more appealing than someone with the courage to fight for their goals. Size and age won't matter if we fill that stage with people who have the drive to push through their real weaknesses. Every person at home will want to work hard along with them."

Lauren considered my idea. "Confidence . . . is sexy."

"It's brilliant," Jared said.

"It really is," she said, zeroing in on me. "But how can we pull it off quick enough to curb Friday's boycott?"

"Easy." My own confidence flowed through me. "Friday's program is still a big mystery."

"We've kept everything a secret!" Lauren practically squealed the words, her relief exuding onto the rest of us. "No one has seen a glimpse of our Waterfall Collection, and the only person on the MaxFit99 ads so far is Jared, because we haven't finished auditions yet."

"Exactly. Tomorrow, after you pick the new cast, we do a quick photo shoot of everyone wearing the Waterfall Collection. Then we spam the entire world with ads for the twenty-four hours leading up to the promo. No one will guess we reconsidered our casting choices last minute, because who could pull together an entire marketing campaign overnight?"

"Can you?" Lauren asked, cocking her head. "In only a few hours?"

My eyes darted to Daisy, whose mouth hung open. Lauren should have posed that question to the marketing team. Instead, she stayed focused on me.

"Come on, we all know you do Daisy's work," Lauren said.

Daisy's skin turned as white as the wall behind her, then she lifted her chin and spoke straight to Jared. "Are you sure you want to put your future in Bee's hands? After all, she got fired from her last job for bad marketing."

All heads turned to me, awkwardness and shock on their faces. Daisy didn't usually insult me publicly or cause a scene where others could see. Punishments usually came later, quietly, like a knife hidden inside a jacket, stabbing where only the two of us could see. This was something different, a knee-jerk reaction to scare me back into my corner. This was war.

But I was tired of backing down.

Lauren ignored Daisy completely. "Bailey, can you make the ads?"

"Definitely."

The color finally returned to Lauren's face. "Let's pray this works. Our only hurdle now is picking a diverse enough cast. They're still all too slender."

"I'll do it," Stella said.

"Ew," Daisy mumbled.

I pressed my arm against Stella's, trying to send confidence through our connection. "She's perfectly qualified. Not only is she a certified personal trainer, but she taught a popular high fitness class back in Ohio. Let her audition this afternoon, you'll see what I mean."

"Great idea," Jared said, leaning forward on his elbows. "Come audition, I'll give you a shot."

He finally ended the meeting, and we all gathered our things. But as we did, Cinnamon's voice floated above the cubicles, and back through

Bailey in the Corner

the door, loud enough for half the office to hear. "Did you see her clothes? Moms of teenagers shouldn't dress like they're still in their twenties."

"She's trying to get Jared's attention," Daisy replied.

"Yeah, trying to sleep her way to the top."

My blood turned cold as my eyes darted to Jared, still in his chair. He raised an eyebrow, listening.

"Not just trying," Daisy's cool voice said. "She already is. How else would she be getting so much attention?"

Lauren shook her head. "Ignore her."

But I couldn't stand one more second of Daisy rubbing my reputation in the dirt. She thought I was a failure? I'd prove her wrong once and for all.

"Hey, Jared?" He was already looking at me. "Add my name to your list. Today, I'm auditioning."

Chapter 18

Stella fell straight into a panic attack the second we reached the fabrication room. She collapsed into a chair at the end of a long white table, clutching her chest. "What if I screw up? Or what if I suck on camera? Without me, the whole show could fail!"

"Bailey's auditioning too," Lyneeka said, massaging her shoulders. "She won't let you make a fool of yourself."

Nervous excitement twisted through my chest, my heart pounding. I still couldn't believe I signed up. "I couldn't stand listening to Daisy for one more second. I want to prove to the entire staff I'm more than Daisy's sidekick."

Stella crossed her legs, shooting me a smug look. "You're perfect for this."

I left them to their sewing and walked back to my desk, but my excitement shrank with each step. What was I thinking? Daisy and I *never* tried for the same goal. I'd learned that lesson the hard way, when we worked at Lucky 7 Gym and my first Ballroom Cardio class was a smash hit. People had filled my mirrored classroom wall-to-wall, then crowded in the hall. Only Daisy refused to participate. She'd leaned against the front mirror, stoic. She'd taught the class before mine, but only a dozen attendees had come.

When the hour ended, people swarmed with enough compliments that my jaw hurt from smiling. That night she left the gym without me,

Bailey in the Corner

stranding me and Mia since my car was broken down. She didn't pick us up the next morning either. I had to walk the six miles, carrying my toddler on my hip, arriving three hours late. This lasted two weeks until she deemed my punishment sufficient—the same day my car came back from the shop.

Since then, I'd never gone after something Daisy also wanted. It wasn't worth the battle.

I sank into my chair and pulled out my phone to text Marco, but at the last second, I called him instead. My nerves were an electrical storm of emotion—annoyance at Daisy, excitement for auditioning, dread that Jared wouldn't pick me, and more dread that he would.

"Bailey!"

"Either you're a bad influence, or these pants are laced with magic. I volunteered to audition for MaxFit99."

"Seriously? That's huge!"

"Is it, though?" I searched for the words to explain how complicated this all felt, but I couldn't do it justice. No matter how much I wanted freedom from Daisy, her punishments wouldn't go away.

Marco must have heard the anxiety in my voice, because he tried to lighten the mood. "Has Jared seen you in your magic pants yet?"

It didn't help.

"Yeah. And then Daisy told him I was trying to sleep with him."

Marco paused and I held my breath, praying he could send a miracle solution through the phone. Suddenly, he laughed. "You two really did go to war. You know what? Let's turn that back around on her. Let's make *him* want to sleep with *you*."

"I don't understand."

Marco laughed again. "The best way to make a guy want you is to let him see you with another man. Don't go anywhere, I'm on my way."

Marco hung up and I stared at my phone. What just happened?

After that, Marco didn't respond to my texts. As the minutes ticked by, my stomach fluttered. I brushed through my long hair, twice, and reapplied my lip gloss. Then I jumped when his voice echoed across the building.

But Daisy beat me to him.

"Marco! What are you doing here?"

I turned the corner right as she wrapped her arms around his neck and pulled him into the longest, most intimate kiss. I ducked into the nearest cubicle, nauseous. But half the staff, including Jared, watched her stake her claim on the strikingly sexy man with a silver cane.

They also witnessed what he said next.

"I'm actually here to see Bailey."

I popped up from my hiding place and Daisy's eyes darkened enough to match Marco's black outfit. But when his gaze landed on mine, his whole face lit up.

"You look amazing," he said so everyone could hear. Then he turned to Jared, shaking his hand like an old friend.

"I'm Marco," he said. "Love your show."

Jared's eyes darted to mine, then back to Marco, appraising. "Thanks. You lift?"

"When I can. You have a solid program. More technical than Michael Kay. He's too gimmicky."

"Couldn't agree more," Jared said. "What do you do, Marco?"

"I sell diamonds, and I coach ballroom when I'm in town."

"Diamonds? I bet that's interesting."

"Never boring, that's for sure. Lots of travel. I bet you travel a lot too."

"Fitness conferences, mostly. What gym do you use?"

Marco rubbed the back of his neck. "Whatever they've got in hotels. I'm not home enough to pay for a local membership."

Was this how men sized each other up?

"Good for you for sticking with it," Jared said. "Hotel gyms can be rough. We have a decent one in the warehouse. Use it anytime you're in town. No charge."

Bailey in the Corner

"Hey, thanks. Bailey and I need to work through a few dance steps, can we borrow the stage? You're welcome to watch."

Jared glanced at his wrist. "We don't start filming for a few hours, that should be fine. Tell the stage crew I okayed it."

"Thanks, Jared."

Marco strolled toward me. Nervous electricity zinged through my stomach as every head in the room followed him. His face stayed professional, but his eyes filled with laughter. Or excitement? He was playing a game I didn't understand.

"Are they still watching?" he whispered. I could smell the faint hint of his cologne, an expensive version of piña colada.

I nodded, whispering back, "We're dancing?"

"Absolutely."

We grabbed my ballroom shoes from my desk, but by the time we reached the gym, the entire office staff had already arrived, pretending to look busy, crowding amidst the stage equipment while their curious eyes never left Marco's dark hair, his black clothes, his confident grin. Camera men, sound guys, and the lighting crew scurried around, prepping for the auditions. Lyneeka wheeled in a cart of clothes and makeup, and hopeful auditioners leaned against walls or stretched their muscles. Marco whispered to the sound guy, then once we'd changed our shoes, he led me to the center of the wide, empty stage.

No sign of Daisy. But she would certainly come—she wouldn't let me make a spectacle with her boyfriend. This would boost our war to an entirely new level.

The warehouse lights shut off, dropping the enormous room into black, then the stage lights snapped on.

"You okay?" Marco whispered.

Still no sign of Daisy. But why would this dance make Jared want me? He wasn't even here.

Marco placed me in front of him in dance position, his hand around my waist, my fingers wrapped over his bicep, our hips locked together. Then he paused, not moving.

"What are we doing?" I whispered, trying to ignore the gathering crowd.

"Wait for it."

"Wait for what?"

He said nothing, just held still as everyone in the room watched.

Then, the gym door opened, letting in a sliver of light, and Jared stepped in, leaning casually against a pillar.

"Is he here?"

"Yes," I whispered, breathless.

Marco nodded to the sound guy, who hit play on what must have been Marco's phone connected to the sound system. Our first song exploded over the loudspeakers. The intro pulsed through the floor, up into my feet, into my bones, until all that existed was the drumming heart of the music and Marco's hand on my back. Even the worry about Daisy's war flickered away, buried under the vibrations. The rest of the employees filed into the room, drawn by the mysterious music, but I only heard Marco's voice in my ear.

"Do you remember our lesson on Monday, when I said we could dance the Rhumba without it being too intimate?"

"Yeah."

"Forget everything I said. Just feel the music and move with the emotion of the songs."

I leaned back to frown at him. "The emotion?"

Mischief twinkled in Marco's eyes. "Make it sexy. Jared's watching."

The song's intro ended and Marco pulled my hand down, swinging me into the first step of the dance. I wanted to object, to argue that I wasn't the least bit sexy, but then I saw Jared's eyes glued to my body and I finally understood Marco's plan.

Confidence is sexy.

Bailey in the Corner

This dance was my chance to finally catch Jared's attention, and thanks to these magic pants, I could do it.

As I twisted into the first step, I knew instantly this version of our routine would be different. Sure, the footwork hadn't changed, but everything else had. Marco danced without a trace of his rigid professionalism. His body flowed loosely, pulling me an extra inch toward him so our shoulders brushed together as his hand slid across my waist. His body flowed sensually with the song, from his feet to his knees to his hips, and it only took me a second to catch on.

We overexaggerated every step, every movement, beaming at the crowd when they clapped after the first floor-drop. At the lift at the end of the Cha-Cha, he barely had to lift his eyebrows for me to nod agreement to his modification. Instead of wrapping my foot around his ankle, I kicked my entire leg around his waist. He grabbed the back of my thigh to hold me firmly in place, lunged into a low dip, his face mere inches above mine, then pivoted into a spin that lifted my back leg off the floor.

Marco set me gently down, sweat glistening across his forehead as he released his hold on my body. Once we were facing the audience, he rolled up the sleeves of his black button-up, winking at the crowd. I couldn't believe he was even here, that Marco abandoned work in the middle of the day, and ruined his perfectly pressed clothes—for me.

The music boomed into Samba and my nerves kicked into gear. On my formation team in college, we never danced flashy—we danced stiffly, formally, so every couple perfectly matched. Solo dancing required a level of showmanship I'd never tried. To make it worse, much of Samba was danced side-by-side, not touching. I couldn't even hide behind Marco.

He must have sensed my anxiety because he nodded encouragingly as we started the first steps, five feet apart. "You've got this," he mouthed.

And then, an overwhelming realization crashed into me. All day long I'd assumed my new confidence came from my outfit, that these clothes had elevated me into a person worthy of respect. But then I locked eyes with Marco. It wasn't the pants. It was never the pants.

It was Marco.

I'd found the courage to believe in myself because *he* believed in me first. No one had encouraged me in years—maybe since my dad died. Daisy certainly hadn't.

All this time, did I just need someone in my corner?

Something inside me clicked into place. Something in his smile, his eyes, did too. When he swung around behind me, pressing his stomach into my back for Samba rolls, I leaned firmly into him as if I could send my emotions straight into his chest, my heart beating against his. He answered by snaking his right arm around my waist and pulling me tighter, locking his fingers around mine.

I raised my left hand into the air, and he wrapped his other hand around my palm as we took our first step into the Samba rolls. We leaned to the side as one, his knee pressed into the back of my knee, his arm running the length of mine. And then we spun, locking our feet together, twisting like a top, gravity drawing us together until I couldn't tell where I ended and he began.

The Samba rolls finished, but I didn't want to let go. I twisted in place to face him as the music faded into Rhumba, his left cheek resting against my forehead, left arms out. As the drums thumped their new, agonizingly slow rhythm, his fingers trailed down my exposed forearm, leaving fairy dust down my skin.

His hand paused tentatively on my cheek, the bass drum beating through our feet, and we held still, inches apart, waiting for our cue to take the next step. We both breathed heavily, the air mingling between us, our mouths inches apart. Every surface of his body sparked against mine, his hip against my stomach, our thighs connected all the way down to our knees. His fingers pressed against my back, each one holding me exactly where I needed to be, firm, gentle, safe.

But when the first Rhumba step came and I lifted my right foot to slide my toe across the floor, Marco didn't move. He held perfectly still.

Bailey in the Corner

When I lifted my head from his shoulder, I found his eyes boring into mine. They'd changed again. They glowed with burning intensity, full of a question he couldn't ask out loud—at least until he called things off with Daisy.

He didn't dance. He only waited for my answer.

My answer?

I knew what my brain would say. It would scream that I was trying to impress Jared, *not* Marco. That Daisy would be furious, that we could never chase after the same thing. Or the same man. But as Rhumba music vibrated through my ears and blood pounded through my veins, Jared and Daisy faded away in the background. My rational thoughts were nothing but white noise, but I could *feel.* I felt Marco's hand pressed solidly against my back. I felt his fingers warming the skin beneath my shirt. I felt a gravity pulling me to him, like a rope around our middles pulling us together. He gave me confidence, made me feel *seen,* encouraged me to escape my self-imposed prison and step out into the light.

Where Marco was, I wanted to be.

My lips turned up, giving my answer to his question, and he smiled back. Not a stage smile for the crowd, but one just for me. It penetrated my eyes and my hands and my heart. And then, never once breaking eye contact, he launched me into the Rhumba, picking up with the music like he'd built our pause into the dance. Each time a step drew me away, he ended it half a second early, pulling me back against his body, like he wanted more time touching me. Every body part connected as we spun, even ones that weren't supposed to, but with Marco it felt natural, familiar. The dance was no longer for the entertainment of the crowd, but only for the two of us.

Marco and me.

Us.

And when the dance drew to a close, when he should have released me into a spin that landed us side-by-side for a bow, he turned me toward his body instead. He released my hands and caught my waist, wrapping both arms around me, my hands pressed against his chest, his face an inch from mine.

The music ended, but neither of us moved. So much had changed in this unspoken conversation. I didn't want it to end. When I rested my forehead against his, his eyes dropped to my lips. Marco's mouth turned up slightly and he inched closer.

The room erupted into applause.

We both jumped.

Marco released my waist, but he caught my hand and held it tight. I squeezed back, keeping our conversation alive.

Jared reached us first. Despite five years working together, he felt like a stranger after the last three days with Marco.

After the last five minutes.

"Incredible," he said, and Marco had to drop my fingers to shake Jared's hand, but he stayed close to my side, always maintaining contact. "Come on, I'll get you a drink. We have excellent supplements."

Marco didn't move until I nodded. "You go, I'll be there in a sec."

The men walked away but I couldn't tear my eyes from their backs. I'd loved Jared for so long, but had Marco almost kissed me? I leaned over, resting my hands on my knees. Having them in the same room felt . . . uneven. Threw my world out of balance. But why? The answer came easily enough.

I was falling for Marco Esposito.

And not a cutesy little crush but falling head-first-off-a-cliff.

This was very, very bad.

Daisy stalked across the stage, fists clenched tight. "What the hell was that?" she shrieked, the fire in her eyes burning hot enough to ignite the entire building.

I glared right back. "We were practicing Mia's dance routine."

"You're teaching Mia to dance like a stripper? You practically had sex on the stage!"

Bailey in the Corner

The muscles in my neck stiffened. "Why do you care? You don't even like him, you're using him like a toy."

"He's mine," she hissed. "And if you're sleeping with him, I'll destroy every single thing you care about."

"You're just jealous that he likes me."

The color drained from Daisy's face, but she leaned in until we stood eye-to-eye. "He's mine," she hissed again. "I already warned you, you can't win this war. Back off, or I'll go straight to Dom and tell him the truth about Mia."

The entire world stopped.

"What did you say?"

"You heard me. I'll tell him he's Mia's dad. I'll even help him demand custody."

"You promised," I whispered.

"You give me no reason to keep it."

An iron claw crushed my ribs. My heart pounded wildly, my skin ice cold. Never in a million years did I think she'd take it this far. She couldn't tell Dominic. I had to stop her.

So, I took a deep breath . . . and backed down. "Marco's all yours, I promise. There's nothing between us anyway; it was all for show."

Her eyes narrowed. "Good. Because I'm keeping him, long-term. If you touch him again, if you betray me, I'll do the exact same thing to you."

Without another word, Daisy strode to Marco's side and wrapped her body against his. Marco's eyes shot to mine, clearly panicked. He wanted me to rescue him, extract him, but my feet wouldn't move.

They couldn't.

If Daisy and I both pursued Marco, she'd destroy my entire life.

Our war was over. I'd lost. And that could never change.

She didn't even truly like him, but she knew I *did,* and that was enough. She'd make sure I never had him.

Or she'd go after Mia.

The realization stung like ice water dumped over my head. I let it wash away the memory of Marco's fingers trailing down my skin, his breath against my cheek, his eyes on my lips. None of it could stay, everything had to be erased.

Marco still watched me, biting his lip with concern. But when Jared headed my way, determination in his gaze, I focused on him instead. He was what I'd always wanted, right? We'd put on this whole production to catch his attention, and here it was. I had it. I concentrated on his six feet of solid muscles, and his determination to succeed, which I'd always admired. I focused on how his jawline jutted into a firm square, the silver streaks peppering his black hair. And his eyes, always so intense, so focused.

And now they focused on me.

I love Jared. I've always loved him. This is exactly what I want.

"Can we talk?" he said. "Somewhere private, like my office?"

Every inch of me wanted to run back into Marco's arms. But I didn't. I let Jared place his hand on my back, let him guide me toward the door. And as I felt Marco's gaze on my skin, I squashed my desire to look back.

Chapter 19

Jared deposited me on the navy-blue leather couch in his office. He sat at the other end, leaving an empty cushion between us, and lounged back. My eyes swept the room, taking it all in. The office was bigger than my living room, with a giant desk in the far corner and windows covering the two back walls. A table filled the center, big enough for four, and our couch filled the rest. But what drew my attention, what I'd never noticed any time I'd refilled his printer paper, were the frames covering every inch of his walls: photos of Jared with the governor, pictures with Olympic champions, articles announcing his shows and the records he'd broken.

And in the very center, a glowing review written by Fearless Felicity.

"Impressive," I squeaked. *Starstruck* didn't begin to describe how I felt.

Jared's eyes never left me. They scanned every inch of my body—my turquoise outfit, my flowing hair, every detail of my face. But not in a predatory way. He appraised me the way he would study a contract.

"What's impressive," Jared said, "is everything on the internet when I google your name. You're a certified personal trainer? You taught the famous Ballroom Cardio classes at Lucky 7? I attended a few, by the way. I can't believe I didn't recognize you." His words came out fast. "And you wrote the Lucky 7 newsletter? I read it every day until they suddenly stopped. What happened?"

I swallowed. Twice. "I got a job here."

"We don't even have your resume on file. If we'd known who you were, we wouldn't have stuck you with filling the crockpots."

A wave of nausea flowed through me. "I like my job."

"You're ridiculously overqualified." Jared scooted closer until his knee brushed against mine. "Your internet presence completely vanished five years ago, but you've been here all along. Are you hiding from something?"

"No." That *something* knew exactly where to find me.

Jared's deep blue eyes settled on mine, his voice low. "Then let's get you into the spotlight where you belong. Be my assistant in today's auditions. If you do as well as I think you will, you could even apply to lead your own show."

The racing train in my head slammed on its brakes, sirens screaming. Daisy wanted her own show. That was *her* dream. I stood, backing away. "Daisy's already your assistant. I'm just auditioning, remember?"

Jared stood too. "I remember, but I don't want Daisy's help. If you're my assistant, you can help people with their form and audition at the same time."

My legs grew so heavy they wobbled under my weight. I wasn't allowed to go after the same thing Daisy wanted. Signing up to audition jabbed at her enough, but taking her spot as assistant? Applying for my own show? After she'd threatened to tell Dominic about Mia?

Jared stepped toward me. "So, will you help me today?"

I'd already walked away from Marco. Angering her again would make that sacrifice meaningless. There was no line Daisy wouldn't cross to get her revenge.

I couldn't risk Mia's safety.

"You can't give me something you already promised to Daisy."

"But you're better than her."

It didn't matter.

"Bailey," Jared's brow creased, his eyes earnest, "I've been watching you all week. You're the best lifter in our gym, and Lauren says you're the

Bailey in the Corner

glue holding this office together. If you want to be in MaxFit99, you don't even have to audition. It's yours."

So much of me wanted to jump up and claim that spot. But the rest of me wouldn't dare, not with Daisy's threat hanging above me. The next words hurt as they blew out of my lungs. "I don't want it. Thanks, though."

Jared raised one surprised eyebrow. "Then why are you auditioning?"

I squirmed backward. "Only to support Stella. You can't put me in the real show."

"That doesn't make sense."

"I know, but it's important."

Jared crossed his arms. "Does this have to do with Daisy?"

"No." I said it too quickly and he tilted his head.

"Will you at least still use the microphone and give cues while you audition? We can give you a headset mic, to be with Stella and do form checks at the same time."

Would that keep Daisy from feeling too threatened?

"I'll make you a deal. I'll do form-checks during the audition—I'll even do it the entire three months of MaxFit99—but in return, you have to keep Daisy in the show."

My body turned cold as I said it, but it had to be done. If Jared accepted my deal, Daisy and I would both win. She would beat me in the auditions, but I could still support Stella.

"Daisy?" His lips pressed together and he stared into the distance. "Lauren wouldn't like it. Some days Daisy is great, but other days . . ."

"She cares about being an Influencer more than anything else." I hoped he could see how earnestly I meant it. "She won't screw this up." Not with earning her own show on the line.

Jared finally nodded. "Deal." He led me to the door, but leaned casually against the wooden frame. "But I'd still rather have you."

Was he flirting with me? I cleared my throat. I'd dreamed about Jared ever since Daisy first showed me his YouTube channel. Why was I backing away?

The answer came quickly enough. Even though his arm was almost brushing mine, no shivers tingled across my skin, no butterflies filled my stomach. It felt nothing like Marco's warm fingers trailing across my back, his hand on my hip, his soft breath on my cheek.

I tried to push away the thoughts, to remember that Daisy had already claimed him.

"Don't be a stranger," Jared said, smiling. "My office is always open."

I left in a daze, fumbling the twelve steps to my cubicle. I needed a minute alone to process everything I'd just given up—Marco and MaxFit99—and that Jared had finally flirted with me. But as I reached my desk, I stopped short. My cubicle wasn't empty.

Marco sat in my raggedy swivel chair, his cane against the wall, the knob reflecting the ceiling lights. The scent of piña colada cologne floated in the air.

"You can't be here," I said, refusing to step closer.

But Marco jumped up and closed the gap, stopping inches before me. His black hair fell slightly over one eye, mussed up from our dance. "Why not?"

"What if Daisy sees?"

"I don't care." His nearly black eyes pierced mine, like he was searching for something in my face. He took my hand. "Where did you go after we danced?"

Daisy's laugh echoed over the cubicles.

"You really can't be here," I said again. "You're Daisy's boyfriend."

He blinked. "No matter how many times you say that, it's still not true. Never was."

"She'll never let me have you."

"*Let* you? Like she gets to choose?"

I flinched. His words sounded ridiculous, but that didn't make them untrue. With a painful breath, I released Marco's hand. "She always chooses. She always wins."

Bailey in the Corner

Marco took my waist instead, giving a half-shrug. "But you never had me on your side, helping you stand up to her. What do *you* want, Bailey?"

What did I want? It didn't matter, not with Mia's welfare on the line. "I want you to leave."

"Wait, seriously?"

No, but the rest didn't matter. Daisy wouldn't let me have it. "Please, just go."

Marco took a slow, deep breath, his eyes scanning every inch of my face. Confusion etched across his forehead. Then he dropped my waist and took a small step back, like he was hoping I'd stop him. When I didn't, he frowned deeper and left my cubicle, glancing back as he walked away. With every step he took, the temperature dropped.

The second he disappeared, a wave of regret washed through me. I wanted to run after him, chase him down. Take back everything I'd said.

But Daisy's laugh echoed through the office again and I glared at the ceiling, hating that sound, hating Daisy's power.

Hating that hollow look in Marco's eyes.

Chapter 20

In the gym, preparations for the final round of auditions were in full swing, the noises and clangs ridiculously loud. Hoping to help, I made Green Fizz for the auditioners, but Lyneeka interrupted me.

"That's my job today." She pulled the cold water bottles out of my hands. "If you're in the show, we need to practice without you backstage."

I didn't bother explaining I'd already given my spot to Daisy. I just let her hand me a bottle of liquid energy, plus another one for Stella, who anxiously paced the warehouse, wringing her hands.

"I don't know if I can do this." Stella rubbed her arms, fidgeted with the hem of her shorts, then chugged her Green Fizz. "What if I screw up? Daisy won't go easy on me."

I took her empty bottle. "We both know you'll rock this. As soon as your muscles get a pump, you'll coast right through."

"You think so?"

"Absolutely."

Stella gave a shaky laugh, then we distributed earpieces to everyone auditioning. Even Lauren took one, pressing the little plastic and metal bud inside her ear, saying she was curious as to who followed my cues. I hooked a headset around my ear with a tiny microphone poking across my cheek, so light and small I almost couldn't feel it.

Bailey in the Corner

Nerves grew high as the giant countdown reached one minute. We all took our spots on the stage. Nineteen people bounced with energy, ready to audition.

Except Jared never arrived.

Neither did Daisy.

"Anyone seen them?" Lauren asked.

"I was with Jared in his office an hour ago," I said.

"Go see if he's still in there." Lauren double-checked her watch. "Maybe he lost track of the time."

The light was off in Jared's office, the room silent. I checked the fabrication room, where a few focused tailors continued to sew. After yelling into the men's bathroom, I checked the parking lot where his blue Audi still sat. Drizzling rain pierced my skin, and I rubbed my arms. If he hadn't left the building, where else could he be?

Laughter came from the alley around back. I jogged around the corner and froze, too stunned to interrupt. Not three feet away stood Jared, in all his shirtless glory, with his arms wrapped tightly around a woman, their lips locked in the kind of kiss I definitely didn't want to witness.

Neither of them noticed me, even when I scuffed my feet to get their attention.

"Hey, Jared?"

The woman jumped back with a yelp, wiping her mouth on her arm, face as red as her curls.

"Daisy?" The word slipped out before I could stop it. "You're kissing Jared? What about Marco?"

"I can kiss whoever I want," she said.

"You can't claim them both!"

"Watch me."

But Jared whirled around, pulling his shirt from under his arm and sliding it back over his head. "Bailey!" He closed the space between us in two broad steps, his shoes crunching on the gravel. "This isn't what it looks like."

"It's exactly what it looks like."

"It's not. There's nothing going on between us."

"Sure there is," Daisy said with a wicked grin.

"You can kiss whoever you want," I said, unable to look at his face. "We just need to get inside for the audition."

"Please, believe me. I don't want you to think I'm a scumbag." He spoke with surprising sincerity. Was Jared DiMaggio begging for my attention? His eyebrows pulled together, pained, and Daisy scowled.

"Let's just go inside," I said.

Jared led the way to the gym. But it fell hauntingly silent when we entered.

Suddenly, I realized why. I lifted a hand to the light-as-air microphone attached to my ear. They'd heard our entire conversation. I replayed our words in my head, my stomach twisting. I hadn't said anything bad, had I?

"Let's go!" Lauren yelled, clapping her hands. "We're behind!"

I'd never been so grateful for chaos.

"Was he really making out with Daisy?" Stella whispered when I took my spot at the front corner of the stage, where I had a clear view of everyone. I nodded. I didn't want to say anything out loud, since the entire room was connected to my mic.

"Slut," Daisy said as she passed—as if I had done more than interrupt *her* kissing in an alley. "You're really going through with this audition?" She said it loud enough for the entire room to hear.

I didn't answer. There was no use fighting when I already knew she'd win a spot and I wouldn't.

"Of course she is," Stella said. "Bailey's an amazing lifter."

But Daisy twisted back to face me. "Just tell me you're not hoping to win your own show." She cringed. "Don't forget what happened last time you taught your own class."

Bailey in the Corner

My eyes darted around the room. Everyone was still watching, listening, and my throat squeezed tighter. "Daisy, stop. I'm no threat to your spot on the show."

She stared me down. "In the twenty years I've known you, Bee, you've never been a threat to me."

"Woah," Stella whispered as Daisy strolled away to take her spot at the front of the stage. "Harsh."

"It's fine."

"It's not fine," Stella growled. "But whatever, you'll prove her wrong."

Instead of arguing, I swapped my weights out for heavier ones. The heavier I lifted, the more aggression I'd burn off. Right now, that was exactly what I needed.

"Ten seconds!" the stage manager yelled, and everyone flipped on their smiles. "Three, two, one . . ."

"Welcome back to MaxFit99!" Jared spoke into the camera like we were broadcasting to the entire world. "Today we're working our upper bodies and core, so let's begin with our warmup."

We moved quickly through activation exercises, then the workout began in earnest. At first, muscles fresh, I pushed my weights with all the fury I could muster. Fatigue kicked in and my muscles burned, but I didn't stop. When my body realized I wouldn't back down, oxygen filled my veins and a wave of endorphins flushed through my limbs. On the next set of bicep curls, I bumped up my weights. My arms burned, my muscles swelled, and I pushed harder, hitting a new personal record.

"Perfect form," Jared said, stopping beside me. I tried to ignore him, but he eyed the number stamped into my dumbbell and grinned. "Did you put something special in your Green Fizz today?"

I laughed, the combination of his approval and my endorphins melting my aggression.

"Shoulder presses are next," Daisy said to the group, so I bumped up my weights again and focused on my form. Glutes tight, core tense, back straight with no arch, shoulders down, no shrugging when I pushed the dumbbell above my head.

"Number two," I whispered into my mic, reading the number pinned to a woman's shirt, "don't let your arms droop in front of your ears when you press." The woman fixed her form and Jared nodded his approval. "Seventeen," I whispered, "you're arching your back. Tighten your core or drop to lower weights on the next set. I don't want you to injure your back."

By the end of the second set of shoulder presses, everyone's form looked perfect. But when I stopped talking through the mic, Daisy took over out loud.

"Number six, drop your elbows to your ribs between each press. You'll build more muscle with bigger arm movements."

My eyes shot to Jared, whose eyes locked on mine—Daisy was wrong. But only eight reps remained, so did it matter? But half the auditioners, including Stella, had followed Daisy's recommendation. Jared gave me the tiniest nod.

"Sorry, guys," I whispered into the mic, "I'm going to disagree." Daisy's head snapped around, but I kept going. "Dropping your elbows releases the tension in your shoulders—you'll build muscle slower. Keeping them above parallel increases your time under tension. It's harder, but you'll get better results."

Jared nodded again right as the clock hit zero for the first break. The little red light on the camera turned off and dumbbells thumped to the stage floor.

"Great job, everyone," Jared said. "Grab a quick drink, you've got two minutes."

Stella came straight to my side. "How am I doing?"

"Amazing."

The second segment progressed similarly to the first. Daisy demonstrated lifts, Jared weaved between rows, and I gave quiet cues through the mic. Fortunately, Daisy didn't cause any scenes and I lost

Bailey in the Corner

myself in my workout, shaking off the stresses from her and Jared. I hit two more personal records and couldn't stop laughing over how strong I'd become without realizing it.

Jared knelt beside me at the end of the segment as I lay on my back, working my triceps by doing skull crushers.

"Do you see," Jared said into the camera, "how Bailey keeps her elbows squeezed together and pointed toward the ceiling? That's perfect form."

He shot me a grin before he walked away, and endorphins rushed through my system. When it came to lifting, Jared knew everything. Earning his approval made my body temperature rise. I chugged half a bottle of ice water during the next break.

The third segment focused mostly on chest presses. This time, Jared squatted beside me immediately.

"No one matches," he whispered, pulling me to my feet with rough fingers. "I don't care which presses they do, but I need them to look uniform, and to lift safely."

I put my hand over the mic so it wouldn't pick up my voice. "Can you show me?"

Jared grabbed my dumbbells, lay on the ground, and quickly demonstrated. Then we stood together in the corner as I coached the group through each press, adjusting the angles of their arms and hands. By the end of the third set, they moved in unison.

"Perfect," Jared said, bumping his fist against mine.

We ended the final segment with a burnout, one minute of every exercise to fully fatigue our muscles. As the clock counted toward zero, I pretended like the camera was live and we were performing for the world. Adrenaline pumped into each of my last reps, like the old days at Lucky 7 Gym when people squished into my classroom to join me, or the ballroom performances in college where thousands watched from the audience.

LINDSAY HILLER

For a moment, I regretted my deal with Jared. On stage I felt at home, courageous. But I ignored it. Daisy had to win the big stuff, like MaxFit99, so she wouldn't follow through with her threat about Dominic.

Daisy had to win.

My endorphins fizzled into nothing, and Jared ended the show. Everyone put their equipment away and rushed off for Purple Protein or Blue Juice.

Someone flipped on the glaring warehouse lights and I searched for my own drink. Lyneeka stood behind the kitchen counter fanning herself with a paper plate. Empty powder packets littered the floor, crunching under our feet, and costume pieces and hairbrushes covered the counter.

"What happened back here?" I asked. "Did a hurricane blow through?"

"It's your fault," Lyneeka said, fanning herself harder. "I didn't realize how much you do offstage."

Before I could reply, my phone buzzed and Marco's name flashed across the screen. My heart leapt into my throat.

How did the audition go?

I glanced around, but Daisy still stood far away. Was I allowed to talk to him? Even though I'd told Daisy she could have him?

Stella kicked butt.

I bet you did better.

I didn't respond, but my heart pounded when he sent another text.

Can we talk about what happened earlier today?

There's nothing to say.

Yes there is. I know we were feeling the same thing when we danced. But what happened after? Why'd you send me away?

I read his messages a second time, breathless, then found Daisy watching me from across the warehouse. She pressed her lips together, like she knew exactly what my phone said. I tucked it quickly into my pocket without responding.

Nothing had changed—Daisy still wouldn't let me have him.

Chapter 21

By the time Lyneeka and I cleaned up the gym, the office had emptied for the night. With three hours to kill before ballroom rehearsals, I headed to the fabrication room to turn my secret clothes into costumes. I paused halfway there, though, when something shattered in the conference room, followed by an angry shriek.

I dropped my box and ran toward the sound.

Lauren sat in her usual spot, photos of the MaxFit99 candidates laid in neat rows across the table. But Lauren wasn't looking at them. A glass plate lay in pieces below the far wall, and she'd pulled her legs up against her chest in her chair.

I knocked tentatively on the door. "You okay?"

Lauren scooped up her mug and hurled it at me. I ducked, covering my head. The cup smashed into the wall, shattering violently and raining ceramic shards onto my skin.

"What the hell?" I shouted.

"That's for your shitty advice about standing up to Christian. I got his response two minutes ago. He said, *Screw you, I'm signing Michael Kay.*"

My blood ran cold. "He used those words?"

"No, I summarized." Lauren wrinkled her nose as my blood pounded through my limbs. "I never should have listened to you, the stupid crockpot girl."

Stupid?

I brushed ceramic shards off my arms and stomach. "Just because he's a dick doesn't mean I was wrong."

"You weren't? Even though we just lost our one chance to stay in business?"

"He was pushing you around. All you did was stand up for yourself."

"Like you do with Daisy?"

I exhaled slowly, her words soaking into my skin like acid in my pores. Lauren was right—who was I to offer advice about standing up for myself? It backfired every time. Who cared about demanding respect if it meant everyone lost their jobs?

"I'm so sorry," I said. "I shouldn't have meddled."

Lauren waited a full thirty seconds, then her shoulders finally slumped. "Honestly, though, I don't blame him. Have you seen Michael Kay's new ads? Like, in the last hour? He just announced his new show. Every single episode stars a different celebrity. How can we compete with that?" She dropped her forehead back onto her knees.

"Maybe Christian won't like it. He could still change his mind."

Lauren scowled. "Christian likes family programming. What family wouldn't want to exercise with their favorite movie star? This deal was our last shot to stay afloat. Thanks to the damage from Fearless Felicity's article, we're screwed."

The heat drained from my body. I should have waited until next week to write my article. I should have trusted Lauren to handle Christian the right way. I shouldn't have meddled.

I should have stayed in my corner.

"You know," Lauren mused, "I'm ridiculously unqualified to run this company. It was supposed to be a side gig until our real careers took off, but then Jared's YouTube channel blew up and he needed me to manage it. Now we're a forty-employee company but neither of us know what we're doing."

"You need an assistant."

Bailey in the Corner

"I need a whole team of assistants. And a huge raise." Lauren smoothed back her hair, then dug two caramels out of her bag. She passed one to me and the sugar melted deliciously onto my tongue.

"Jared helps you out with the business stuff though, right?"

Lauren choked on her candy. "No. Things fall apart when he tries to contribute. Like this stupid live-streaming idea."

All this time, I'd assumed Jared was the mastermind behind JD Fitness. Maybe I'd given credit to the wrong person.

"If it makes you feel better," I said, "my job doesn't fit me, either. I have a degree in journalism plus years of experience writing for newspapers and Lucky 7 Gym. I don't know how I ended up filling crockpots and restocking printer paper."

Lauren cocked her head. "I thought Daisy wrote the Lucky 7 newsletter."

"Nope. That was mine."

Lauren pulled up Daisy's resume on her laptop and read it out loud. "Founder and author of the Lucky 7 Gym newsletter."

"She wrote a couple articles at the end, I did the rest."

"She took credit for your work?" Lauren pushed buttons on her keyboard, then frowned. "I don't have a resume for you. Who interviewed you?"

"No one. I didn't even apply. Daisy just pulled some strings."

"But *she* took the marketing job, while *you* took an entry-level position? Isn't that backward?"

I stared at the table, unwilling to describe my convoluted firing from Lucky 7 Gym. My newsletter subscribers had quadrupled, and my Ballroom Cardio classes drew unbelievable crowds, so Doug made me assistant manager—a promotion Daisy felt should have gone to her.

I'd taken something she wanted.

I needed to act fast, give her something of mine to ebb her anger—something that hurt me.

So, I told the entire staff that she secretly wrote my newsletter articles for me.

Doug looked betrayed, but I breathed easier. Daisy no longer needed to punish me. But with the "truth" out in the open, Doug officially passed the newsletter to her.

Devastated, I snuck into Lucky 7 Gym's server room that smelled of old socks and copied the gym's email list onto a flash drive. Then I deleted the entire thing from the company files. Every name, every email address, every past article—gone. I'd built that distribution list from nothing. If Daisy wanted to hijack my newsletter, she could do the same thing herself.

Doug couldn't prove I'd deleted the emails, but he still fired me the next day. Within a week, Daisy got us both jobs at JD Fitness.

But six months later, in the safety of my bedroom, I uploaded the Lucky 7 Gym contacts into my brand-new anonymous email account. Then I wrote an article about establishing healthy boundaries and trust with your friends and gym professionals. I triple-checked it for anything hinting at my identity, wanting this new blog to be completely anonymous.

When I reached the signature line, I stopped, my fingers trembling. What would Daisy do if she caught me with this email list? I hated feeling so scared, *all the time.* But as I re-read my article, my hands steadied. Bailey might be scared of every single thing, but the author of this article didn't sound like it. She sounded . . . fearless.

I signed the article "Fearless Felicity" and hit send.

Lauren scanned her laptop screen, reading Daisy's resume out loud. "Why do I get the feeling Daisy didn't do half the things listed on here?"

I leaned in to look. "Because she didn't. That's my resume, but with Daisy's name on top."

Lauren scratched her chin. "I feel like maybe I should fire her. Or at least make you two switch jobs."

"No! I'm fine where I am."

"Being the errand girl?"

I winced. "Someone has to fill the crockpots."

Bailey in the Corner

She shook her head, but tossed me a stack of papers, sending the rows of photographs on the table fluttering. "Once we're all fired, maybe this guy will hire you instead."

I flipped through an assortment of ads for a fitness program, starring a French man with overly Photoshopped muscles. "Is this Michael Kay?"

"The one and only. That's his new program."

I skimmed through the ads, stopping on the final page—a team photo of their full cast. "Hang on." I slid into the chair beside hers, pushing aside her taffy wrappers. Then I set the paper in front of her. "What does every person on this page have in common?"

"They're all beautiful?" she moaned.

"Actually, yes." My heart started pounding, a thread of possibility lacing through its rhythm. "Michael Kay has made the same mistake we almost made—every person on their new cast is perfectly fit. But what's our slogan?"

"'Fitness for Everyone?'"

"Yes. He's taking the opposite approach. Fearless Felicity said we need *more* diversity in our casts—different body styles, different ages, different fitness levels. But what's Michael Kay doing?"

Lauren's eyes widened. "He's only putting fit, famous people on his stage."

"Exactly. Fans may enjoy his new show, but they'll relate to ours more."

Lauren's pulse still thumped on her temple, but she stopped digging her fingers into her scalp. "Do you think Christian would see it that way?"

"Maybe, if you explain it to him. And I still think you should insist that he treats you with respect."

Lauren nodded, the hint of a smile teasing the corners of her mouth. "It's worth a shot." Then she squared her shoulders with a confidence that made her seem taller than her tiny frame, and smoothed out the rows of photos on the table. "While you're here, any thoughts on who I should pick for MaxFit99? You know what we're looking for better than I do."

I tried not to grin as we sorted through the pictures, discussing their fitness levels and backgrounds. In the end, we settled on two separate groups of five, half men and half women, between the ages of twenty and fifty-seven. Each cast had two seasoned lifters, three with moderate experience, and one beginner.

Stella made the first group as a seasoned lifter.

Daisy made the second.

"You're not in either cast yet," Lauren said, writing my name on a sticky note, ready to add to a pile. "Which group do you want?"

"None."

"Why not? Honestly, you should take Daisy's spot. She has it coming."

My voice stuck in my throat. I knew I had to refuse, but I didn't want to.

Lauren handed me my sticky note. "Your choice."

I held it over Daisy's stack, but my fingers froze, trembling. This was my chance to make a name for myself outside of Daisy, to prove to everyone that I was valuable without her. But it didn't erase Daisy's threat to tell Dominic about Mia.

Lauren stood silently, waiting for me to stick my name to the top of a pile.

"You know what? I'm happy filling crockpots. Daisy worked hard for that spot; I can't take it from her."

Lauren tilted her head. "Are you sure? We could use you."

I wrinkled up the sticky note and tossed it into the trash. "Teaching was always Daisy's thing."

Lauren sank back into her chair, arms dangling over its sides like she didn't have the strength to lift them. "It doesn't matter anyway. Thanks to Fearless Felicity, we might not earn enough money on Friday to ever start filming." She closed her eyes, her worry lines softening. "After all these years, this is how JD Fitness ends. I didn't think I'd be so sad to see it go."

Bailey in the Corner

She'd given up her career, her life, her happiness, to keep Jared's dream alive, and it would all dissolve in two days, thanks to Fearless Felicity.

Thanks to me.

Forty people would lose their jobs. Lauren's sacrifices would mean nothing. It would be my fault—unless I found a way to fix it.

But how?

"What if I could save JD Fitness . . . ?"

Lauren opened her eyes.

"What if, hypothetically, I could get in touch with Fearless Felicity? What if she reached out to Christian? Or promoted Friday's show?"

Lauren stayed motionless as she soaked up my words, her eyes red-rimmed and glossy. "You know Fearless Felicity? Personally?"

"Sort of. I know how to contact her. I might be able to convince her."

"That would save us." Her voice caught in her throat, but at the hopeful sheen in her eyes, my own plan formed. First, I'd need to write a blog post supporting JD Fitness's new program. Then, if Lauren sent her email to Christian, and Felicity sent one too . . . But it would mean breaking my cardinal rule—breaking Felicity's rule. But if it could save the company? Rescue Lauren from closing our doors forever? It was worth the risk.

For the first time in her entire existence, Felicity needed to respond to an email.

"I can't promise anything."

Lauren nodded, her head bobbing so quickly her hair fluttered. "Thank you for trying," Lauren whispered. "I can't thank you enough."

I rose and headed toward the door, already planning what kind of article to write so I didn't give my identity away.

"Will you tell me who she is," Lauren asked, "if I promise to never tell?"

I paused, halfway out the door. "She would literally kill me."

Half of Lauren's mouth tilted up. "It was worth a shot. Now shoo. I need to email Christian, then find some real food. I've had nothing but candy for days."

Chapter 22

Lyneeka and Stella were hard at work sewing Waterfall clothes when I darted into the noisy fabrication room. I still needed to sew a dress.

"Can I use the big table? To cut fabric?"

"Go ahead," Lyneeka said, and I pulled my homemade pattern out of my bag, along with a selection of red, orange and black clothes. I cut through the sides of three shirts, spread them across the table, and pinned the pattern pieces to the fabric. The matching pants I saved, to use on Jackson's shirt.

My phone beeped.

Is The Silver Salmon okay for dinner? Daisy said it's your favorite.

I cringed but didn't bother correcting him.

Sure, whatever sounds good to you and the kids. Mia knows what I like.

"What are you working on?" Lyneeka asked.

"Mia's dress for her audition. It's a Latin medley so I'm trying to make it colorful."

"Oh, we know all about the dance," Lyneeka said, winking at Stella. "We all saw you 'practicing' with Marco this afternoon."

My face grew hot. "It wasn't like that."

"Yes, it *was*," Stella said. "But you had chemistry on stage with Jared today too—if you can forget about him kissing Daisy. The way you two partnered up to help us with chest presses?"

"Jared's never touched me like he was touching Daisy." But the heat from my skin could have lit my clothes on fire.

"You don't need to touch to have chemistry," Lyneeka said. "But you're going to have to pick one, or you'll lose them both."

"I don't know about that," I said, putting aside my pins and grabbing my sewing scissors. "But I *do* know Stella killed it on stage today. You were the only person who didn't need any help through the mic."

"You think so?" Stella put down her fabric and pressed her hands to her cheeks. "I'm so nervous! I wish they would announce the new cast already. The wait is killing me."

I tapped my chin, excitement bubbling up inside me. "Suppose, hypothetically, ten minutes ago I helped Lauren pick the official cast. Would you want to know?"

"Yes!" Stella squealed. "Did I make it?"

"Yup! You were the easiest choice."

Stella jumped up and down, then raced to my table and threw her arms around me. But she pulled away abruptly, all excitement draining from her face. "What if people hate me? Do they want a big girl working out on their TV?"

I squeezed her arm. "All they'll see is a crazy strong woman with unbelievable courage. Nothing else."

"Courage?" Stella blinked. "What courage? I'm terrified!"

"Having courage doesn't mean you aren't scared. It means you put yourself out there even when it scares you to death. You already proved yourself in Ohio. Now you're doing it again, right here. You show up every day, you're sticking to your guns, and you're proving people like Daisy wrong. In my book, that's as courageous as it gets."

Lyneeka nodded as the tension drained from Stella's face.

"I wish I was more like you," Stella said. "Watching you on stage today, doing your workout *while* coaching everyone else? You're the bravest of us all."

Bailey in the Corner

I cringed. I wasn't courageous. In fact, I was a phony in every part of my life. Lies had become so familiar that I hardly knew the real "me." How could Stella look up to me when "me" barely existed? I had no courage. If I did, I'd have put my name on the cast list with Stella. And I wouldn't have sent Marco away.

"Can I see your dress?" she asked, as I finished cutting my fabric.

I laid the pieces out, a black bodice with a wide, ruffled skirt that fanned in the back but split up the front for easier dancing. Lyneeka joined us as I pinned fabric panels together.

"I'll attach the colored pieces to Mia's skirt and Jackson's sleeves," I explained.

"Beautiful," Stella said. "I watched a dance show where every time the music changed, the dancer's outfit transformed too. I wonder if you could do that with Mia's dress."

"I don't understand."

Stella had me hold the black bodice up against my body while she explained. "They're starting with Cha-Cha, right? What if the main skirt is pinned tightly against her upper body, so it looks like part of the shirt, with only a small, flashy skirt around her legs. Then when the music changes to Samba, she pulls it free and the skirt tumbles down into a wide, ruffly dress."

Lyneeka grabbed a box of snaps from my sewing kit and pushed them toward me. "You could snap the main skirt on at the waist instead of sewing it. So, when the music changes to Rhumba, she can yank the skirt off completely to reveal a third outfit underneath it all."

"Would that work?" I laid the dress pieces on the table, choosing different segments for three contrasting looks. "Three separate skirts in one dress?"

"With a big reveal for each one!" Stella squealed. "It would wow the judges."

"You're right," I said, as the idea came together. "This is brilliant. But I doubt I could sew it in time. The kids arrive in an hour and I'm still pinning fabric."

Lyneeka pulled the bodice pieces toward her. "I could help you for an hour. I don't mind staying later to finish up the Waterfall stuff. I'm curious how this dress will turn out."

"You'd do that? When you're already working late?"

"You do so much around here. I can return the favor."

"I'll help too," Stella said. "Tell me what to do."

"Thank you, both of you!"

Lyneeka got to work on the body of the dress, while Stella and I tackled the three-piece skirt.

"We're going to need more fabric," I said. "That bag over there has scraps from cut-up old clothes. Can you pick some with similar texture, while I sew these together?"

Stella dumped the bag onto the next table, then laid out the six remaining outfits. She brushed her fingers over them, getting a feel for each fabric, but stopped when she reached the fourth. "Where did you get this?"

I glanced at the loose yellow shirt in her hands. "I don't remember. It's Craig Mill Athletics, so probably their store in St. Louis."

"No, you didn't." Then she held up the shirt beside it. "And where did you get this one?" Stella's eyes narrowed, scrutinizing the clothes, then scrutinizing me.

I cleared my throat. "I don't remember, it's probably old."

"It's from last year—the StrongGirl Collection that Spirit Sports didn't end up releasing."

"What do you mean?"

"I'm a sucker for athletic clothes. I spend way too much money on them. Spirit Sports marketed the heck out of this line, but filed for bankruptcy before the clothes went into production. I never got the chance to buy it. In fact . . ." Stella scrunched her forehead, "the only time I ever

Bailey in the Corner

saw these clothes, outside of Spirit Sports ads, was when Fearless Felicity posted a picture of the promo pair they sent her."

Lyneeka's eyes shot up, and the whirring of her sewing machine slowed until a hollow silence filled the room.

I lowered the pins in my hand. "What are you trying to say?"

"I'm not sure." She pressed the clothes against her chest. "Bailey . . . Are you Fearless Felicity?"

My heart erupted into a frantic rhythm making it impossible to breathe. "Of course not."

But Stella's eyes widened. "Daisy made fun of my size, then that same night Felicity wrote an article against fat-shaming. It was you. You're her." Stella dropped the shirts and closed the space between us, excitement lighting up her whole body. "No one else could own these clothes!"

Too many emotions battled within me. Obviously, I couldn't admit to being Felicity, couldn't risk it getting back to Daisy. I'd held this secret so close to my chest for so many years, Felicity was an inherent part of me. Her secret defined a large chunk of my life. Giving her up meant giving up my only slice of independence.

Except that Stella wasn't Daisy. She wouldn't try to use Felicity for her own gain. In fact, the excitement in her eyes held no hint of selfishness, only awe at knowing the real me.

The real me?

Felicity.

Maybe I'd gone all these years without making friends because I'd kept the *real* me a secret. Had I never let anyone see me? Or know me? Maybe if Stella knew my secret, I wouldn't feel like a liar all the time, like a phony. It was half tempting, half terrifying.

In the end, I didn't have to answer—my silence told Stella everything. Her voice dropped to a whisper. "Holy shit, you really are her."

I hid my face in my hands, then peeked out between my fingers. "Swear to me, you'll never tell a soul. Not one person."

"I swear."

"Me neither," Lyneeka said, "but *she* might." She pointed to the open door, where Lauren stood, jaw dropped.

"You have to tell Jared."

The walls spun and I gripped the table. "No."

"Yes." She lurched into the room. "You can single-handedly save JD Fitness. You can blast us above every other company in the world. Do you have any idea how much influence Fearless Felicity has?"

"Of course she does," Lyneeka drawled, coming to stand beside me. She folded her arms, glaring at Lauren.

"Jared will give you any job you want, promote you, pay you anything. He'll make you the face of the company, right by his side. Why keep this a secret?"

"Because it's mine." The words scratched at my dry throat. "I want to keep it that way."

"But you could be world-famous."

"I don't want to be famous! I stay hidden for a reason."

Stella's eyebrows squished together in confusion. "Why, though? Weren't you kind of famous at your last job?"

"And you wrote the Lucky 7 Gym newsletter," Lauren added. "But here you've refused every chance to grow."

"I don't get it either," Lyneeka said. "It sounds like you used to enjoy the spotlight, but now you pretend to be just the crockpot girl. Why the change?"

"Was it Daisy?" Lauren asked.

My fingers turned to ice, the cold spreading up through my arms and shoulders. If I moved too much, I'd shatter. "Daisy can never know," I croaked. "Promise me, she will never find out."

Lyneeka and Stella nodded, but Lauren chewed her bottom lip. Her loyalty to Jared was fierce.

"Let's make a deal," I said to her. "If you promise to keep my secret, I'll promise to consider telling Jared. No guarantees, but maybe."

Bailey in the Corner

Lauren hesitated, then nodded. It would have to be good enough.

"Sorry about Tuesday's article," I added. "I wrote it because Daisy was awful to Stella. I didn't expect it to hurt the company."

"No one could have predicted it," Lauren said. "Fortunately, you can fix it."

"I'll write that article tonight. Hopefully it makes up for the first one."

"Thanks." Lauren walked away, muttering something about dinner, but stopped at the pile of outgoing shipping boxes near the door. She pulled one out and brought it back to me with a smirk. "Guess we don't need to mail this to"—she read the label—"Florida. May as well save on postage."

I tucked the box under the table with my purse. "I'll leave a spectacular review."

"You'd better," she said as she left, "even if you don't like the clothes."

Everyone laughed except me. Five minutes after sharing my secret, people were already telling Felicity what to say. Not that I wouldn't have left a five-star review for the Waterfall Collection, or that Lauren didn't have good intentions, but what would happen if I didn't like a JD Fitness product? I'd always had the freedom to be brutally honest in my reviews, no repercussions. But now . . . ?

Lyneeka returned to sewing Mia's dress, and Stella picked two outfits from my bag to cut into the second layer of skirt. She didn't pick the limited editions.

"Is it weird that I'm fangirling over you?" she asked.

"Yup." But I wasn't in the mood to joke around. My eyes kept darting to the door. Would Lauren keep my secret?

"I still can't believe you're cutting up these clothes. Jared would drool if he saw you in them." She paused, then grinned. "Marco too."

I focused on the skirt pieces so she couldn't see me flustered. "I can never wear those clothes in public. Especially since it only took you six seconds to figure me out. Mia's dress needs them more than the box hiding in the back of my closet."

But Stella's words from earlier bounced around in my head. Did Jared and I really have chemistry on the stage today? I knew Marco and I did, though Daisy still wouldn't let me keep him. But if she was committed to her relationship with Marco, why was she kissing Jared?

But then the door opened, and the kids ran in, followed by Marco carrying a giant bag of takeout. It didn't say "The Silver Salmon" on the side. It said "Frenchie's" in elegant cursive letters. His eyes met mine, his face lit up, and my heart skipped a beat. Every single thought of Jared vanished.

Chapter 23

Frenchie's? He brought Frenchie's? Garlic and spices danced through the air. I grinned as he set the food down on the center of the long table. I couldn't stop.

"How are you?" he asked, voice low. His fingers lightly brushed my back, filling my mind with images of our dance. Had that only been hours ago? It felt like ages.

"I thought you were getting seafood."

"Mia told me you hate The Silver Salmon. You should have said something. She said Frenchie's is your favorite." He searched my face. Was he nervous? "I didn't know what you liked, so I got everything."

My heart pounded too loudly to answer. Yes, Frenchie's was my favorite. But the fact that he'd changed his plans for me, gone out of his way to get what I'd want. No one ever went out of their way for me. "You didn't have to do that."

"I wanted to." Then he turned to Stella and Lyneeka, keeping his fingers on my back. "I brought enough for you two."

"I knew I liked you," Lyneeka said, sidling up to the table. Stella followed behind her, laughter in her eyes.

"What?" I mouthed.

"You have to pick," she mouthed back, as if Marco couldn't see her.

Fire burned in my cheeks. She was right, though. Despite Jared's moment in the alley with Daisy, we'd connected today. But now that

Marco stood beside me, I couldn't help my hyper awareness of his arm brushing against my shoulder, his tropical cologne, his fingers lingering on my back. Marco had never touched me this long unless we were dancing. Sirens screamed in my head—what if Daisy caught me? But his gravity pulled me closer.

Marco felt it too. I could tell by the way he held my gaze, how his eyes asked a familiar question. If I reached out my hand, he would take it.

And Daisy wasn't here to stop me.

"Hey, Mom, are you going to eat?" Mia's voice broke the spell as she dug into the pasta, her plastic fork scraping against the cardboard box.

Marco grinned, a hint of pink in his cheeks. "Shall we?"

We joined them at the table and Marco jumped into conversation with Stella, asking about her audition. Soon, he had the entire table laughing while I sighed with contentment, eating a plate of margherita pasta. He'd ordered my favorite dish.

"We'll finish up the dress," Lyneeka said, when the food had disappeared. "You guys get to dancing."

"I can't thank you enough," I said.

She shooed us off to the gym with a wave.

We put on our ballroom shoes and Marco plugged his music into the sound system. He used a tiny remote to queue the song. The kids took their positions on the stage, then Marco held out his hand. "Want to dance?"

I stared at his fingers, knowing this invitation was different than all the other times. The ultra-focused version of Marco wasn't here today. Neither was the sexy Marco from this afternoon, but he was somewhere in between.

I glanced at the metal door, closed, unmoving.

Daisy wasn't here.

I was playing with fire.

But my heart pounded against my lungs and I couldn't stop my fingers from clasping his.

Bailey in the Corner

I nodded, and Marco pulled me into the opening Cha-Cha position, one hand around my waist, the other around my fingers. He held me closer than normal, his posture a fraction less rigid. I leaned into him, knowing full well I was too distracted to do any real dancing.

"How was your afternoon?" he asked as the routine began.

"Honestly, I don't remember." With Marco this close, I could barely remember my name. "How was yours?"

The steps separated us before he had a chance to answer, but when we came together again he said, "I can't remember."

We both laughed and the kids gave us weird looks. He spun me in a tight circle and his hand trailed around my waist and across my stomach, leaving goosebumps everywhere he touched. When he stopped me, my hip locked tightly against his, our sides pushed firmly together, just like they had in the afternoon. He exhaled heavily into my hair, our chests rising and falling together, until he spun me away and I collided with Mia.

We both tumbled to the floor, and I snorted a laugh. Mia scowled, and she yanked the stereo remote from Marco's pocket.

"I think they cooked a little something extra into their pasta," she muttered to Jackson. They returned to their places and she restarted the song.

Marco pulled me into dance position, but when the kids began their routine, we did not. He held me there, his body against mine from our ribs all the way to our knees. I could feel his heart pounding. Or was it mine?

"I lied," he said, barely whispering into my ear.

"About what?"

"I remember exactly how my afternoon went. I got nothing done."

"Why?" My voice came out breathless.

"All I could think about was you. Our dance. I replayed it over and over in my mind." He pulled away just enough that he could look into my eyes, his black hair falling over his forehead. "You're all I've thought about for the last six hours." His gaze dropped to my lips. That string of gravity urged me closer. "Can I take you on a date? Tonight, after practice?"

My breath hitched. I knew exactly what my answer should be. What Daisy expected it to be. Her words from this afternoon echoed through the room. *I think I'm going to keep him . . . Long term . . .* And the meaning behind her words: *If I can't have him, neither can you.*

Fire.

I was playing with Daisy's fire. But Marco's cologne was intoxicating, the warmth of his skin, the beat of our hearts.

I knew better.

And Daisy's threat still rang in my ears.

But no one had ever looked at me the way Marco did, like he *saw* me, knew me, wanted to learn more. How could I push that away? With Marco, I didn't need to be anything other than myself. I didn't need to hide pieces of my personality, to pretend to be less, to compartmentalize who I was. There was no Felicity, no Bee, no "crockpot girl," no "ugly clothes girl." I didn't need to pretend to be anything. Or pretend *not* to be anything.

With Marco, I was simply Bailey.

"Tonight," I whispered. "Let's do it."

Marco sighed and my heart pounded. "What made you change your mind? You sent me away this afternoon."

The answer came instantly. "You brought me Frenchie's."

He dropped our dance position and took my chin delicately between his fingers. We'd been this close a million times, but now we didn't even pretend to dance—we both knew exactly what we wanted. His eyes returned to my lips and I slid my hands around his waist, pulling him into me. I tilted my face up as he leaned forward.

With a crash, the warehouse door flew open, the metal handle slamming into the wall.

Daisy stalked into the gym.

Bailey in the Corner

My blood froze, lungs too cold to take a breath. I leapt out of Marco's arms and turned abruptly toward the kids, as if coaching occupied my full attention. As if guilt wasn't written across my face. Across my body.

Daisy's narrow eyes stayed glued to mine as she slid straight up to Mia, who was mid Cha-Cha with Jackson, and pulled her into a hug.

"Hey, sweet girl, it's been forever! How's my favorite niece? My brother's outside. He wants to watch your practice."

It was like she'd planned this, like she knew what she'd find when she burst through that door. I'd finally pushed Daisy too far. I'd sharpened her axe by being stupid with Marco. If I refused to let Dominic watch, I'd push Daisy even farther over the edge. But if I said yes? If I let her bring Dominic into Mia's life?

"No," I whispered. "Dominic can't come."

Marco raised an eyebrow, but Daisy held my gaze, as if waiting for me to back down.

I didn't.

I couldn't.

I'd always told Mia if she wanted to know about her dad, I'd tell her everything. But she'd never asked, never shown any emotion besides a deep-rooted disgust for the father who never came around. And now was not the time to tell her, not with her audition on the line.

Telling Mia was one thing.

Telling Dominic was another.

He could ask for custody and ruin all her plans. The fact that he was even in the same building made me stumble sideways until I crashed into a tall, narrow stage lamp.

Marco rushed to my side, steadying me. "What's going on?" he asked, but I pushed him away, put three feet between us. Couldn't he see he was making it worse?

Daisy grinned as she strolled across the stage, wrapped her arms around Marco's waist and rested her head on his shoulder. She knew she'd won. Marco's eyes darted to mine for the briefest second, confused, alarmed, but he didn't push her away. Everyone just watched me, waiting for my next move.

My next move? What would upset Daisy the least?

"The kids need to practice," I squeaked.

Marco peeled himself out of Daisy's grasp and retrieved the remote from Mia as Daisy took a spot next to the stage.

"What's going on?" Marco whispered when we'd moved far enough away. "Are you okay?"

But I didn't answer, keeping my focus solely on the kids. They danced their routine until Marco paused the music, walking them through the transition into Samba.

"Ohhh," Daisy said, popping out of her chair. "That twist looks fun. Marco, honey, will you teach me?" She put her hand in Marco's and stood expectantly in front of him.

His eyes darted to mine and I nodded, desperately trying to send him a message. *Do whatever she wants. Keep her happy.* He walked her through a basic Samba step, then turned the music back on for the kids. Three seconds in, she interrupted again, taking the remote from Marco and pausing the music. "Teach me that one too!" Marco walked her through the next piece, but she stopped halfway through and scooted up next to Mia. "Remember that day you beat up a kid at school? The boy who kept calling you 'shorty'?"

Mia nodded but gave a sidelong glance to Jackson.

Daisy patted her head, overly innocent. She knew how much it worried me when Mia got in fights at school. She was reminding me who held all the power.

Daisy turned her attention to Marco. "Mia was hanging out with a rough crowd, kept getting into trouble, so Bee finally stuck her in dance to keep her off the streets. Signed her up for three hours after school, every single day. Didn't want her to end up a pregnant teenager or something, you know?"

Bailey in the Corner

Marco's eyes met mine, her dig at my own pregnancy not lost on either of us. She was wrong, though, about Mia's dancing. One day after school I'd found her engrossed in the outdated TV in our living room, face too close to the screen, watching a professional ballroom competition. The awe in her expression brought back my own college days—the exhilaration of dancing, showing off for the judges. I couldn't blame her for wanting it. Fortunately for Mia, Fearless Felicity's promo checks had picked up momentum and I could afford to sign her up.

"It's almost nine," Mia whispered, after Daisy had monopolized Marco's attention for a full hour. "We've hardly practiced anything."

Daisy was trying to flirt with Marco by stealing the stereo remote. I crossed the stage and plucked it from Daisy's hand.

"I need Marco. The kids need to practice."

"He's *my* boyfriend," Daisy said. "Not yours."

Fortunately, Marco stepped beside me. "The kids are on a tight deadline. Can I teach you another day?"

"Sure thing, honey." She gave a falsely sweet laugh, then returned to her chair. But when Marco held out his hand to me, I couldn't take it. Not with Daisy right there, watching, calculating. I was so stupid to let him think *we* were a possibility.

Marco frowned as I took a step back, out of his reach. And when the kids resumed dancing, Jackson and Mia fumbled through the steps, unable to focus. Daisy cheered and whistled at every dip or spin, creating a constant distraction.

Finally, I paused the music. "Let's take a break. Want to see your costumes?"

Chapter 24

When we entered the fabrication room, Stella and Lyneeka were hard at work on Waterfall clothes. Mia and Jackson's finished costumes sat in a neat pile on the table. Seeing Daisy behind us, Stella darted to the cutting table and shoved the scraps of Fearless Felicity's clothes back into their bag. She closed it tight before Daisy could see.

I mouthed *thank you,* and she winked, right as Lyneeka held up Mia's dress.

"It's better than I imagined," I said, grateful for the distraction from Marco and Daisy, and Mia pressed her hands to her cheeks in awe. I rubbed the black bodice between my fingers, then trailed my hand down to the orange, yellow, red, and pink ruffles. It would fan widely when Mia spun, but the split in the front would keep her legs from tangling. "I can't thank you enough."

"Just wait until you see it on her," Lyneeka said.

Both kids raced to the bathroom to change, then returned, bubbling with excitement.

"I'm not sure how it works," Mia admitted, so Stella demonstrated.

"For the first dance, you'll wear it exactly as is. But when the music changes to Samba," she turned to Jackson, "you'll open the snaps on both her shoulders while Mia unties the ribbon holding the extra fabric tight to her chest. Watch this." A thick, brilliantly colored Samba skirt fell from Mia's torso to swirl around her knees.

Bailey in the Corner

"That's incredible!" Daisy gushed, pushing to Mia's side. "You're stunning."

"That's not all," Stella said. "The entire skirt is attached by snaps. So, when the third song comes on, you will spin in a quick circle while Jackson tugs on your dress. The entire ruffly skirt will come off."

Stella tugged on the bottom and it unsnapped into her hands with a *pop, pop, pop*, leaving Mia wearing nothing but the black leotard and a sheer, burgundy skirt that brushed the floor with a slit up one thigh for ease of dancing.

"It's incredible," Mia whispered, and I squeezed Lyneeka's arm in appreciation.

"Let me try!" Daisy grabbed the skirt and turned Mia in a slow circle, reattaching each snap then clipping the top layer back up to her shoulders. Then she yanked on the top, ripping off the skirt with an excited squeal. "So much fun! Let's do it again."

"Careful," Lyneeka said, rescuing the pieces from Daisy. "It's one-of-a-kind, we don't want to rip it. And Jackson will be removing the skirt, so he should be the one practicing."

"Good point." Daisy winked mischievously at him. "Nothing like having an excuse to rip a pretty girl's clothes off."

Jackson turned an unhealthy shade of red and Mia scooted two steps away from Daisy.

"Who needs more Blue Juice?" I asked, searching for a distraction. Both kids perked up, so I handed them powder packets and room-temperature water bottles from a crate against the wall. They picked a table far away from Daisy, but she strolled over and slid between them. Marco took a step closer to me, but I moved away. We never should have gotten so close.

"This stuff is so good," Jackson said. "I wonder why JD Fitness doesn't sell more of it."

"Crappy marketing department," I muttered.

Daisy checked her watch and squeaked, "Oh no, Dom's waiting for me! Love you all, but I've gotta go."

I'd never heard happier words.

She kissed Mia's cheek, then Jackson's. He wiped his face with his arm, but Daisy laughed and sashayed toward the door, glancing back at Marco. "See you soon, babe!"

No one moved when the door closed behind her. We all stared, like she might burst back in. But once Daisy's BMW fired up outside, I knelt in front of the kids. "Are you guys okay?"

Jackson scowled at the table. "Is she always like that?"

"A bitch?" Mia grunted. "Yeah, she is."

"Mia!" I said, but it was half-hearted. Had she always felt this way? "I thought you liked Daisy."

"She's always been a bitch. And I'm not even paying you a dollar for it."

I hugged them both, exhaling with relief. "Anytime someone makes you feel uncomfortable, you can come to me. That includes you, Jackson—day or night."

Marco put his hand on my shoulder, easing the exhaustion that washed through me. "You guys can come to me too," he said, only to frown when I scooted away. "You okay?"

"Daisy's always worse when her brother's in town." I couldn't meet Marco's eyes, ashamed to tell him the rest. "I don't want Dominic around the kids, ever."

"Okay." Marco flexed his fingers, like he still wanted to reach out and touch me. "But I don't understand why I'm keeping up the charade of dating her. Is there something you're not telling me?"

But the women joined us before I could answer. I touched Stella's arm. "Thanks for hiding my fabric."

"No problem. You know Daisy acts like that because she's threatened by you, right?"

"By me? Not a chance."

Bailey in the Corner

"Oh, yes she is," Lyneeka agreed. "You're the capable one, and she knows it. She's afraid if you figure it out, you'll stop doing everything for her."

"It's true," Stella said, tapping her fingers in a drumbeat on the table. "That's why she tries to make you feel crappy all the time. She doesn't want you to discover how valuable you are and kick her out of the spotlight."

"Why are you friends with her?" Lyneeka asked.

But how could I explain Daisy's hold over me? That her brother was Mia's father? That as long as I cared about Mia's welfare, Daisy called the shots—including in my relationship with Marco, or lack thereof.

"She helped me with Mia's dad," I said, skipping over every detail, "a long time ago."

Jackson turned to Mia. "Have you ever met your dad?"

Mia took a long slurp of Blue Juice. "Nope. My mom says I can anytime, but I don't want to. Pretty sure he's a dick."

Marco's eyes settled on mine, but I had a hard time meeting them. Then he glanced at the door Daisy had vanished through. I could feel him putting together why I didn't want Daisy's brother in here. My face burned hot.

"I get it," Jackson said. "My dad's a loser too."

"Do you guys want to go practice in your costumes?" I asked, but after the night they'd had, they both groaned. I grabbed two boxes of Blue Juice powder packets off the shelf. "If you can nail the costume transitions in the next half hour, you can each take one of these home."

Jackson perked up right away, and he and Mia hurried off to the gym. After a final thanks to the women, Marco and I followed slowly behind, neither of us saying anything. I felt his confusion. His questions. He had no idea what Daisy could do, how much she could hurt me.

"Need a brush?" I asked Mia. The kids were re-cleaning the bottoms of their shoes.

"No thanks, I have one." Mia took Jackson's brush, then scraped the gunk off. "I just keep it in Jackson's bag."

They climbed to their feet, all signs of prior stress evaporating, then practiced revealing Mia's skirt in slow motion.

I dropped into the chair left behind by Daisy, and Marco pulled another one beside me, so close his leg pressed against mine. He watched me, rather than the kids, but I couldn't return his gaze. This close together, with the smell of his cologne between us, I didn't trust myself to make good choices.

I scooted my chair six inches away.

Marco sighed and folded his arms, leaning back. "The costumes are amazing," he finally said. "Did you say you learned in college?"

My shoulders relaxed. This subject was safe. "My mom taught me. Then when I joined the ballroom team, me and another girl made the team costumes."

"You must have been pretty skilled."

"Not at first. At the end of my sophomore year, the entire side of my dress split open while waltzing—during a performance." I shook my head as laughter bubbled up in my chest. "I jumped off the stage quick, but half the guys on the team stopped to stare. They crashed into each other like dominoes!"

Marco winced as he pulled out his phone. "Was there a video?"

"Sure was. It was all over YouTube for a while. Fortunately, you could hardly see me, it's mostly the guys tumbling into a heap. But I learned a valuable lesson about sewing quality seams that day."

"I'm sorry in advance for this." Then he interrupted the kids and called Jackson over. "Do you remember that video of the waltz team, when the girl's dress splits, and all the guys fall off the stage?"

"For sure."

Mia burst out laughing. "That was totally my mom. I show that video to everyone!"

Bailey in the Corner

"No way!" Jackson leaned onto Marco's shoulder as he cackled. "That's one of our favorites."

Perhaps I should have been bothered, but seeing Jackson so close to his uncle, and laughing rather than scowling, made my heart happy.

Sorry, Marco mouthed, but the video really was funny. You couldn't see anything but my bare shoulders. The guys tumbled like a bunch of penguins slipping on ice.

"Ready to keep dancing?" Jackson finally asked, wiping tears from his eyes. "I want to get the costume thing down perfectly, so I don't hurt you on stage."

My mom-heart doubled in size as they walked back out on the floor. Watching Mia dance with a partner who cared about her well-being made my chest nearly burst.

Two years ago, after Mia joined the competition team, she had risen quickly to the highest level, then beyond. At ten years old, she'd outdanced every teenager and most of the instructors. That was when Bruno's mom approached me in the studio lobby about coaching Mia independently and them competing together on the weekends. After two months of grueling practices, we traveled to their first competition. The four of us slid into the bleachers of a stuffy high school gym, waiting for their turn to go out on the floor.

I can't find my shoe brush, Mia said. *Bruno, can I borrow yours?*

His face turned a sickly shade of purple that matched the satin ruffles on his shoulders. *I don't want your gross fingers touching my things. Have you washed your hands yet?*

Yes, twice.

Good.

They performed beautifully during their first two dances, earning them a spot in the finals. Bruno made her wash her hands again before he'd touch her, and Mia silently obeyed, her face set to hide her emotions. When she returned, Bruno glared at her feet.

You painted your toenails red?

Yes.

Your dress is purple. Why didn't you coordinate? Mia's entire body shrank inside itself. *And remove your braces before our next competition. They make your mouth look huge.*

I turned to Nadia, furious, but she only shrugged, agreeing with her horrible son.

From now on, I said, *we will coach the kids together. And Bruno will treat my daughter with respect.*

Twenty minutes later, Mia and Bruno were awarded the overall gold medal in their division. Daisy showed up right after they finished, just in time to snap a picture with Mia.

I leaned closer to Marco. "Thanks for bringing Jackson into her life. She needed him."

Marco angled his chair toward mine and leaned closer too, his eyes hopeful, his voice low. "Thanks for helping me connect with him. But I wish you'd tell me why I'm still pretending to date Daisy. I'll keep doing it, but why can't I date you instead?"

Daisy.

The weight of her, my worry, my fears. All of it dragged me down, a rainstorm that never ended. It was the same old sirens, wailing in my head. Marco and I couldn't be together . . . Daisy wouldn't let us . . . It all sounded so tired, so old, so exhausting. I'd fought this battle so long, I hardly had the strength to keep going, to convince Marco to stay away.

But nothing had changed.

I leaned away from his piercing brown eyes. "We'll never work."

Marco gave me a blank look. "Because of Daisy? Can't we just avoid her?"

I closed my eyes, the ache growing in my chest from the truth he didn't understand. "She's unavoidable."

He rubbed his face in both his hands. "Why don't you tell her you're done? Is she holding something over your head so you can't leave? Controlling you somehow?"

Bailey in the Corner

"It's so much more complicated than that."

"Is it, though? You have it stuck in your head that she gets to make all your decisions. But what would happen if you just walked away?"

My eyes snapped to his. "I can't. Untangling myself from her would have . . . consequences. She'd lash out." She'd bring Dominic straight to my door.

Marco stood. "I've given you advice the last two nights. Want more?"

I nodded, barely.

"Stop worrying about what Daisy, or anyone else, thinks of you. Just be yourself. Anyone who says differently is toxic."

"But if I walk away from Daisy, she wins!" I stood too, my chair legs scraping against the cement. The kids stopped dancing, watching us. "If I walk away, Daisy keeps my marketing job, she takes Jared's show, she takes my friends, she takes you." She'd also take Mia, at least every other weekend. Maybe even every other week. She'd give her to the most dangerous person imaginable. "I lose everything. She wins!"

"She's already taking those things, because you're letting her. It's okay if you win sometimes too."

"You don't understand, Marco. It's her or me, every time. Never both of us."

"You can't both succeed?"

"No!" My voice rose an octave. "If I don't take the spot on Jared's show, she'll rub it in my face that I wasn't qualified. But if I take it, she'll say I stole her dream out from under her. It's the same with you and me. If I walk away from you, she gets what she wants. But if I stay, if we go on even one date . . ." I didn't finish. I couldn't. I didn't want to face it.

"Bailey, that's a terrible way to live."

"I know!" I shouted. "I've been living it for twenty years!" I wrapped my arms around my body like I could protect myself from the truth. Marco reached for me, but I twisted back. It wasn't worth it. I couldn't risk unleashing Daisy's wrath. He held my gaze and we stared at each other, both breathing hard, until the kids turned off their music to change their shoes.

"Ready to go?" Mia asked softly.

Neither of us moved for five seconds. Ten. His eyes swam with confusion. With questions. But I finally slipped into my sneakers, doing my best to avoid the strained silence between Marco and me.

As we headed toward the exit, I tossed Jackson a box of Blue Juice packets. "Practice hard tomorrow night, and I'll give you another one." He grinned and waved as the kids disappeared through the glass door to the parking lot.

But Marco paused, his lips pinched together, his hand on the door. "What will it take to get you out from under her thumb? How can I help you?"

Was there anything he could do? Any way out?

Through the glass door, Mia laughed at something Jackson said. She exuded happiness, so carefree. I couldn't let Daisy ruin this. Even if I told Marco every shameful detail of Mia's conception, he couldn't change any of the facts. He couldn't rewrite history. He couldn't make Dominic any less Mia's father, or any less terrifying.

"It's impossible," I said. "*We're* impossible."

Marco recoiled like I'd struck him. "She's controlling you. And you're allowing it."

The weight of his words settled onto my shoulders, like chains pulling me into Daisy's dungeon. "I know."

After a sullen goodbye, Mia and I drove home in silence. She hopped into the shower upstairs and I slumped into our ancient striped brown sofa that smelled faintly of popcorn. I opened my laptop and stared blankly at the screen, Marco's words marching a solemn parade through my head. *She's controlling you. And you're allowing it.* He was right, but it had always been this way. What other choice did I have?

Bailey in the Corner

I forced myself to write the Fearless Felicity article I'd promised Lauren, then an awkward email to Christian. How did you offer unsolicited advice about a fitness company to a major TV exec?

After my latest blog post, JD Fitness offered me insider information about Friday's big reveal of their upcoming program. I was extremely impressed. I'll admit right up front, I judged them wrong when I accused them of a lack of diversity.

I cringed as I clicked send, then slipped into a pair of pajamas. Our breakfast mess still sat on the table, but the drama of the day had zapped all my energy.

The clock said eleven when I finally said goodnight to Mia, but both our phones beeped wildly as I walked out of her room. She'd received six texts from Marco, and I got four. I didn't have a chance to read them before my phone rang.

"Hey," I said. "Everything okay?"

"No." Marco's voice shook as he spoke. "Jackson disappeared from his room. He's gone."

Chapter 25

Mia crowded close to the phone, her hair still wet from her shower. "What happened?" I asked.

"I'll fill you in later. I just wanted to check if you've heard from him. He must have turned off his phone because we can't ping his location."

"No, but we'll help search. We'll find him, Marco. He'll be okay."

I hung up, my mind racing through the places he could be. The bus station? The airport? Maybe the JD Fitness building.

"Mom," Mia said, tugging my arm. "Look."

She pointed to the tree outside the window, where the bedroom light reflected off a pair of eyes between the limbs of the big oak tree. I pulled open the window and freezing wind wafted in.

Jackson clung to a thin branch in nothing but a T-shirt and pajama bottoms, his eyes as hollow as Daisy's had been twenty years ago when she appeared in that same tree. Jackson didn't move, he just watched us, eyes watering from either the wind or something deeper.

"You said I could come if I needed help?"

"Always." I helped him climb inside, then I wrapped my arms tightly around his cold body, my heart pounding with relief. Jackson shook with sobs, his tears soaking my shoulder. "You're okay," I whispered into his hair.

"I want my dad to come back."

"I know."

Bailey in the Corner

After a long time, Jackson stepped awkwardly away and wiped his face with his arm. "Sorry to just show up."

"Don't be. You're not the first one who's come through that window. Come downstairs, let's get you warmed up."

Mia popped popcorn while Jackson walked down the long hall and sank onto the couch under a warm blanket. He turned on *The Truman Show*—a classic 90's movie. As they settled in, I sent Marco a quick text.

I found him. He's at my house.

We're on our way, he texted back immediately. *My sister's with me. I can't thank you enough.*

A few minutes later he stepped into my entryway, eyes dark, cheeks sagging, and Jackson bolted off the couch, down the hall, straight into Marco's arms.

"I'm sorry," Jackson sobbed. "I shouldn't have left."

Marco kept holding him, but his eyes met mine and held them, his gratitude clear. A moment later, he opened the door for someone who could only be Jackson's mom. She had the same dark eyes, narrow face, and when she saw Jackson, she collapsed against the scratched-up door frame.

"I'm sorry, Mom," Jackson said, letting her wrap him in a hug.

She thanked me, over and over.

"I'm just glad he's safe," I said.

After a few minutes, she turned to Marco. "I've got to get to work, can you take Jackson home?"

Marco frowned. "It's the middle of the night."

"I had to take a double shift." With one last kiss on Jackson's head, she disappeared into the night.

Marco led Jackson to my small kitchen, which consisted of nothing more than a stove, a fridge, and a round wooden table. I cleared this morning's dirty dishes, then gave them space while they spoke in low tones.

"Is he okay?" Mia whispered when I joined her in the living room.

"I think so."

Half an hour later, Jackson slumped down beside Mia, and Marco motioned me into the kitchen. He pulled me straight into a hug.

"Thank you so much for finding him."

I soaked in the warmth of Marco's body, the summery smell of his cologne. As I held him, the tension in his back slowly released. "I didn't do much, he just showed up in Mia's window."

Marco exhaled a slow breath into my hair. "But thanks for being a safe person for him to run to."

"What happened?"

He pulled away and lowered himself into a chair. I sat across the table while he searched for words, concern etched in every line of his expression.

"After practice tonight, Daisy was in the parking lot."

My blood ran cold. Daisy did this?

"She said she wanted to talk about our relationship."

I cringed. This was my fault for asking him to keep up the charade. "Yikes."

"I had Jackson with me, so I told her it wasn't a good time. For a few seconds she seemed annoyed, but then her good mood came back, like she'd flipped a switch. She hopped in my passenger seat saying we could talk after I dropped him off."

My heart beat heavy with dread. This sounded too familiar. "Was she smiling? A big cheerful smile?"

"Yeah, like she'd never been happier. It was strange."

"That's what she does when she's plotting," I said softly.

"She didn't speak to me the whole drive to Jackson's house, she only chatted with him. She asked about his friends and his hobbies, but then she brought up his dad." Marco rubbed his eyes with his fists. "She told him about her brother moving away, how she rode the bus all the way to Georgia and convinced him to come home. By the time he climbed out of the car, Jackson was looking up bus schedules on his phone. Every time I

Bailey in the Corner

told Daisy to stop talking, she brushed me off like it was nothing, but then she slipped him a wad of cash for a bus ticket, right there in my car."

"Oh no," I whispered. "What did you do?"

"I kicked her out."

"Did she go?"

"Yeah. But then she kissed me on the cheek and told me to pick her up at eight on Friday for dinner. Obviously, I told her no, I said we were over forever. But she just smiled that cheerful smile. Ten minutes later, my sister called in a panic saying Jackson had disappeared. We searched everywhere. I kept thinking it was my fault, for kicking her out near Jackson's house, like she was getting back at me."

I reached across the table and pulled Marco's unsteady hand into mine. "Marco, look at me." Red-rimmed eyes searched my face. "There's nothing you could have done to stop her. When Daisy decides to hurt you, you can't predict it."

"Sure, but she didn't just hurt me, she hurt Jackson. And my sister." The last of the color drained from his face. "If I don't go on that date with her on Friday, will she do something worse? I can't let her hurt Jackson again."

I looked down the hall to Mia on the couch. "I know exactly how you feel. I've lived with this same fear for so long."

"You tried to tell me, but I didn't listen. I'm so sorry."

"And I'm sorry I dragged you and Jackson into the middle of this. If I didn't like you so much, she wouldn't be trying so hard to keep you to herself."

Marco's eyes stayed heavy. "You didn't drag me in. I dated Daisy weeks before I met you. You warned me she would lash out. I didn't want you to be right." He pulled his fingers out of mine, then stared at my empty hand, his shoulders slumped.

"Want to know what happened between me and Daisy? How she controls me the way she does?"

Marco looked up, nodding.

I told him everything, starting with the day she moved into town in eighth grade, how desperate I'd been for a friend and how special Daisy made me feel. I told him how everything changed when Daisy's father died and left her in Dominic's care. The abuse, the drugs, how she eventually ran away to my house—but how she'd punish me anytime my success outpaced hers.

"She likes me best when I stay in my corner," I explained. "I do her work and it makes her look good."

Then I told him about my parent's car accident during our senior year of college, and my years of depression with Daisy as my only lifeline.

And my one reckless night with Daisy's brother.

"We never told him about Mia," I whispered. "We didn't even need to discuss it. We both knew he could never find out."

"And that's changed?" Marco asked, glancing down the hall toward the kids.

"Never, until this week. Not until she ditched me on my birthday, and I got tired of living in her shadow. When she saw us dance this afternoon, it tipped her over the edge. She said if we're not friends anymore, she'll tell Dominic everything."

Marco exhaled a long, slow breath. "That's why you sent me away."

I could hardly look at him, ashamed of myself for being so weak, for letting Daisy control my life. "What else could I do?"

Marco nodded, like he finally understood. I'd never told someone the whole story, or any of it. I felt a little lighter to no longer carry it alone, but also heavier that I'd pulled Marco into the middle of it. Now she controlled him too.

"I'm just sorry she lashed out on Jackson," I said. "I was so focused on protecting Mia, I didn't think to keep an eye on Jackson too."

"Me neither," he said. "But I'm glad I finally understand."

"I'll never let her hurt Jackson again."

"Or Mia," Marco said. "We have to protect them."

Bailey in the Corner

His words hung in the air, heavy with the future we'd have to sacrifice.

"Are you guys ever going to join us?" Mia yelled, as the kids burst into laughter at something in the movie.

I turned back to Marco and tried to muster up some optimism. "At least we know, right this minute, all four of us are together and safe."

"And Daisy isn't here."

"Exactly."

"Just one night?" His words hung in the air, an invitation, a promise. A deadline.

"Just one night," I whispered.

Marco took my hand again, pulling me to my feet. He pressed our entwined fingers against his chest, then kissed the back of my hand. My heart fluttered as he led me to my long, leather sectional. He pulled me close against him under a cozy, plush blanket, my back against his chest, his arm around my shoulder, and his other hand still closed around mine.

I settled into him, basking in his warmth and in the comfort of his touch. Even if it was only temporary, even if it only lasted one night, I would enjoy it while I could. I hadn't been close to a man like this since that reckless night with Dominic. This felt nothing like that, this felt . . . safe.

Twenty minutes later, Mia paused the movie to pop another round of popcorn, and Marco sighed. "This is nice, I haven't had a movie night since I was a kid."

"We do them every Friday night," Mia said from the kitchen. "You should come."

I didn't look at Marco. I didn't want to see the truth reflecting in his eyes. This would be our one and only night together.

"My mom and I watch movies too," Jackson said. "You can join us."

"I'd like that," Marco said. "I travel so much, I forget how nice it is to slow down and spend time with people."

"Did you ever want your own kids?" Mia asked, setting the popcorn on the coffee table.

"Yeah, sure. My ex and I talked about it sometimes, but we both traveled for work and neither of us were ready to stop. But now that I'm almost forty, it's probably too late."

"Lame," Mia said, starting the movie back up.

No one spoke again until it ended. The kids had both fallen deeply asleep on the couch, but neither Marco nor I moved to wake them. He kept his arms wrapped tightly around me, like he could extend the night if he held still for one more second.

My phone beeped and I opened a text from Daisy.

I know things are weird with us, but I'd love to chat. I had the best night with Marco, we're officially a couple! And you never told me how sweet Jackson is. We're basically best friends!

Marco took a deep, slow breath behind me. "She'll never let us be together, will she?"

The unspoken answer floated in the silence between us. "I'm sorry."

"Me too." Marco climbed out from behind me. Avoiding my gaze, he picked up the popcorn bowls and carried them to the kitchen, rinsing them in the sink. I followed behind him, folding our blanket that was no longer warm. "With me out of the picture, I guess you're free to pursue Jared. How did it go with him today? Did our dance finally catch his attention?"

We were moving on? Already? Jared felt like an intruder in my mind, encroaching on the warmth that Marco had built up inside me.

"I guess," I said.

The mood had changed. Marco stood taller, stiffer, like casual-Marco had disappeared and professional-Marco took his place.

"Did he ask you out?" he asked.

"No, but I helped him with today's auditions."

Marco nodded again, then walked to the front door and put on his shoes and coat.

"But then I caught him making out with Daisy," I added.

Bailey in the Corner

Marco twirled around, disgust on his face. "Seriously?"

I nodded.

"I don't know who's worse," he growled, hands balled into fists. "Daisy, for staking a ridiculous claim on me while making out with him, or Jared for treating you like shit."

"There's nothing between him and me," I said, weirdly defensive. "It's not like he was unfaithful, he doesn't owe me anything."

"He was a dick. Why are you making excuses for him?"

"I'm not."

"Yes, you are!" He ran his hand through his hair until it splayed all around. "Just like you do with Daisy."

"You're way off." I'd loved Jared my entire adult life, while Marco knew nothing about him.

Marco's jaw twitched, like he was biting back words. "Then answer this. You're doing all these things to prove how valuable you are to him, but what's he doing to prove himself to you?"

I crossed my arms, trying to shrink smaller. "He's a celebrity, Marco, and I'm the crockpot girl. Only one of us has any *proving* to do."

"That's bullshit." He stormed toward me but stopped halfway across the kitchen. Then the fury dropped from his face and his body sagged, his eyes pleading. "Did he like you before you put on expensive clothes? Did he bother to pay attention? Because I did. I couldn't care less if you're the crockpot girl. You're incredible, and you deserve to be pursued as much as anyone else."

His words knocked the air out of my lungs. My arms fell to my sides, and I just stood there, struggling to form words. "You don't get it," I finally said. "He's *Jared DiMaggio.* He's pursued by hundreds of women every day. Why would he notice me? And if you and I aren't dating, what difference does it make?"

The last of the anger drained from Marco's face. He ran another agitated hand through his hair until it draped over his eye. Somehow, even in the middle of our argument, he managed to look sexy. "You're right," he said. "I can't date you. But that doesn't mean I want you to end up with a scumbag. He doesn't deserve you."

I didn't know how to respond. I wasn't sure if I should be angry or flattered, so I settled for silence. He watched me too, his body tense, like he couldn't decide if he wanted to run toward me or away.

"I don't like fighting," I whispered.

Marco sighed. "Me neither."

"Then why are we doing it?"

He thought for a long time, rubbing his forehead. "It's because we're not being ourselves."

"What does that mean?"

"All my life, my dad tried to tell me who to be. He wanted to pick my hobbies, my college major, my career. I hated it. I was miserable every day, until I finally stood my ground and picked my own path. But here I am, and it's happening all over again."

"You're not being yourself?"

"No!" Marco banged his palm against the wall, then rubbed both hands angrily over his face. "Daisy's pulling the strings in both of our lives. We're miserable! You're so scared of her wrath, you're constantly making excuses for her shitty behavior. And I'm standing all the way across the room when all I want is to walk over there and kiss you. But I can't!"

Everything fell silent; even the beat of my heart stopped for one long second.

Two seconds.

Three.

Screw Daisy.

Bolting across the room, I pulled Marco's lips against mine. He melted instantly into me, wrapping his arms around my waist, deepening the kiss. Every emotion I'd refused to let myself feel exploded into my chest. All the desire I'd refused to acknowledge, all the longing I'd suppressed. It flooded back through me, and I dug my fingers into his hair,

Bailey in the Corner

parting my lips and tasting his tongue. He staggered back against the wall, groaning, pulling me with him and slipping his hands under the bottom of my shirt, rubbing them against the bare skin at the small of my back.

Then the kiss changed. Marco slowed down, his lips turning soft as his urgency faded into hesitation. He paused, pulling an inch away, his eyes asking an unspoken question like his body had when we'd danced.

Was this real? Could we make it work?

I was tired of saying no. Tired of sacrificing my happiness to spare other peoples' feelings. This time, my answer was yes. I arched into him and he responded instantly, pressing his warm lips against mine. Our bodies fit together perfectly, and Marco trailed his fingers slowly up each bump on my spine, then back down the soft skin between them. He kissed my chin, then my jaw, then the space behind my ear before pressing his lips gently back against mine.

I never wanted it to end. I wanted an entire night right here in this moment. I wanted a hundred nights, a lifetime of them. Marco must have had the same thought because he held perfectly still, both of us suspended in time, like the moment might last forever.

Then Marco glanced at the door.

Did he even realize he'd done it? No, but I knew that glance. The nervousness in his eyes, the fear that someone was watching, the relief that we were still alone.

He was watching for Daisy.

We both were.

Because we were both scared.

As long as Daisy was in our lives, we'd never escape that fear of being caught. We'd never be free. Never be truly together.

"This is stupid," I growled. "I worked so hard this week, crawling out from under Daisy's thumb. I hate that she's pushing me back down."

Marco sighed. "I hate it too."

"She only has this power over us because we allow it."

His eyes danced between mine. "What are you saying? What about Mia and Jackson?"

"If she touches either of those kids again, I'll kill her myself. But I'm not hiding away while she controls my life anymore."

The corners of his lips turned up. "Do you have a plan?"

There was only one option, and it made my entire body tremble. "We call her bluff. We live our lives however the hell we want, then face the consequences. When she realizes we aren't backing down, she'll eventually give up, right?"

Marco cocked his head, worry in his eyes. "But what about Dominic? Can you risk letting him ruin your life?"

With a heavy breath, I stepped back. "He's already ruining my life and he's not even here. I can't live in this corner forever, and Mia can't live with Daisy breathing down her neck. The only thing standing between us and our freedom is Daisy's threat about Dominic taking custody. To move forward, I need to remove that threat."

"You want to tell Dominic?"

"No. But maybe I talk to an attorney, tell them the whole story. What if Dominic has no parental rights after all?"

"You've never checked?"

I rubbed my forehead. "Honestly, I've been too afraid of the answer to ask. I've worried that if I tell someone, it puts the information out in the world and it could find its way back to Dominic. But I'm tired of hiding, and this seems like a good place to start."

Marco smiled. "I like this plan. Do you have a family attorney? I know a great one. Want me to reach out to him?"

My heart swelled knowing I wasn't alone in this. It felt less daunting. "That would be amazing."

He sent a quick text, then received an immediate response.

"He's free for a lunch consultation tomorrow."

My heart pounded with excitement, and fear. "So soon?"

"I called in a favor."

Bailey in the Corner

"Thank you, Marco."

He trailed his fingers up my arm, leaving goosebumps across my skin. "Anything, for you."

"But how do we keep the kids safe until I figure this out? If Daisy catches wind, she'll go after them again. What if she does something even worse than she did tonight? What if she ruins their audition?"

Marco pulled me into a hug and I rested my cheek against his warm chest.

"I can't believe I'm saying this," he said, "but we probably need to keep the charade going a little bit longer. Just until you have answers."

"You'd do that?" I pulled back, but found only sincerity in his eyes.

If he was willing to be her fake boyfriend, I could return to my corner and keep the peace with Daisy. Just until I had answers. Until lunch tomorrow.

Marco pressed his lips against mine, one last time. "Like I said, I'd do anything for you."

Chapter 26

The next morning, I reached for my usual scuffed leggings and faded T-shirt. I needed to stay in my corner, stay off Daisy's radar. But I couldn't bring myself to wear them.

I dug my box of secret clothes from behind the false wall in my closet, then picked a pair of white, sparkling leggings with red lightning bolts down the sides, with a matching sports bra and tank top. It felt silky smooth between my fingers, and even better on my body. Fortunately, they were a few years old and widely purchased, which meant they wouldn't draw too much attention.

When I stepped in front of the mirror, the red brought out my barely-visible freckles, and the white accented my pale skin. I blew-dry my hair and curled the ends, spraying them into place until I felt ten years younger. I could hardly believe how powerful I felt. After lunch today, the pieces would be in motion. I was doing it. I was *really* doing it.

Soon, I'd be free of Daisy forever.

Half an hour later, I dropped Mia off at the junior high and drove toward JD Fitness. "Perfect Day" by Collective Soul came on the radio like a sign from the 90's fitness gods, and I sang along to every word. Mia would have been proud.

I stepped out of the car, cautiously optimistic, maybe even excited, and I pulled up Fearless Felicity's blog before walking into the office. I typed a quick post and hit send, blasting it out to all six million of my subscribers.

Life's always better when you're honest about who you are. Be yourself, guys, and don't be ashamed. You deserve to be seen.

Then I walked inside, ready to hide in my mundane cubicle until my lunch meeting.

But it turned out, I couldn't.

Sitting on my tiny little desk was the largest bouquet of brilliantly red roses I'd ever seen. There had to be at least two dozen, perfectly arranged in a gold-and-black vase with a matching gold card. My heart skipped a beat, then another. I pulled the card from between the gloriously soft petals and froze, a cold knife plunging into my chest.

They were from Jared.

And he'd addressed the note to Fearless Felicity.

Jared reached my desk before I had time to process my shock. He whirled me around, beaming.

"Your blog post last night was perfect!" He spoke with so much enthusiasm, people in the nearest ten cubicles likely heard him. "The entire internet's excited about JD Fitness again. We might actually pull through!"

My mouth dried out. I yanked him down the hall and into his office, shutting the door behind us with a crash. "Lauren told you?"

"Yeah, last night." He could barely hold still. "You're really Fearless Felicity? You single-handedly saved us from a world-wide boycott! How can we repay you?"

It took all my effort not to violently tremble. "I don't want anything."

"Then I'll give it to you anyway. I have so many plans. Your days of invisibility are over."

"Jared, stop." For so many years, I'd waited for someone to say those words, for the world to find out Felicity's identity and celebrate everything I'd created. But this wasn't how I'd imagined it. The cover girl for JD Fitness? Completely controlled by the marketing department's decisions?

By Daisy's marketing department?

By Daisy?

I wanted to feel angry, or even betrayed, that Lauren gave me up, but all I felt was exposed. My perfectly private, truly authentic secret identity was gone. Ruined. This didn't feel like a celebration, it felt like they were stripping me of myself.

"You should have told me about Fearless Felicity long ago. People will take advantage of her, but I can protect you."

I swallowed hard. "Nobody knows about me."

"Secrets always get out."

"It can't. You have to swear not to tell *anyone*."

"I can't promise that."

"Yes you can!"

He cocked his head. "Is this because of Daisy? Lauren said you were fighting."

I closed my eyes, unsure how to respond to his over-simplified question. "Daisy can never find out."

"Deal. I'll never tell her. But I'll need to tell my attorney, my publicist, and probably the marketing team."

"Daisy manages the marketing team."

"Oh, right." He lit up again. "But not anymore, come look!"

With an extra skip in his step, he wrenched open his door and led me to the spare executive office, the one we'd always used for storage. A new silver name plaque said *Bailey Dupree, VP of Marketing*.

He led me inside the newly emptied office. It smelled of fresh paint and a large desk filled the middle, with three computer monitors in a neat row, plus a blue leather couch that matched the one in his office. A giant floor-to-ceiling window gave a view to the park across the street, and a smaller one opened directly to my old cubicle across the hall.

"Do you like it?"

"What's it for?"

"For you! Lauren says you're great with journalism and promotions, and with the influence of Felicity behind you, you're a perfect VP."

Bailey in the Corner

I yanked the door closed, slamming it harder than I'd intended. "You can't mention Felicity around the office."

Jared nodded. "Right, got it. And your promotion comes with a raise! A big one. Grab your things from your old cubicle and you'll be all set." He grinned expectantly, wrenching the door back open. "I'll let you settle in, then I'll send Lauren over."

"Jared, wait—"

I had to convince him to keep my secret. Had to make sure he understood. But he marched out, and the big white walls closed in around me. What was happening? I'd set out to have an invisible morning, but by nine thirty I already had a major promotion and a giant vase of flowers from my celebrity crush.

And to make it worse, after five years of pining over Jared, he'd finally given me his full attention—but it wasn't because he liked me, it was because he liked Fearless Felicity. He was using me for her influence over the fitness world.

I needed to stop him, before he got out of control.

Racing down the hall, I turned the handle on Jared's door, but it was locked. Voices seeped through, like he was talking on speaker phone. I trudged slowly back to my new office, then let out a shriek of frustration and yanked a handful of my curled hair.

"Ow," I groaned, my scalp burning in protest.

Instead, I sank into my new, plush office chair, which was a million times cozier than the one in my cubicle. Then I logged into my company account on my shiny new computer. Not only were my three monitors a major upgrade from my old laptop, but I suddenly had unrestricted access to all company files.

Even Daisy didn't have that much access.

How would she handle my new VP position? This would undo all my plans to keep her happy. She would congratulate me, give me her brilliant smile, then take out her rage on Mia. Or Jackson or Stella or Marco.

I had to fix this.

LINDSAY HILLER

No one knew about my promotion yet. The second Jared finished his meeting I'd turn it down. But Cinnamon passed my window and froze like a statue, staring at the two dozen roses in my old cubicle.

Please don't read the card.

Then she turned around and froze again, her eyes darting to the nameplate on my door, then to my face. With a gasp, she sprinted off, only to return ten seconds later with Daisy, who took it all in, slowly, her eyebrows drawing together in a deeply pained look. Like I'd punched her in the chest, then again in the gut.

I jumped to my feet. "Daisy, this isn't what it looks like."

She leaned against my doorframe, filing her nails with a pocket-sized file, then blowing the dust onto my clean floor. "It's exactly what it looks like. Who'd you sleep with to get it?"

Cinnamon answered for me. "Jared, obviously."

"While trying to steal Marco? When did you become such a slut?"

Her words sliced into me, an axe through my chest. Did she not know me at all? In all our years, I'd never intentionally hurt her. *She* was the one dating Marco while making out with Jared. But when I tried to protest, she spun on the heel of her cross trainers and vanished.

The next two hours brought a constant stream of spectators. Daisy must have told them everything because I could feel rumors about Jared and me bleeding through the cold walls. Every time another face peered in, I shrank, cowering, second-guessing every decision that led me here. Had I dug this hole with my own ugly ambition? I'd started this fight with Daisy, after all. And with these new clothes, and coaching during Jared's workouts, and falling for Daisy's boyfriend . . . Look what it had gotten me—a promotion, recognition, Jared's attention. Everything I'd always wanted, right here in my hand.

And I hated every bit of it.

At eleven, when Jared still hadn't emerged from his office, I caved and called Marco. He didn't answer, so I texted Mia, but she didn't respond either. Then Daisy walked past my office for the ten thousandth

Bailey in the Corner

time, and I couldn't sit there any longer. I tossed my bouquet in the dumpster out back and flushed the little card down the toilet, then went on a hunt for Lauren.

It took me twenty minutes to find her, in the one place I didn't expect—her own office, right next to Jared's. She slumped behind her enormous desk with her face in her hands, the air stale and cold, and when I knocked, she turned as pale as my ugliest shirt.

Her voice came out hoarse and low. "I'm so sorry."

"Why'd you tell him?"

Lauren lifted her head, eyes wide with shame, until I figured out the answer on my own.

"You're in love with Jared."

She buried her eyes in her hands and I sank into a chair, all my questions about Lauren clicking into place.

"You finally make sense. All the long hours, the late nights, the years at this job you hate in an industry you don't care about."

Lauren peeked through her fingers, face riddled with shame. "I'm so pathetic."

"You're not . . . But I'm starting to think you could do better than him."

"He's not that bad." Lauren rubbed her forehead. "He's driven and focused, which means sometimes he plows people over to reach his goals. But I'm the same way, which is why we work well together."

"You don't plow people over."

"I threw a mug at your face."

"Good point," I said, which made Lauren a fraction less pale, but the stress lines around her eyes had grown so deep they reached her bones. When was the last time she slept? And why didn't Jared stay late with her, every single night, trying to keep the company from bankruptcy? In fact, he hardly seemed stressed at all. He didn't worry over landing the TV contract either, he just assumed Lauren would make it happen. "Does he always push the stressful stuff onto you?"

"He didn't use to, but it's gotten worse over the years."

And there it was.

Daisy had gotten worse over the years too. Lauren needed to be free of Jared as much as I needed to escape Daisy, or we would both drown together.

"I shouldn't have told him about Fearless Felicity," Lauren said. "The second I said it, I'd wished I could take it back."

"Then why'd you do it?"

"I thought if I saved the company, he might finally notice me, realize I'm here, jumping up and down, waving my arms to get his attention. But now he only thinks about you. Has he shown you your new office yet?"

"I hate it."

"Has Daisy seen it?"

"She's the reason I hate it."

Lauren nodded like she genuinely understood. "I imagine she wasn't always so awful. When did it get this bad?"

I had to think for a while, back to the moment when she'd finally erased the last traces of Bailey and left me only as Bee. It was the day we started working at JD fitness. The day I realized the only way to survive was to let Daisy win *everything*. That was the day I swapped out my nice clothes for ragged ones.

Daisy had approved wholeheartedly.

"Too long ago," I told Lauren.

"Why have you let it go on?"

Before I said the words, I knew how pathetic they would sound. "To keep the peace. But I've enabled her for so long now, I doubt Daisy realizes what's happening anymore."

"Bailey . . ." Lauren folded her hands on her desk, bumping a pen that rolled slowly across the smooth wood. "Everyone knows when they're being an ass. And everyone knows it's not okay. Don't act like you're anything other than the victim. You deserve better."

"You deserve better too," I said.

Bailey in the Corner

"Believe me, I know."

"Will you do something for me? Try to keep him from telling anyone about Felicity?"

"Of course. And again, I'm so sorry. I wish I could take it back."

"Any word from Christian? Will he reconsider JD Fitness?"

Lauren shook her head, chewing absently on the tip of a pen. "Nothing."

I left Lauren's office a few minutes later, tried Jared's door again, then found Stella in the fabrication room, sweating over a giant stack of fabric. The thrumming of a half dozen sewing machines made the floor vibrate through my shoes, and Stella didn't hear me approach. "Hey."

She lit up, and the urge to cry smothered me. Today had turned into the opposite of what I'd hoped for, and her friendly face was too much.

"You got promoted," she said. "Congratulations!"

"Thanks, I think."

"You're not happy about it?"

I buried my face in my hands. "Lauren told Jared about you-know-what."

Stella's eyes widened. "She shouldn't have done that. Are you a total celebrity now?"

"In his eyes, yeah. He doesn't understand why I want it kept secret."

"Well, if your life suddenly blows up, I'll still be here for you. Want to get lunch and talk about it?"

I desperately wanted to. I wanted to tell her everything, just like I'd told Marco. But my meeting with the attorney was in half an hour.

That same minute, though, Jared poked his head into the mail room. "Don't go anywhere, Bailey, you and I have a lunch date."

The second he disappeared, Stella shrieked, jumping up and down. "A lunch date with Jared? Tell me every single detail when you get back."

Despite her excitement, unease crept down my spine. I needed to meet with Marco's attorney, but I also needed a serious conversation with

Jared. The longer I waited, the more time he had to tell people about Fearless Felicity.

With a groan, I pulled out my phone and sent Marco a text.

I'm so sorry, can you reschedule lunch? Something's come up and it can't wait.

A few minutes later, I climbed into the passenger seat of Jared's Audi. It still smelled brand new, and the leather racing seats hugged my body. This was my first time alone with him outside work, and I wasn't sure what to say. Where should I put my hands? My purse?

He sounded completely at ease as he pulled out. "How's your new office?"

"Big. And empty."

Jared laughed. "Don't worry, you'll fill it. And once these auditions end, we'll have more time to train you."

"Look, Jared—"

But he cranked the radio to an 80's song I didn't know until we pulled into Le Chateau, a historic mansion converted into a fancy French restaurant. When we walked inside, a live three-piece orchestra was playing a quiet melody from one corner, and servers in tuxedos carried wine glasses with gloved hands. They sat us at a table in the dead center, with fluted glasses and flaming candles and way too many forks around my plate. My gym clothes looked ridiculously out of place, especially since Jared had donned slacks and a sport coat. But no one looked twice, including all the people who knew Jared by name.

They came to our table in droves, everyone wanting to shake his hand. He introduced me every time, a model of good manners. "This is Bailey, our new VP of Marketing," or "Bailey's the new face of JD Fitness," or "She's the brightest employee to walk through our doors."

His words were flattering, but I was grateful when our server arrived and people finally left us alone. The entire menu was in French. I copied Jared's order and tried to bring up Fearless Felicity. But then Jared's phone beeped.

Bailey in the Corner

"One sec, I've waited all morning for this call."

Fifteen minutes later, his phone was still at his ear when our food arrived. He slid his plate away, scribbling notes about a fundraiser on a notepad. I pushed my food around with my fork. It was chicken in a fancy sauce, but I didn't recognize the grains or veggies. They tasted fine, but as the clock ticked by, my appetite shriveled.

Forty-five minutes into his phone call, I'd eaten all I could, drank three cups of diet soda, and our candles had died out. Why were we even here? Clearly, he didn't want to spend real time with me. Was he showing me off? Letting everyone see us together before he announced Felicity's identity? Last week, all I'd wanted was a date with Jared DiMaggio. But now? Did I want to be his arm candy? His "brightest employee"?

Ten minutes later, I asked our server for the check, then slid it across the table to Jared. After twenty more, he led me back to his car, still on the phone. By the time we reached the office, two hours had passed, and he finally hung up.

"Great lunch," he said. "Very productive. Let's do it again tomorrow."

Seriously?

Yes, he was completely serious. He'd had a productive meal, with no clue that mine was a waste of time. I'd sacrificed my attorney meeting for this! Lauren had said he was so focused sometimes he plowed people over. Was this what she meant?

Jared disappeared inside his office and locked the door again, leaving me alone in the hall between my new office and my old cubicle. I paused between my two desks, then finally sank into the barely padded chair of my cubicle, setting my phone beside me.

At least this little box of an office felt familiar. As VP of Marketing, what exactly was my job? The accounting team could easily take over payroll, and anyone could count powder packets and fill crockpots. But to be honest, I liked knowing my tasks held the company together. But now how would I spend my days? As Felicity full time?

Before I could stew over the question too much, Stella burst around the corner.

"Come quick!" She grabbed my arm and yanked me back the way she came. "Lauren posted the official MaxFit99 cast list, and you're on it!"

Chapter 27

That couldn't be possible. Jared and I had made a deal—he would give Daisy my spot if I stayed on the microphone. We sprinted to the cafeteria door where the cast lists had been taped, two papers side-by-side, and we shoved through the crowd. Sure enough, the first name in Group A was Stella. The first name in Group B was mine.

Daisy wasn't listed at all.

Why wouldn't they include her? Only one other cast member from the JD Fitness staff made the list—a man who worked in the warehouse. Every other name came from outside the office. Dread soaked through me like a rainstorm, heavy and cold. Even if I gave Daisy my spot, the damage was already done. There'd be no undoing her humiliation. Maybe I could talk to Jared or Lauren, get them to switch someone out for Daisy before she saw the list.

Lauren walked by and I grabbed her arm. "Why did you give me Daisy's spot?"

"You're the better person for the job."

She moved away, revealing Daisy standing behind her, watching the whole thing. Her eyes darted to the list and my heart raced, faster and faster.

"Daisy, I told them to pick you."

For the first time in twenty years, tears filled her eyes. Not the calculated kind, with a phony smile and fiery eyes, but genuine sadness.

No, not sadness. Devastation.

"You've ruined everything," she said. "MaxFit99 was my chance to earn my own show, to become a full-time JD Fitness Trainer. This was *my* dream, and you destroyed it."

She was right. In the last six hours, I'd stripped her of her position as head of marketing, her future on MaxFit99, and her chance to prove herself to Jared. These were Daisy's biggest dreams, and I stole them from her.

"I didn't mean to," I said, but fury erupted across her face.

"Yes, you did, just like you stole everything else that matters to me. But this is the last straw. Time to return the favor."

"What does that mean?" I asked, my throat restricting.

She pulled her phone from her pocket. "It means I'm telling Dom everything, right now."

"Daisy, don't!"

But she scrolled through her contacts until she reached his name.

Panic coursed through me. "It won't do any good, I'm already meeting with an attorney. When we're done, Dom won't have any rights to Mia!"

Daisy paused, then a grin slid over her face. "Who needs rights? We'll just drive to the studio and take her. Everything you care about will disappear in a flash, just like mine did today."

Then she whirled around and stormed away, pressing her phone against her ear.

I couldn't think. Couldn't breathe. Stella said something to me, but her words didn't register. I needed to talk to Mia, *right now.*

I sprinted back to my desk to grab my phone, but froze. It wasn't on the desk where I'd left it. Dropping to my knees I searched the floor, the drawers, inside my purse. It wasn't anywhere. Instead, I checked my laptop for the dance studio's number and asked the receptionist to grab Mia from her class.

"Mom?" Mia's voice sounded in my ear.

Bailey in the Corner

My fingers shook with relief and I collapsed into my chair. "Listen very closely," I said. "Absolutely do not leave the dance studio with Daisy or her brother today, do you understand?"

"What's going on?"

I hesitated. How much to tell her? With Mia's audition coming up tomorrow, I didn't want to spook her too much. "She's acting especially crazy today. Just please, don't leave with anyone except Marco, okay? Promise?"

"Sure, Mom."

After giving similar instructions to the receptionist, I finally hung up. But I only felt marginally better. Daisy had threatened to kidnap my child.

Kidnap.

How had we reached this point? It didn't feel real. I wanted to talk to Marco, to explain everything and reschedule that meeting with his attorney, but where the hell was my phone? Before I could search again, Lauren found me, pointedly avoiding my eyes.

"Jared wants you."

"Right now?"

She shifted her weight. "Yeah."

Calling Marco would have to wait. Lauren's awkwardness worsened when we entered Jared's office. Not only did she lock the door behind us, but she tucked a gym towel into the crack between the door and the floor, soundproofing the room. My lungs grew heavy. This could only mean one thing.

It was time to talk about Felicity.

Jared pulled three chairs around the small table in the center of the room, and we each picked one. His countenance was the opposite of Lauren's. He bounced in his chair, brimming with enthusiasm. Then he removed his sport coat and rubbed his hands together.

"It's time to brainstorm Fearless Felicity's next articles." He scratched her name on a piece of paper. "Here's what I'm thinking: we'll start with a rave review of tomorrow's promo workout, specifically addressing the points she made against us on Tuesday. That should bring back any fans who were still on the fence and spark new interest from her subscribers."

He paused to scribble notes.

"Next, we'll have her review the Waterfall Collection. Has Felicity received the promo outfits we mailed?"

My stomach soured with every word he spoke, but I nodded. The box still sat in the trunk of my car.

"Perfect. I expect we'll sell a ton when they're released on Friday, but when sales taper off, we'll have Felicity post her review to start a second wave. That should keep numbers up for quite a while. Any questions so far?"

Neither of us reacted. Lauren stared at the table.

Jared pushed on. "After that, we should focus on Blue Juice. It's our best supplement, but weirdly, it hardly sells. Maybe people don't know about it. One carefully placed article from Felicity should solve that problem. Of course, you'll have to write a few unrelated articles in between, so no one suspects you work for us. How often do you usually post?"

"Once a week."

"Let's ramp it up to every other day, at least for a while. We need to take advantage of Felicity's supposedly unbiased opinion before the world figures out who you are. After that, they'll know you work for me, and you'll lose your credibility as an independent Influencer. We need to sell as much product as we can before that happens."

My stomach twisted. "You talk like it's inevitable. Why tell anyone?"

"That's how publicity works. Secrecy drums up curiosity, then you use a big reveal to cash out."

"What if I don't want to cash out?"

His face wrinkled with pity. "It's unavoidable. In fact, you two are my marketing gurus. Start planning the best time to announce your identity. Maybe at the release of next quarter's show? Plan out a detailed

Bailey in the Corner

timeline, then draft your next few articles and have it all to me by tomorrow morning. I want plenty of time to review and make changes."

Lauren finally met my eyes. *I'm sorry,* she mouthed.

"Does that work?" Jared asked, looking only at me. He needed a real confirmation. He needed to know if I'd roll with his plan. Like I hadn't yet handed all the keys to Felicity over to him. On some level, I still had a choice.

But what would happen if I said no? Would he reveal my identity anyway, when it suited him best? Would he send me back to the corner where "crockpot girl" belonged? Or would he fire me completely?

Maybe I still controlled Felicity, but Jared controlled everything else. It felt dangerously similar to my relationship with Daisy. After all my effort to escape her grasp, did I want to entangle myself in someone else's?

On the other hand, I'd wanted to feel important, wanted people to see how hard I worked and how much I contributed. If they knew about Felicity, I wouldn't have to hide anymore. No one would doubt I deserved my big executive office. No one would accuse me of sleeping with the boss.

I had no idea what choice to make.

All I knew was I needed to protect Mia. That meant minimizing Daisy's anger until we worked out the situation with Dominic—and she was already furious. Losing her spot on MaxFit99 had been hard enough, but if she learned Felicity's identity? She'd explode. My only chance of postponing Jared's announcement was to stay as close to him as possible.

Jared watched me, unmoving, anticipating.

"That sounds good," I said.

But the second I said the words, I hated them.

"Great!" Relief dripped from Jared's eyes. He plopped a file of printed pictures onto the table. "Now let's talk about your outfit for tomorrow's live workout. I'm thinking this one."

He spread pictures of Waterfall Collection items across the round table, then pointed to one in the center. The low-waisted spandex shorts shimmered like purple water. The single-shoulder sports bra dipped low in the front with a vertical gap cut between the breasts. The model wearing the outfit, Daisy of course, pulled it off perfectly. But the thought of my twelve-year-old daughter seeing me show so much cleavage made me squirm.

"You can pick it up from the fabrication room anytime," Jared said. "I'll let Lyneeka know, and you can choose any color. Then, I'm thinking this one for Stella." He pointed to an outfit identical to mine, but with high-waisted shorts. "We need to make her prettier, and this option is the most slimming. Thoughts?"

Lauren looked as offended as I felt.

I finally found my voice. "Not only do you sound pig-headed, but that's discrimination. You can't say things like that."

Lauren nodded in agreement, but Jared stayed focused on the pictures.

"Actually, I can, since we're hiring her as a performer. It sounds cold-hearted, but I care about what sells, not what spares people's feelings." Jared's phone rang and he glanced at the screen. "I need to take this. Can you guys finish up in Bailey's office?" He gathered the papers and shoved us out of the room.

Lauren finally spoke when we reached my office door. "Thanks for speaking up about Stella's clothes. What do we tell her?"

I opened the file he'd shoved in my arms and stared at Jared's selection. "We tell Stella to wear whatever the hell she wants. She deserves to feel confident on that stage."

Lauren grinned. "Perfect."

We walked to the fabrication room and found a flurry of people picking through piles of Waterfall clothes.

Lyneeka met us at the door. "Photoshoot for the new cast is in an hour. Once you pick an outfit, I'll do your hair and makeup."

I chose knee-length shorts and a simple sports bra *without* a slit between the breasts in a shimmering shade of pale red. Stella picked

Bailey in the Corner

something similar, but with a Waterfall tank over her bra, her tiger tattoo growling from her shoulder.

"You look stunning," I said, as Lyneeka attacked Stella's hair. "Want to see what Jared picked out for us?"

I showed her the pictures and she burst into laughter. "My boobs would fall out in twelve seconds."

"I like what you picked much better."

"You too."

An hour later, the eleven of us posed for pictures on the stage. Each time the camera clicked, my stress level calmed. Most of today had become a train wreck, but standing with the cast of MaxFit99, I'd found the one silver lining.

When the photoshoot ended, I searched for my phone to call Marco. I wanted to explain why I'd bailed on our lunch meeting, and I wanted to tell him about my roller coaster of a day. But my phone was still missing. Even when I pinged it from my watch, it couldn't be located. I must have left it in Jared's car.

Jared was nowhere to be found, so I spent the next two hours turning the photoshoot pictures into last-minute MaxFit99 ads. Then I moved my things from my cubicle into my new office.

At six-thirty, I couldn't stay in one place. I wanted to see Mia, of course, and to check in on Jackson about last night. But seeing Marco . . . my nerves tingled from my ears to toes.

But at seven-fifteen, they hadn't arrived and my anxiety skyrocketed. Had Daisy taken Mia? Convinced her to get in Dominic's car? I called Mia's cell from my desk phone and groaned in relief when she answered.

But the news wasn't great. She was still at the dance studio. Jackson hadn't been there all afternoon, and Marco never picked her up.

"Just be patient," I said. "They know how important this last practice is."

"I'm trying." But worry laced Mia's voice. Without tonight's rehearsal, they had no chance of nailing their audition. And without my phone, Marco couldn't contact me. Mia asked the front desk for his number and I wrote it on a sticky note, but when I called him, it went straight to voicemail.

When the clock hit eight-thirty, I finally faced the truth.

Mia wasn't missing.

Marco and Jackson were.

Chapter 28

Where were they?

My car roared to life, but I didn't shift it out of park. I didn't do anything but sit there in the JD Fitness parking lot, stagnant, my keychains hanging from the ignition, swinging, hitting the dash in rhythm.

Tick, tick, tick.

I focused on that noise, clung to it.

Were they okay?

Had Daisy done something to delay them? Had she meddled with Jackson? Or had he run away again? Whatever had happened, it was my fault.

And where the hell was my phone?

I had one job. One, single job—to spend the week helping Mia prepare for the biggest night of her life. But what did I do instead? Started an epic battle with Daisy, fell for her boyfriend, and opened the door for Daisy to ruin everything.

I clenched the steering wheel until my knuckles ached, then slammed my palms onto the dash. Why didn't I wait until next week to stand up for myself? Why couldn't I keep my hands off her boyfriend? I'd done this dance with Daisy for twenty years—I could have held out a few more days. Now my little girl was stuck in a parking lot, alone, waiting for me to pick her up. Her world was crumbling, and the blame fell solely on me.

When I reached the dance studio's parking lot, Mia ran, crying, into my arms. A sob lurched into my throat too. Until the moment I saw her, felt her petite body, I hadn't realized the depth of my fear that Daisy would take her.

"Where are they?" Mia cried.

"I don't know." I held her tight.

"How could they not show up?"

"I don't know, sweetie. I just don't know."

On the way home, Mia didn't turn the radio to her usual 90's station. She stared out the window, eerily quiet, both feet on the seat, arms around her knees.

"Do you think Jackson will still audition?" Mia spoke softly, like she was afraid if anyone heard, her words might come true.

"I hope so." But I didn't sound reassuring.

Mia retreated to her bedroom as soon as we reached home, so I perched on the end of her bed. My eyes kept darting to her window, hoping Jackson's face might appear in the oak tree.

"They'll come tomorrow," she said, climbing into bed. She spoke with a steely determination, but her voice cracked on the last word.

"Definitely. And you'll steal the show."

She pulled the fluffy covers up to her chin and I kissed her forehead, my heart breaking as I turned out the light. This time of night, Mia was usually doing homework or watching movies, music blaring, lights on. But tonight, the house stayed dark. With a blanket around my shoulders, I sank onto the couch in the same corner I'd curled up with Marco only one night before.

The cushions felt too cold, too empty.

I moved to the kitchen instead, remembering Marco washing the dishes two feet away, how he'd held my hand, the warmth of his lips. But even with an attorney's help, had Daisy become too ingrained in my life to untangle all her threads? Could we truly be free of her? I'd have to move away, vanish overnight without a forwarding address. And even then,

Bailey in the Corner

she'd hunt me down, because without my help she'd be exposed as an incompetent phony.

She would never let that happen.

Which was why she kept pulling my strings and punishing me when I stepped out of line.

My question now was, after taking MaxFit99 from her, was she punishing me by detaining Marco tonight? She'd already told the staff I'd slept with Jared, then turned my new office into a zoo. Was she telling Dominic about Mia right now? Would they come to my door tonight while Mia slept?

Someone knocked on the door.

My heart lurched.

Marco and Jackson?

Or Dominic?

My hand flew to my mouth, the air stopping in my lungs. I was almost too scared to answer.

But when I flung open the door, it was Daisy—with a tub of caramel ice cream, and a bleeding, swollen eye.

Frosty air gusted into the house, carrying the smell of rain and wet leaves. I shivered. Daisy did too, wearing nothing but her leggings and a sports bra, like she'd run away from somewhere in a hurry. A single drop of blood leaked from the slit under her rapidly swelling eye.

Finally, she held out the caramel ice cream. "A peace offering?"

"I don't like caramel ice cream."

Daisy's eyebrows quirked in surprise. "It's your favorite."

"It's *your* favorite. I've always hated it."

She lowered the ice cream against her goosebump-riddled stomach and her chin quivered. "I've been such a bitch, haven't I?"

The wind blew again. I didn't want her inside, but I couldn't leave her out there without real clothes. We'd done this dance a thousand times; I knew exactly how our conversation would go. She would apologize and shower me with praise, I would forgive her, and we'd start the whole, miserable cycle over again.

But not this time.

"Make yourself something warm," I said, pointing to the kitchen. "I'll grab you a sweater."

When I came back, she'd made us both cinnamon tea.

"I wasn't sure if you wanted any." She spoke timidly, like she wasn't sure of her place in my home anymore. She added a dollop of milk to mine, exactly how I liked it, then sat across from me, warming her fingers on her mug.

"Do you want to tell me who gave you that black eye?"

Daisy touched her face. "Is it purple already?"

"Almost. Did Dom hit you?"

She kept her eyes glued to the table, but her fingers trembled enough that her metal ring tapped against her cup.

"Did he grab your arm too? You have bruises around your wrist."

Daisy hid her hands in her lap. "It was my fault."

"No, it wasn't. Every time he hurts you, it's his fault. When will you stop letting him back into your house?"

"I don't want to talk about it."

I folded my arms and leaned back in my chair. "Fine. What do you want to talk about?"

Daisy sighed with her entire body, a tear rolling down her cheek. "Us, Bee. I miss you. What's happening? This week has been a disaster."

The answer felt so huge, so complex. How could I wrap twenty years of emotional abuse into one short conversation? Maybe if I started with something simpler. "Why'd you ditch me on my birthday?"

Daisy crumpled in her chair. "I shouldn't have done that. Or told people you slept with Jared, or any of it. I don't know what got into me." She leaned over the table and sobbed into her arms, *real* tears for the second time today. I'd never seen Daisy like this, a completely honest,

Bailey in the Corner

emotional mess. She was always calculating, always plotting, but this time?

She was different.

Maybe she'd hit rock bottom.

Maybe she was finally tired of this dance with her brother. Maybe she was finally ready to take control of her life. A spark of hope ignited in my chest and I reached across the table and took her hand. She didn't look up, but she squeezed my fingers.

"Dom flipped out when he saw Jared's cast list."

"He was mad you weren't on it?"

"Yeah."

I put my other hand over hers too. "Did you remind him you've already starred in three of Jared's shows?"

"It doesn't matter. He said he's sick of his sister taking second place."

"Second place? You win at everything! Who does he think keeps beating you?"

Daisy finally raised her eyes, mascara streaking down her cheeks. "You. You're better than me at everything. Why else would I sabotage you? It's because he knows how perfect you are."

I pulled my hands out of hers. "Was that supposed to be a compliment?"

Daisy shook her head, "No, you're right. That was awful." She stood and paced across the kitchen. "I don't know what's wrong with me. I get like this every time he comes home. He makes me feel like the worst sort of failure, then I do stupid, desperate things to earn his approval, but I end up with him more disappointed than ever. I can't win, Bee. How do I make him happy?"

Catching her shoulders, I held her inches from my face. She looked so lost, so fragile, no signs of fire anywhere.

"You don't," I said. "You could become queen of the world and it still wouldn't be enough. Why are you trying so hard?"

"Because he has all Daddy's money. If I want any, he says I have to prove I'm worth it."

"That's disgusting. Who made him in charge of deciding your worthiness?"

Daisy lifted one shoulder. "Dad did, before he died."

"Forget about it. You have a good job; you don't need a penny of that money."

She blinked three times, like she couldn't understand my words. But then she took a deep breath. "Then what do I do?"

"You stop defining yourself by what he thinks. All that matters is what *you* think about yourself. You're an excellent personal trainer, you're fantastic on stage, and you're even getting the hang of making ads."

Daisy snorted.

"Okay, not really with the ads. But the rest is more than enough to make a successful career."

"And when he tells me I'm not enough?"

"You let it go."

Another round of tears dripped from her eyes, so I pulled Daisy into a hug. She gasped for air and clung to me, her fingernails digging into my back like I might evaporate if she let go too soon. I held on until her tears finally slowed.

"I'm so sorry," she sighed, "for everything. You're always there, every time he knocks me down, and I don't deserve it. I'll kick him out tonight. And I'll take away his key."

"That's a good plan."

Except she'd made that promise a dozen times before. Hundreds, maybe. So, as she popped a bag of popcorn and dumped it into a bowl for us to share, my insides squirmed. Would this be any different than the other times? I'd never seen her so raw, so real. But would that be enough? Could our friendship survive?

Did I want it to?

Bailey in the Corner

Would she give me the freedom to make my own choices? Or would she keep dangling Dominic above our heads as a permanent threat?

"Did you tell your brother about Mia?" I whispered.

"Of course not." Daisy's eyes held mine. "No matter how mad I got, I would never hurt Mia that way."

Relief poured through me like a waterfall. "Thank you."

When Daisy finally stood to leave, I stopped her right inside the door. "You're kicking Dom out, right?"

"He'll be gone by morning, I promise." She smiled, a real genuine smile, and nudged me with her elbow. "And with your new fancy job, everyone will be jealous I was your best friend *before* you became rich and famous."

"Do you need a ride home?"

Daisy opened the door and a gust of frigid air swirled through the entryway. "I'll walk—I need time to figure out what to say to Dom."

"It's three miles, in the middle of the night."

"I'll be fine, if I can borrow this sweater."

She waved goodbye and ducked out into the cold, using her phone as a flashlight. I closed the door quietly behind her and leaned against it, clueless how to process all my thoughts. I guess we were friends again? But even if she sent Dominic away for good, how long until she tried to push me back into my corner? Still, my goal today had been to appease Daisy until I met with an attorney. If nothing else, I'd accomplished that.

But I felt uneasy.

Typically, I'd write a blog post and let Felicity's fearless personality hash through my experiences, but Jared wanted to save my next post for a review of tomorrow's YouTube show.

Felicity was officially gone.

And with my revived friendship with Daisy, so was all the freedom I'd won back this week.

I'd handed it back to her on a silver platter.

Chapter 29

Neither of us touched our breakfasts, and I couldn't even manage giving Mia a half-hearted pep talk on the way to school. After dropping her off, I arrived to work early, my protein shake and a slice of toast untouched. The building was still empty, the air cold, so I slipped into my new office without bothering to turn on the light. It smelled faintly of old storage and musty cardboard boxes. Besides filling the crockpots, I had nothing to do but stare at my computer screen and dread every single part of today.

Eventually Jared and Lauren arrived; I could hear her shrieking down the hall.

"What the hell were you thinking, making today a *live* broadcast? We only picked our cast yesterday!"

"The show will be authentic," Jared's voice shot back.

"Authentically shitty. When we crash and burn, it'll be *your* fault."

"There's always the TV deal."

"The TV deal? Christian emailed me late last night. He's getting on a plane in an hour to come watch us make a fool of ourselves. I'm already humiliated, and his plane hasn't even taken off!"

Felicity's email had worked, then? Christian was coming here? Today? It didn't make me feel any better. It was just one more way to fail.

The office slowly filled with noise, everyone buzzing with excitement for today's live show. The stage crew scurried past my office with a flurry

Bailey in the Corner

of questions for Jared. New cast members wandered in and Lyneeka dressed them in Waterfall clothes and plastered their faces with stage makeup.

An alarm buzzed through the building—Jared's way of marking the countdown to a new show. Eight a.m. The live show started at one.

Daisy hadn't arrived yet.

The roar of an engine rumbled into the parking lot. I peeked out the lobby door, my stomach dropping. A shiny new red Mustang GT500 had stopped right in front of the door, parked across the two handicap spaces in a diagonal. Daisy stepped out of the driver's seat wearing a matching red jacket and shades.

Her brother climbed out of the passenger seat.

Over six feet tall, Dominic Rose towered over everyone, and the Polynesian tribal tattoos lacing up his arms and neck made his presence all the more menacing. He tucked his hands casually into the pockets of his faded black jeans, but nothing hid the barely controlled hostility simmering in his eyes.

Daisy bee-lined straight for me, pulling me into a hug in front of everyone.

"He gave me the car this morning," she whispered. "I'll still kick him out, I promise."

Then she linked her arm in mine and pulled me to the center of the crowd. Everyone gawked at the car, while Dominic leaned casually against the passenger door. Even Jared grazed his fingers down the sleek white racing stripe.

"Is he sticking around?" I asked, quietly so Dominic wouldn't hear.

Daisy winced. "He wants to watch the show. I couldn't say no after a gift like this."

Stella kept looking at me, then at Daisy.

Daisy followed me inside a few minutes later. She removed her sunglasses, revealing makeup caked over her black eye. The purple peeked out underneath, but she smiled brightly. "I brought office-warming gifts."

Dominic entered my office behind her, and I sucked in a breath. He said nothing. Neither did I. But his eyes trailed up every inch of my navy leggings and my blue sports bra-tank top combo.

My skin crawled.

Daisy revealed a three-foot canvas picture of our first Homecoming dance, me in that pea-green dress, and Daisy in her leather boots and flame-red skirt. "This is to remember how our friendship started," she said, and she hung the picture in the dead center of my wall.

Next, she set a candy bowl on my desk and dumped in a large bag of Hot Tamales. "In case you need comfort food."

At least it wasn't caramel ice cream.

"And finally . . ." She handed me a puke bag, the kind they keep on airplanes for motion sickness.

"What's this for?"

Daisy burst into giggles. "It was a joke! Remember how scared you were that first time you performed in college? You kept saying you were going to be sick, so I brought that puke bag, just in case."

Had she forgotten I'd performed hundreds of times in college? Then hundreds more at Lucky 7 Gym?

She propped up the bag on my desk as Dominic dunked his giant fist into my bowl of Hot Tamales. The two of them filled up my entire office, every square inch, leaving no room for me. The weird thing was, it all felt familiar, expected even. Was this how I'd lived the past twenty years? Because I could hardly stand another minute.

Another buzz rang through the building. Nine a.m. Four hours until showtime.

Lauren raced frantically past my door, her skin as white as the walls, so I jumped out of my chair and followed, grateful for an excuse to escape. Lauren slid into her desk chair, grinding her teeth and pulling violently at her hair.

"Lauren, stop!"

She didn't.

Bailey in the Corner

I grabbed her hands, putting my face right in front of hers. "Take a deep breath." I inhaled, slow and steady, until she mimicked my actions and her shoulders relaxed. "Now, tell me what's going on."

"Christian will be here in a couple of hours. But half our cast hasn't shown up!"

"Did we give them an arrival time?"

Lauren froze, then yanked her hands out of mine and resumed pulling her hair. "This is too much, Bailey. I can't do everything, all the time. I need an assistant. Or six."

I grabbed her hands again, clasping them as hard as I could. This time, she took a slow breath on her own.

"I'm panicking. What do I do?"

"First, you keep your cool." I spoke in my calmest, slowest voice. "No more pulling your hair or you'll be bald before you're fifty. Second, do you have their phone numbers in your files? Can you call them?"

"Phone numbers?" She sounded dazed. "Sure, I can do that."

"Perfect. You get them to the building, and I'll send them to Lyneeka to get ready. No stress, no hair pulling. Deal?"

Lauren nodded, then dug through the files on her desk before looking sharply back at me. "Wait, why aren't *you* in hair and makeup? Get there, right now! Go! Go! Go!"

I let her shoo me out the door, but my own stress was creeping into my chest. I didn't want us to fail either, but with Christian on his way, and only half the cast in the building, plus Dominic's overbearing presence? I followed my own advice and took a slow, steady breath.

It didn't help.

The fabrication room had been repurposed as the staging area for the cast, and heaps of Waterfall clothes in every color were piled on tables and in corners. Lyneeka and two others dashed frantically between the mounds, putting together outfits for the six cast members who had arrived so far. With only one dressing room, she had taped together boxes to form shades for people to change behind, and if someone's outfit didn't fit, the fabrication team frantically dug through the piles to find them something else. Lyneeka stood at the edge of it all, barking out orders.

"About time you arrived," she said. "I was about to send Stella to hunt you down."

But Stella sat rigid at a far-off table, already in her Waterfall outfit, staring blankly into the distance.

"Is she okay?" I asked Lyneeka.

"Scared to death. Barely said a word all morning."

I crossed the room and squeezed Stella's trembling arm. "Hey."

"I'm freaking out."

"Have you eaten?"

She shook her head, but finally looked at me. "Looks like you and Daisy are friends again."

"She showed up at my house last night. It was . . . confusing."

"If you want to talk, I'm here."

"Thanks. Now let's get some food in you."

I made her a Neon Nutrition shake. She forced me to drink one too, and my stomach churned. Maybe I'd need Daisy's puke bag after all. Then Lyneeka pulled me over to get dressed.

"Jared set these aside for you." She pointed to the Waterfall clothes from his photo—the one-strap bra with the slit between the breasts. He'd paired them with short shorts, not even the knee-length ones I'd worn yesterday.

"Doesn't he realize I'm thirty-five? I don't think he wants the camera guy zooming in on my veiny legs."

"I just want you to feel good about what you're wearing," Lyneeka said. "Whatever you pick, I'll back you up."

The alarm buzzed through the office again, marking ten o'clock. That meant one hour until Christian's plane landed, two hours before the cast's on-stage warm up, and three hours before the camera would broadcast live to the world. My stomach twisted and I searched for the nearest garbage can in case my shake came back up. Then I found my outfit from the

Bailey in the Corner

photoshoot last night, the double-strapped bra and the knee-length leggings.

But I paused when I picked them up. Two other girls already wore the same outfit in different colors. Jared needed Fearless Felicity to review *all* the clothes in the Waterfall Collection, and she couldn't do that if someone didn't wear them on screen. My lungs sank deep into my stomach, the air turning murky and thick. Jared controlled Felicity, and therefore controlled everything, whether I liked it or not.

I set down the leggings and picked up Jared's ensemble, drawing the line at the short shorts. And the color. I swapped them out for pink, then slid into knee-length shorts and Jared's favorite bra.

"Looking good," Lyneeka said, when I stepped out from behind her cardboard dressing room.

"If my boobs don't fall out."

Lyneeka snickered. "Good thinking with the color swap, this one matches your skin. Shall we do your hair?"

"I can," Daisy said, strolling in. Dominic followed behind, leaning casually against the wall. He still didn't speak, but his sharp eyes took in every detail. Why was he here, after all this time? After all these years of staying away?

Daisy wore her black leggings and a pale green shirt—the exact color scheme I'd worn on Monday, when she took my birthday dress and ditched me. And I now wore the same pink she'd used for Monday's MaxFit99 audition.

We'd switched places.

The irony wasn't lost on me.

Daisy assessed every inch of my outfit. "Looking hot, mama! Did Jared pick this out?" Her praise didn't lift my mood. It only reminded me I now had two powerful people controlling my life, instead of one. Even when I picked an outfit, the credit went to someone else. "I like the pink. Now you just need hair and makeup to match."

She swiped the comb from Lyneeka, then guided me into a chair. Lyneeka raised an eyebrow, but I shook my head, not wanting to fight. I'd worn my long hair down the last three days, and it had held curls surprisingly well. Hopefully Daisy would do something similar for the show.

"So," Daisy said as she brushed, "have you nailed down your on-screen personality?"

"My what?"

"Think of yourself as an actress. For the next twelve weeks, you can be anybody you want, as long as you stay consistent. It looks weird if your personality keeps changing."

"Change my personality?"

"It's essential. In one show, I played the badass bodybuilder. In another, I was a total ditz. Jared laughed a million times, it was fun! What will you be? A pro soccer player? A gym rat?"

"Just myself, I guess."

Daisy stopped brushing. "Seriously? Way too boring." She swapped the brush out for a comb and spray bottle. "If I'd known you were auditioning, I could have given you on-stage tips, like how to stand so the camera gets the best angle. It's too late for today, but I'll train you this weekend." She walked around me, assessing my hair, then nodded. "Perfect. What do you think?"

She handed me a mirror. Daisy had braided my hair down my back, exactly like I'd worn it every day for the last five years.

Every day except this week.

"Um . . ."

She sprayed a gallon of hairspray over my head. Now, even if I tried to take out the braid, I couldn't redo it without a shower. The Bailey I'd become over the past week was gone.

Bee had officially returned.

After caking my face with makeup that smelled like mustard, Daisy declared me finished. She held up a mirror and a stranger stared back at

Bailey in the Corner

me, with pasty skin, eyeshadow up to my eyebrows, and hot pink cheeks. Not a stranger, a clown. Daisy beamed as I tried not to grimace, though a shiver shot up my spine.

"Cold?" Jared entered the room and took off his navy-blue sport coat, wrapping it around my shoulders.

"I'm fine, thanks." But when I tried to shrug it off, he insisted, then he stood next to Daisy to study me.

"She looks good, right?" Daisy asked.

"Absolutely. Can't wait to see her on stage."

The alarm buzzed again. Only two hours until showtime, one hour to be on stage, and Christian would arrive any second. Jared hurried out with Daisy on his heels, but she stopped at the door.

"Bee? Dom and I are hitting The Silver Salmon for lunch, want something?"

Seafood? From my least favorite restaurant? I shook my head.

The second she left, I escaped from Jared's jacket and hung it on the back of my chair. Lyneeka and I watched through the giant window as Daisy and Dominic climbed into her new Mustang, laughing. How would it feel to be Dominic? To have a sister so devoted she would drop everything to please you—even when you treated her like toilet scum.

All it took was the perfect gift to make her crawl back.

But I'd crawled back to Daisy as pathetically as she had to Dominic, and she didn't even buy me a car.

When Lyneeka ushered the cast toward the gym, I didn't move.

"I'm done," I whispered.

"What was that?" Lyneeka asked, coming closer.

"I'm done, forever. I can't live like this anymore. With or without an attorney, I won't spend one more second in her shadow—I don't even care that I stole her spot on MaxFit99."

"Stole?"

The confusion in her voice made me pause. At no point had I intentionally stolen anything from Daisy. I'd always loved performing and

241

teaching. I'd loved my ballroom years, and teaching my class at Lucky 7 Gym.

"You're right, I didn't steal anything. I auditioned for this because I wanted it." It felt good to declare it out loud.

"And you're an excellent office manager, even if you give the credit to Daisy."

"You know about that?"

"Everyone knows about that. You earned this spot, fair and square, so stop feeling guilty for succeeding."

"I don't. Not anymore."

Lyneeka's face split into a smile. "I've been waiting five long years to hear you say that. I almost booted her out of here listening to her lecture you. Not to mention, you look like a clown."

"Please tell me you can fix it."

"Sure can. I can fix your hair too."

She lowered me into a chair and handed me a makeup wipe, then moved behind me and unbraided my hair, spraying it with water when the hairspray crunched. I cleaned one eye, then grabbed another wipe and worked on the other while Lyneeka attacked my hair with a curling iron.

"Thanks, Lyneeka."

"It's the least I can do after how many times you've saved us this week. Everyone can see how hard you're working. With your new slogan for MaxFit99 and then Fearless Felicity, I'm just glad you finally have a job title where you can clean things up around here."

"Daisy won't see it that way."

"I know, but what you two have isn't healthy, honey. Or normal. And you've faced her alone way too long. But you're not alone anymore. Lots of us don't have much family, so we've come together to make our own—and you're one of us now. We'll have your back. You'll never face Daisy alone again."

A warmth trickled into my chest as she winked at me.

"It'll be a bloody battle," I warned. "She won't let me go easily."

Bailey in the Corner

"That's for sure. She has her hooks in you deep and won't go down without a fight. But this time, you won't be fighting alone."

A burst of hope slammed against the inside of my ribs. "You know what's funny? All these years, I've only tried to help her."

"These things are always complicated, aren't they? But you can't save her if she doesn't want to be saved. Sometimes, all you can do is let people go. But are you sure you're ready for it?"

She ditched you on your birthday. She called you a slut. She told everyone you slept with Jared. She attacked Jackson and threatened Mia.

I wanted freedom like I wanted air to breathe, so much I might suffocate without it. Even if she retaliated, even if she went straight to Dominic, I wouldn't go down without a fight. Mia and I were tough, we'd find a way to survive. To thrive.

"Absolutely."

"Good, because we need you right now. Desperately."

"What do you mean?"

Lyneeka switched to working on my makeup. "The next two hours will determine the future of every single person in this building."

"Because we're going bankrupt?"

"The debt collectors are worse than Lauren lets on. Even with Fearless Felicity's help, if we can't sell our entire stock of Waterfall clothes tonight, our doors won't open on Monday."

"It's that bad?"

"Our final hope is to sign with ZBC, but that's a long shot."

"How can I help?"

Lyneeka rubbed her eyes like she was rubbing away a lifetime of exhaustion. "You can't just *help*—I need you to fix the whole thing. Did you know I was Jared and Lauren's first employee?"

I straightened, surprised. "No."

"Sixteen years ago, they hired me to sew their first line of fitness gear. Since then, hundreds of employees have gone through this building, but not one of them had what you have."

"What's that?"

"The ability to organize our chaos."

Laughter bubbled up from my chest as Lyneeka applied makeup to my clean face. "Jared and Lauren will figure something out."

Lyneeka didn't laugh with me. "Jared's barely more than eye candy. He knows plenty about lifting, but nothing about business. And Lauren melts down at the first sign of stress. But you? Not only do you know the inner workings of every department, but in five years you've never once lost your cool. It's a gift—you're always calm, always steady. You attract unstable people like Daisy and Lauren because you're a solid force in their wavering worlds, but you never swerve off course. You're exactly what this company needs right now. If anyone can save us, it's you."

The funny thing was, she was right.

I already knew what to do because I'd already saved the show three times this week. It was simply a matter of assigning those responsibilities to other people while I was on stage.

But there was still one catch. There was always one catch.

Daisy wouldn't like it.

But I no longer cared.

"If you don't work your magic," Lyneeka said, "we'll all lose our jobs."

But excitement was already rumbling up inside me. Jared's final alarm buzzed through my ears, then slipped under my skin and coursed through my veins like adrenaline. One hour until the camera went live.

My long, curled hair brushed against the bare skin on my back as Lyneeka applied the final touches of my new makeup. She held up a mirror and I looked . . . beautiful. No sign of the clown that had stared back at me half an hour ago. Bee was gone, Bailey had returned. And I was done doing things other people's way. I found my favorite Waterfall tank top, threw it over Jared's ugly sports bra, and rubbed my favorite gloss over my lips. Subtle. *Me.*

"What do you think?" Lyneeka asked. "Can you save us?"

Bailey in the Corner

"Hell yeah. Meet me in my new office in five minutes." With my first genuine smile of the day, I sprinted out of the room.

It was time to rally my troops.

Chapter 30

I found Lauren in her office, the lights off, teetering between panic attack and full-on psychotic meltdown. What had Lyneeka said? Unsteady people need a steady person to cling to? I could be that for her.

I used my most solid, confident voice. "Lauren, I know how to fix this. In my office, now."

Without hesitation, she obeyed.

Stella was already warming up in the gym, but when I waved her over, she came without asking questions. Last but not least, I grabbed Jared from the cafeteria and Daisy from her cubicle, flatly refusing when Dominic offered to join us.

When Lyneeka arrived, all six of us entered my office. Jared sank obliviously onto the couch, but the second Daisy noticed Stella, her face fell dangerously dark. She leaned against the wall and crossed her arms. So much for letting me choose my own friends. Stella leaned against the opposite wall, as far from Daisy as possible.

Lauren slumped behind my desk, her head in her arms, and Lyneeka took the comfy chair in front of it. The last one in, I closed the door behind me with a click, and met each of their eyes.

"Before anyone says anything, I know this is an uncomfortable group of people." Daisy snorted, and Stella scuffed her foot against the ugly carpet. "Hear me out, then you can go."

Bailey in the Corner

Stella and Lyneeka gave me their full attention, and Lauren peeked an eye up over her elbow. Daisy moved to the couch, sitting as close to Jared as she could get, then glared straight up at the ceiling. Pulling them together was already harder than I'd expected. But each had to fill an essential role, or this wouldn't work.

"You're all aware MaxFit99 must pull off a perfect show today," I began, "or JD Fitness will go out of business tomorrow."

Jared snapped to attention, looking surprised.

Lauren lifted her face enough to scowl at him. "Like you didn't know? You're the reason we're in this mess."

"You signed every one of those contracts," he shot back.

"You didn't give me a choice."

"Shut up, both of you," Lyneeka hissed. "Listen to Bailey."

My hands grew clammy, and I knocked, hard, on the table. "Look, I know there's strained relationships in here, but I also know we all want JD Fitness to stay in business. If you're all willing to help, I know how to make that happen."

Lauren perked up, though her leg still bounced erratically under the desk. Stella nodded and Lyneeka motioned for me to continue. Only Daisy still refused to look at anyone. Unfortunately, her part was the most essential. Everything hinged on whether she would cooperate.

"Our biggest hurdle," I said, "will be Christian. Lauren, when will he arrive?"

"Any second. He's in a cab, headed our way."

"Tell me about him. How do we impress him?"

Lauren winced. "His ego's big and he doesn't like to mess around. But he works for a family network so he's looking for family-centered values."

"Those don't go together."

"I know. He'd appreciate a stage full of bodybuilders, but the network won't let him."

"Hopefully our 'Fitness For Everyone' campaign pleases them both—the rest is up to Jared." Everyone turned to him, and Jared's eyebrows lifted. "Christian's your responsibility. You were brilliant at Le Chateau, schmoozing all those execs. I need you to schmooze Christian too. Turn on the charm and show him how important you are, while boosting his ego at the same time."

"Easy," Jared said. "I'll stay by his side till the cameras roll."

"Lyneeka, you're next. We can't have any more bras ripping apart. Double-check all the seams on everyone's outfits, then grab two spares for each cast member. Label them and bring one of your portable changing stations."

"I'll pull the clothes out as soon as we're done here," she said.

"I also need you covering the kitchen. I know it's a project to have Blue Juice ready to go, but put one of your people on it. Christian will think we're amateurs if we leave juice wrappers and water bottles all over the floor."

When I moved to Stella, she was already focused, ready for her assignment.

"Get the zip ties from the stage crew and tie up the cables all over the ground. Then grab the rugs from the lobby and put them over the bundles. No one's allowed to trip."

"Sure thing," Stella said. "I already did it a few days ago."

"Good, because that's not all. Tape X's on the stage floor where each cast member will stand. I don't care if they're visible on camera. Normally, MaxFit99 will have six people on stage and everyone can spread out. But today, both casts will be up there at once. That's a lot of people to pack into one place. We can't have anyone getting injured by anyone else's dumbbells."

"Got it. I'll talk to the cast about keeping their areas organized too."

"Perfect. Thanks, Stella."

Lauren came next. Her face had already turned the same panicky pale as yesterday.

Bailey in the Corner

"You okay?"

She nodded, barely.

"I know the chaos of all this overwhelms you, so your job is to minimize the backstage chaos."

"How do I do that?"

"You're going to scream at the crew, and every extra employee, until they've tidied up every inch of the warehouse. Toss every jacket and gym bag and water bottle into the storage room until Christian's gone. Then make someone sweep the floor until it's spotless. There shouldn't be a single unnecessary item where Christian can see it."

"Minimize chaos. I can do that." The color came back to her face.

"And when the cameras roll and Jared's on stage, stay at Christian's side. Bring him drinks or food, whatever he wants. Pamper him. And never leave him alone."

"Never alone? Okay."

At last, I turned to Daisy, who still glowered at the ceiling. She was the only one not participating, the only one not engaging in the conversation or committing to make this work.

"Daisy?"

She smacked her gum and snarled, "What's my job? Have sex with Christian so he's happy during the show?"

"Of course not. I need you to take my spot on the microphone."

Her eyes dropped to mine, wide with surprise.

"I can't correct form when I'm on stage, and everyone performs better with a coach in their ear. I've seen you train—you're the only one I trust."

Daisy said nothing. She held my gaze, a staring contest I couldn't risk losing. Or winning.

"Fine, I'll do it."

The entire room exhaled.

Then Cinnamon stuck her head through the door and whispered, "Christian just pulled in."

Every eye turned back at me, a sense of purpose shining from each of them. Even Lauren didn't crumble under the pressure.

"This is it," I said. "Showtime. Jared, you're up first."

He ran a hand through his hair and strode confidently out the door. The rest of us exchanged nervous grins, then, one by one, scurried off to fill our posts. Only thirty minutes left until the camera rolled.

Maybe, just maybe, we could pull this off.

Chapter 31

Alone in my office, I took a minute to collect myself. *I can do this. I can do this.*

I tightened my shoelaces, locked my office, and headed to the gym. Daisy was already there, filling cold water bottles with Green Fizz for the cast—I hadn't asked her to do that.

She handed me one and I chugged it, the frigid water freezing my throat and lowering my internal temperature. Just what I needed.

"Good luck," she said. "And don't screw up." She paused, then backtracked. "I didn't mean it that way. I meant, good luck saving us all. Don't be nervous, just focus on making Jared look good."

"I'll be fine."

"Are you sure? Because I can give you tips."

I tossed my water bottle into the empty trashcan. "Daisy, I've got this."

She relaxed. "I know you do." Then she dashed off to distribute earpieces to the cast, while Stella zip-tied all the cables and covered them with mats. Instead of screaming at everyone, Lauren gave quiet orders until the entire backstage shined—I'd never seen her so calm. Lyneeka arrived with a rack of labeled costumes and a giant makeshift changing room. She noticed Lauren's calm demeanor too.

"Don't you ever quit your job," she whispered to me. "You're the best thing to ever happen to that woman."

Stella finished taping X's to the stage floor with painter's tape, and assigned spots to each cast member. At last, I signaled to Daisy that it was safe to fetch Jared and Christian, right as my Green Fizz kicked in.

It began in my fingers, a slight tingle buzzing over the backs of my hands and then spreading up my arms. It hit my face next, like pins and needles in my cheeks. Lots of people avoided pre-workout energy drinks because they couldn't stand the tingles, but I closed my eyes and soaked it in, energy shooting through my limbs.

This workout would be explosive.

Jared and Christian finally arrived and I took my first good look at the man who controlled all our futures. For a TV exec, he looked surprisingly like Jared. Tall, with graying hair and the wide build of someone who spent consistent time in a gym. No wonder the network asked him to choose a fitness program—he knew exactly what to look for.

And we were about to give it to him.

"Five minutes!" the stage manager yelled. I lined a row of weights next to my X on the stage, stretched, then jogged in place, getting my blood flowing.

"Two minutes!"

An excited buzz filled the room, and everyone hurried to their places. Daisy sat on a stool, mic in hand, barely off the front of the stage. Jared removed his sweatshirt and stretched his arms, giving Lauren his place beside Christian. She shot me a thumbs-up, cautiously optimistic, then Stella gave me a nod.

At last, Jared jogged onto the stage, determined, focused. But instead of stopping at his spot in the center, he strode right up to me, took my face in his hands, and kissed my lips. It ended before I could react, but the entire room burst into cheers and hollers. With no time to process it, I laughed along with everyone else as Jared took his place at my left.

"Thirty seconds!"

The warehouse fell silent as the stage crew positioned themselves behind cameras and under lights. Lyneeka stood ready, a handful of

Bailey in the Corner

runners prepared to fetch things if needed. Christian leaned casually against a pillar with his arms folded, his expression filled with curiosity.

We were doing it. We were really doing it. It was time to go live to the world.

"Five! Four! Three!" Then he mouthed, "Two! One!"

Jared beamed into the camera as a tiny red light flicked on.

"Hello, everyone, and welcome to the teaser episode of MaxFit99. We will stream live at four o'clock, every weekday, starting this Monday. We're so glad you've joined us. This will be our best program yet."

Jared took a step back, into the front row of cast members.

"Here at JD Fitness, we believe exercising isn't about looking like a supermodel. Not everyone has the genetics to be shaped the way social media tells us a person *should* look. We also know that life circumstances change constantly. Sometimes, it's easy to eat healthy and make it to the gym, but sometimes it's not. Some of you are at the peak of health, but most people aren't—and that's okay. We believe 'fitness' has no end goal." He squeezed Stella's tattooed shoulder. "It's a lifelong habit, and we want to celebrate every stage of that journey with you.

"This is why, in MaxFit99, we've adopted the slogan, *Fitness for Everyone*. It's also why, on this stage, our cast isn't in perfect shape. We don't want you to feel bad if you don't look like the people on your screen. We want you to see yourself represented, no matter where you are in life. We want you to feel motivated by watching us struggle the same way you are. And most importantly, we want you to celebrate every victory along the way, no matter what it looks like. We're all in this together."

Jared clapped his hands, then returned to my side.

"Before we begin, our new line of fitness gear went live two minutes ago. The Waterfall Collection will sell out fast, so don't waste time! And finally, I want to introduce my number one girl." He put his hand on the small of my back. "This is Bailey. She's a beast in the gym, and she'll be helping me on stage today. Bailey, how are you feeling?"

I blinked, twice, before I answered. Something about that little red light, the one indicating the camera was rolling, made my brain fuzzy.

"Strong," I said. "In fact, I might out-lift you today, Jared."

Christian laughed from his spot against the pillar. Obviously, I couldn't lift heavier than Jared, but people at home liked on-screen banter. Lauren gave us a thumbs-up and rolled her hands. She wanted more.

"You're going to out-lift me?" Jared peered at my dumbbells, then back at his. "I feel a competition coming on."

"Bring it." I rubbed my palms together as adrenaline coursed through me.

"You're on!" He returned to his place. "Let's begin with a warm-up."

We moved quickly through a few exercises designed to pump blood to our muscles, then Jared introduced our first set of lifts.

"Squats," he said, looking at me with a challenge in his eyes. "What are you lifting?"

"Two forties."

Jared grinned appreciatively. "Did you guys hear that? She's going heavy! I'll match her weights." He grabbed new dumbbells off the rack and the workout began in earnest. We did three exercises, ten reps each, for three rounds. By the end, my muscles burned with a solid pump and endorphins flowed through my system.

"It's time for a quick commercial," Jared said, eyes trained on that steady red camera light, "but catch your breath quick because we'll be back in exactly two minutes. We're working our chest and back next."

The red light dimmed, and Jared walked straight to me. "You're amazing!"

"My legs are dying," I groaned. "What was I thinking?"

"Keep it up, you're exactly what we need."

The giant countdown read one minute and fifty seconds, and I couldn't wait to get going again. The cast grabbed pre-mixed Blue Juices from the kitchen, and Lyneeka's team was already filling more. No one tripped on cables, the floor stayed clean, everything was in place.

Bailey in the Corner

Then Lauren darted onto the stage holding out her phone. "Someone's calling my cell and asking for you. It's been ringing nonstop since we started. I keep hanging up so the camera doesn't pick up the vibration, but can you tell him to call back when we're done?" She shoved her phone into my hand as the screen flashed with twelve missed calls.

It vibrated again, flashing a familiar number—I'd written it on a sticky note last night. My lungs lurched. It was Marco. After two days of silence, the wall around my heart collapsed. I pushed the green button and pressed my phone frantically to my ear, as the giant countdown dropped to ninety seconds.

"Marco?"

"Bailey!" His relief sounded as strong as mine. "I've been calling all day, why didn't you answer?"

"My phone's missing. Is everything okay? Where were you last night?"

"I'm so sorry, I wasn't trying to blow you off, but I need your help."

Fear trickled down my spine. "Stop apologizing and tell me what happened."

"Jackson's gone. It's been twenty-four hours, so the police stepped in. He got in a fight with his dad and then he disappeared."

"You should have told me," I whispered. The adrenaline in my veins turned to ice and I scanned the crowded room for Daisy. She wasn't at her stool. Did she cause this? "I would have dropped everything to help."

"I tried." Marco's voice cracked.

"Thirty seconds!" the stage manager yelled.

"I just need to know if you've heard from him. We're getting desperate."

"I'm so sorry, I haven't." The words tasted like tar. Where did he go? And where was Daisy?

Marco didn't answer, but I could hear his breath, quick and heavy.

"Twenty seconds!"

"I have to go," I said, "but I can help search in an hour."

"There's one more thing." Marco hesitated. "Mia's with me."

"She's not in school?"

"She heard about Jackson and cut class, thinking he'd gone to her house. She's freaking out. Can I bring her to you? We're only a few blocks away."

"Of course." Except Dominic was here, somewhere in the building. Everything spun and I grabbed Lauren's shoulder.

"Ten seconds!"

Everyone else was already back on stage. Lauren yanked her phone from my hand and shoved me into my spot right as the countdown hit zero.

Jared spoke into the camera, but I couldn't make out his words. Not with Jackson missing and Mia on her way. But somehow, for the next forty-five minutes, I had to keep smiling.

Everyone dropped to the ground, so I followed, a second behind.

Focus. Focus. Lay on your back. Chest press.

Twelve minutes until the next commercial break.

Get your head in the game.

Compartmentalize.

I couldn't help Jackson from here, so I should just focus on lifting. But the clock moved slower and slower. Where would Jackson have gone? Did he buy that bus ticket to Tennessee, after all? Or was he in my tree, hiding where no one could see him?

Stop.

I trained my eyes on the cold, metal dumbbells in my hands, focused on the muscles in my chest and triceps, pushed the weights up, again and again, going through the motions without hearing a word Jared said.

Maybe I could leave during the next commercial break? Stella could take my spot and I could go help Marco. No, the careers of all these people depended on me knocking this workout out of the park. I had to keep going, had to smile for the camera, had to impress Christian.

Why couldn't I be in two places at once?

Bailey in the Corner

For the next lift, I grabbed a random dumbbell and waited for Jared's cue to begin.

"That's the best you can do?" Jared grinned into the camera as the rest of the cast laughed. My dumbbell weighed five pounds when I should have held twenty.

"Just making sure you're paying attention," I said, trying to sound flirty. But heat crept up my neck as I swapped out my dumbbell for a heavier one. I needed help, desperately. Someone who could keep me from ruining this for everyone.

Daisy.

With the earpiece in my ear, she could talk me through it, keep me focused. I squinted through the bright stage lights and zeroed in on her spot, but Daisy hadn't returned. The microphone sat lonely on the empty stool. In fact, she hadn't given a single cue the entire show. Where was she?

My heart pounded painfully against my lungs. The last time I'd seen her was right before Jared kissed me. She must have seen it . . . And then fled.

My arms grew heavier as fear wrapped around my throat. If she wasn't in the warehouse, where did she go? What was she doing?

The metal gym door cracked open, and Marco slipped inside, followed by Mia. Marco's eyes widened, like he hadn't realized we were filming—or that I was in the show. Lyneeka ushered them silently into the kitchenette and Mia gave me a half-hearted wave, but red splotches covered her face from crying. It took all my self-control not to run off the stage and wrap her in a hug.

Nine minutes until the next break. Nine more minutes to endure this torture.

Then Lauren's voice spoke in my ear.

"Hang in there, Bailey," she whispered into the mic. "I know something's wrong, but I need you to focus. Listen to my voice, I'll walk you through it."

Water sprang to my eyes, but I nodded gratefully. The camera would pick up every detail of a meltdown, so I tried to hold myself together. Fortunately, it was time to lay on our backs for the second set of chest presses. The camera couldn't see my face.

"Breathe in," Lauren said as I lowered the weights, "then out." I pressed them back up. Her words washed through me and I clung to them like a lifeline.

"That's your last one," she said. "Put the weights down and stand up, then grin right at the camera."

Smiling felt impossible—the muscles in my cheeks didn't want to fire. I shook my head the tiniest bit, to let her know I couldn't.

"You're almost done, smile for five minutes."

I closed my eyes and took a deep breath. I'd fake-smiled at Daisy for twenty years. Every time she'd shoved me in my corner, I'd smiled through it, told myself to trust her. Daisy always knew best, after all.

What were five more minutes of pretending?

I stared straight at the camera, plastered on my brightest face, then picked up thirties for the next round of bent-over rows.

"Look at this," Jared said, grinning at the camera. "Bailey's going heavier."

"You're not?" I asked.

Jared leaned back his head and cackled, then swapped out his weights.

"Perfect," Lauren said in my ear. I channeled everything raging inside me into my muscles. "Keep going. Only four minutes."

I finished my tenth rep and dropped the weights with a crash, feeling the pump in the thin muscles between my shoulder blades.

"Only one more set," Lauren said, relief in her voice. "You're doing perfect. Only three more—"

Someone slammed open the metal door, hard enough that it crashed into the cement wall. Every single person jumped. Lauren shrieked, Jared froze, mid-sentence.

Bailey in the Corner

Daisy stalked into the room with Dominic on her heels, a bundle of Felicity's clothes in one hand and my cell phone in the other.

"You bitch!" she shrieked, marching straight onto the stage and tossing a heap of clothes onto the ground. She didn't stop until she stood directly before me, right in front of the camera, for the entire world to see. Then she shoved Mia's dress in my face, the fabric pressing against my cheek. "Why didn't you tell me you're Fearless Felicity?"

Chapter 32

Lauren took immediate action and spoke softly into the mic. "Jared, walk to the far side of the stage, then move to commercial." The camera guy followed him to the left, cutting Daisy out of the shot.

"Time for a quick break," Jared said, "but we'll finish that final set in two minutes, followed by glutes. Get your deadlift weights ready, because the hard work is coming!"

He paused for an extra second, giving Cinnamon enough time to start the Waterfall Collection commercial, then his smile dropped, and he marched to Daisy at the front of the stage. "What the hell are you doing? This is a live broadcast."

Daisy didn't look at him. She stared me down, a mountain of fire raging in her eyes. "While you were in here making out with Jared, your phone filled up with fan mail. You've been Felicity all these years?"

Daisy stole my phone? And snooped through my personal emails? And she must have been digging through my desk if she found Felicity's clothes.

"I don't know what you're talking about," I said, my mouth going dry.

But Daisy raised my phone in the air, then hurled it at the ground. It crunched, grating my ears, and the screen shattered. "All I've ever wanted was to be an Influencer. One word from you, and my career could have exploded. But you refused! Why would you lie?"

Bailey in the Corner

"I never lied!"

"Then what are these?" She pointed to the heap of Felicity's unused clothes on the stage, then shook Mia's dress above her head. "Half of those are special editions, and none of them fit your tiny little budget."

My heart drummed so hard the inside of my chest ached. "Please, give me Mia's dress."

She didn't. "Did you think I was too stupid to figure it out? Or did you want to hoard all the glory?"

"Of course not."

"It's so typical. You only ever think about yourself."

Something inside me snapped. "Fearless Felicity isn't a tool to boost your career, Daisy. She reviews fitness equipment and occasionally vents about her day."

Daisy stepped over my broken phone, crowding closer until she stood in my face. "Then why didn't you tell me about her?"

But I refused to back down, refused to be intimidated. For once, I wouldn't let her push me around. "Because you stole my newsletter at Lucky 7 Gym. I wouldn't let that happen again. Felicity was my one thing *you* couldn't ruin."

Her jaw dropped, but my attention swerved to Dominic, his arrogant strut carrying him onto the stage beside his sister.

"Don't you dare blame *your* lies on me," Daisy said. "This is my dream we're talking about. You could have given it to me, but you didn't. You ruined my life instead, just like you did at Lucky 7."

"Lucky 7?"

She folded her arms, Mia's dress still bundled in one hand. "Doug was going to make you my boss. *My* boss. That promotion should have been mine. I carried you through five years of depression, then suddenly you snapped out of it and Doug gave you everything? It was going to your head, Bee. But you were nothing without me."

A bitter taste filled my mouth, making my lips curl. "Do you hear yourself? All you got me was a crappy receptionist job. In fact, when we came here, you wrote your name on *my* resume when you applied."

Dominic burst out laughing and elbowed his sister. "No wonder they gave you the marketing job."

His voice rolled through my body, low and gravelly, scraping my eardrums with a blast of memories I'd tried to block out.

"Shut up, Dom." Daisy kept her eyes trained on me. "You've stolen so many things from me, you had this coming."

"What have I stolen from you?"

"How about every boy I've ever had real feelings for?"

"Name one."

"Let's see." She held up her fingers as she counted them off. "First Doug, then Marco, and now Jared."

"I didn't steal any of them."

"Like hell you didn't. We all saw you dance like a slut with Marco on Wednesday, then you were making out with Jared on this stage twenty minutes ago."

I glanced to my right, where Marco stood with Mia, his head cocked, Lyneeka whispering into his ear. Daisy likely didn't realize they were in the building.

I refocused on my ex-best friend. "Do you hear what you're saying? You're mad I caught the attention of two men, neither of which I'm dating, while you're legitimately cheating on both. Which of us is the slut, Daisy? Because it's not me."

Dominic laughed again. "She's got you there."

Daisy's eyes darkened and she pointed her finger at my face, an inch away from my nose. "You have everything, and I have nothing. But you still steal everything that ever matters to me."

"What have I stolen?"

"I've lived in your shadow since the day we met." She hissed the words through her teeth, like a snake finally freed from its cage. "You're perfect at everything you do. You're nice and friendly and everybody likes you. I bet no one's ever wondered when you're going to screw up next."

"You're perfectly capable of succeeding, Daisy."

"Not when you're around! My own brother hasn't seen you in a decade, but even he knows you're better than me. I've played second fiddle to you my entire life, and now I finally found a job where I'm the one on top, but you're stealing it away again."

"I'm not stealing anything you didn't take from me first."

"Yes, you are! Trust me, Bee, you've stolen everything."

Trust me.

Her favorite manipulation words.

For the first time in my life, I wasn't going to talk myself into believing her lies. Nothing she said would convince me to grovel at her feet. Those days were over. I glanced to my right and found Mia grinning ear-to-ear. Lyneeka gave me a thumbs-up, and even Marco nodded encouragingly.

But Daisy still glared at me, chest heaving as she gasped for air. I studied her face, her dramatic cheekbones, her red ringlets gathered in a loose ponytail behind her neck, her tanned skin that I would have given anything for.

For twenty years, I'd been jealous of Daisy. All this time, she'd been jealous of me too?

Time slowed down as the puzzle pieces of Daisy Rose slipped into place. I finally understood exactly how her life had brought her to this moment. Daisy had no mother, a dad who never loved her, and an abusive brother with expectations she'd never live up to. She desperately craved acceptance, approval.

I could give her those things.

In fact, I already had. I'd loved her for twenty years.

But it was never enough.

I caught Marco's eyes, remembering the first lesson he ever taught me. *Forge your own path in life, don't follow someone else's.* He'd learned the hard way, and he had the scars on his hands to prove it. Maybe today, I was learning the hard way too.

I couldn't chase Daisy forever.

Stella caught my eye with an encouraging nod. She'd shown me that true friendship wasn't one-sided. Sometimes you needed help, and sometimes you gave it, but true friends never acted selfishly or cruelly.

Lyneeka stood beside her. Just this morning, she'd shown me what belonging to a family felt like. They'd rally together when someone was hurting, they'd have each other's backs.

And then there was Mia. For three years she'd suffered through a dance partner who treated her like scum. Life handed her a gift when Bruno fell down those stairs, and another one when she met Jackson. What kind of example would I set if I handed my life back over to Daisy?

Except now that I knew exactly what Daisy needed, I could save her. She had goodness inside her—I'd glimpsed it last night when she came to my house. If she would leave Dominic behind, we could fix this. Our friendship could survive.

Everything slowed as I hovered, frozen in time, with an impossible choice. How could I abandon Daisy when I knew how to save her? But if I stayed, how could I face my little girl? One option felt like moving forward, and the other felt like going back. Back into Daisy's circle, spinning around and around, tied to a leash I'd wrapped around my own neck.

I couldn't do that again.

I wouldn't.

From this moment on, I'd only move forward.

"I love you," I said to Daisy. "Please, let me get you the help you need. I'll find someone who can teach you how to separate yourself from your brother."

Daisy's face twisted with rage. "Don't act all high and mighty, like I need *you* to save *me*." She threw Mia's dress on top of my broken

Bailey in the Corner

computer and my eyes dropped, scanning it for damage. Daisy noticed. She picked it back up and shook it out. "Is this important to you?"

Mia tensed. Daisy saw it too, her eyes narrowing on my daughter.

"That's Mia's," I whispered, hoping she'd remember a fraction of the love she'd always had for my daughter. For her niece. "It's for her audition."

"I know exactly what it is. What I don't understand is why you lied about the fabric."

"Please, Daisy, put the dress down."

"Sorry, I can't." She turned to Mia, pity dripping from her face. She rubbed the colorful fabric between her fingers, then held it high up in the air with both hands. "This is your mom's fault, for lying to me. I never wanted to hurt you, but I have no other choice."

Heat rushed through my body. "Daisy, don't!"

"Then don't keep secrets!" She pulled the dress in two directions, strain rippling in her jaw, until the sound of splitting fabric rent the silent air.

"No!" Mia shouted, sprinting onto the stage.

But Daisy didn't stop until the dress had torn into two separate pieces, the fabric screaming as it shredded down the middle. Then she dropped them limply onto the ground.

Mia dove on top of them, bundling them protectively in one arm. Then she jumped to her feet, pulled back her free fist, and punched Daisy in the nose, knocking her over. But Mia wasn't done—she straddled Daisy's stomach and punched her again, until Dominic grabbed her small arm and yanked her back. She fought against him, snarling, twisting out of his grasp, until he grabbed her again and heaved her off Daisy.

Mia cried out and a dozen people sprang onto the stage. Marco dove at Dominic first, wrestling Mia away and passing her to me. Jared joined him, shoving Dominic back and holding him off until several members of the stage crew knocked him to his knees and pinned his arms from behind.

I hugged Mia protectively against my chest as Lyneeka and Lauren towered over Daisy to keep her on the ground. Stella examined Mia's wrists and face, making sure she wasn't injured, then joined the other women, creating a barricade between us and Daisy. Mia trembled violently in my arms, still clutching the fragments of her ruined dress tightly against her body.

But Daisy's eyes never left mine. I could see her fury building, her rage, her wildfire. I knew what was coming even as I willed it not to, willed her stay quiet, begged her with my eyes. But it rumbled up through the floor, through her feet, her legs, quaking through her muscles until her body couldn't contain the pent-up pressure.

I'd finally pushed her too far. Now she was going to explode. Wildfire, blazing through the cavernous room to consume us all.

"MIA'S YOUR DAUGHTER!" Daisy shrieked to her brother. "Can't you tell? Look at her, your spitting image. Grab her and let's go, straight to the courthouse. We're taking custody—and suing Bee for hiding her from you."

Dominic froze. Mia froze. The blood in my veins stopped moving.

Then Mia's jaw dropped, her face laced with fear. For twelve long years I'd run from this moment, but here it was. If Dominic wanted his daughter, I had no idea if I could stop him. It landed on my shoulders with the weight of the ocean, pressing me down, squeezing me tighter, smaller. With one call to a lawyer, he could walk away with my little girl, every other week, teaching her how to punch and lie and manipulate. How many times would she come home with black eyes? Bruised arms? Her confidence shredded?

But Mia had other plans.

While I cowered under Daisy's gaze, Mia pulled away from me and pushed through the barricade of women. She coiled back, then spit straight into Dominic's face. "There's no way in hell I'm going anywhere with you." She spun around and shoved her fists on her hips. "Mom, I don't blame you for not telling me who he was. That guy's a dick."

Bailey in the Corner

Dominic said nothing.

I pushed forward and pulled Mia into a hug, squeezing her against me, clinging to her tiny body that encased a spirit so much stronger than mine. Her strength seeped into me and the ocean of pressure lifted. If Mia could be strong, so could I.

"He has parental rights too," Daisy said, her jaw clenched.

But I shook my head. "I always told Mia she could meet her dad any time. Sounds like she's still not interested."

"You can't keep them apart, a judge wouldn't agree."

"Then take it to a judge."

Dominic's eyes bounced between us. Daisy clenched her jaw, but with my secret out in the open, she had nothing left to control me with. The freedom was exhilarating.

"Time to deal with Daisy, once and for all," I whispered to Mia. "Want to help?"

She nodded, then I stood tall, our line of friends—our new family—behind us. Mia stood to my right, and Marco left Dominic in the hands of the stage crew to stand at my left. When I pushed my hand against his, he laced his fingers through mine and didn't let go. Lyneeka put a protective hand on Mia's shoulder and Stella pressed against my arm.

Courage coursed through me, a gift from each of them, as we linked ourselves together. I felt strong, solid, steady—nothing like when Daisy led me on dangerous adventures. All those years, I'd thought she'd been sharing her courage with me, but it felt nothing like this. That had been destructive and exhausting. Maybe, all that time, she wasn't giving me courage. Maybe she was taking it.

"We've all got your back," Lyneeka said.

Daisy took it all in, her eyes widening, lips gaping. "This is how you end our twenty years of friendship? Choosing them over me?"

And just like that, the last strand of Daisy's control snapped.

"No. I'm choosing myself, like I should have done all along."

Chapter 33

One by one, the entire staff of JD Fitness broke into applause, right there on that stage. They clapped for an entire minute, stepping over dumbbells to congratulate me, until the stage manager dropped Dominic's arm and raced back to the camera.

The tiny red light still glowed.

"Shit!" he hollered. "I never turned the camera off."

The entire room froze until the red light finally dimmed, except Dominic, who rose unsteadily to his feet.

My mind reeled, eyes glued to the spot where the light had been. The entire world had heard our conversation. Our ugly history broadcast over the internet. My fight with Daisy. Ripping Mia's dress. My secret identity . . .

Fearless Felicity—no longer a secret.

To my surprise, I wasn't devastated. Felicity was always my outlet to express my hidden self. Now that I had a real family, now that I didn't need to hide myself away, maybe I didn't need to keep that piece of me secret anymore.

Jared, on the other hand, had the opposite reaction. He spewed a string of curse words and sprinted off the stage, crashing through camera equipment until he burst out the door. No one paid him much attention. Instead, I knelt before Mia, who was cradling the fragments of her ruined dress.

Bailey in the Corner

"Can you fix it?"

If Daisy had torn it down a seam, a quick stitch could have put it back together. But she'd ripped it straight through the front. Lyneeka and I exchanged a doubtful look.

Daisy climbed to her feet. "Mia?" She rubbed her eyes like she was coming out of a stupor, then pressed a hand to her chest. "What did I do?" Daisy reached out toward my daughter, but we blocked her way. "Bailey, you have to believe me. I never meant to hurt her."

"Ugh," Dominic groaned. "Pitiful."

Daisy gawked at her brother and her entire body quaked, like the horror of it all—of him—had finally awakened in her. I recognized her expression, the terror that she'd never escape him, because I'd lived it every day for twenty years.

Until today.

"Please, Mia," she begged, barely a whimper. "I'm your aunt, your real biological aunt. All these years your mom wouldn't let me tell you that we're family, but we are and I'd never hurt you."

Mia clenched her teeth. "Too late. And don't act like my mom's the bad guy."

As Daisy shrank back, I stepped beside my daughter and squeezed her shoulders. "Any word from Jackson?"

"My sister called on our way here," Marco said, a tremor in his voice. "Surveillance cameras caught Jackson climbing on a bus, but when it arrived in Tennessee, he wasn't on it anymore."

The room grew suddenly cold. "Do we know where he is?"

"There are a dozen rural stops along the way. He could have gotten off anywhere."

Daisy's eyes jumped back and forth between us. "Wait, Jackson's missing?" At least she had the decency to look ashamed, but everyone ignored her.

"I assume he's not answering his phone?" I asked.

Marco shook his head, his black hair hanging limply over one eye. "It goes straight to voicemail. Either the battery's dead, or he has no reception."

Mia turned straight to Daisy, a storm brewing in her small eyes. "He's a freaking kid. Why would you give him ideas like that?"

Daisy's skin paled, but Dominic laughed, his deep voice rumbling across the stage. "Because he's a weakling," he said. "If Daisy doesn't teach him to be a man, who will?"

Mia launched herself at Dominic, but Marco grabbed her around the waist and pulled her back.

"You've got to stop attacking people," he muttered, but Mia growled.

Daisy crumpled in on herself, sinking to the ground and staring blankly at the floor, right as Jared sprinted back in, tumbled through the camera equipment, and grabbed my shoulders.

"Where's my jacket?" He squeezed me like it might magically appear if he searched hard enough.

"What jacket?"

"The one I put on your shoulders this morning." He peered into my face, his breath smelling like mint gum.

"I left it in the fabrication room. Why?"

"It's gone," he moaned. "My wedding ring's in the pocket, and Daisy announced to the world that I kissed you. I can't go home without it."

I yanked back from his grip. "Jared, you're married?"

"I need that coat!"

Lyneeka pointed toward the back of the gym. "It's in the storage room."

Jared hurried across the warehouse. He dug through the large closet, then sprinted out, his shoes squeaking on the cement as he ran right past Lauren.

"Wait!" she yelled. "We need to finish the show!"

He didn't pause, he just fled. The room erupted into tense conversations—everyone but Lauren, who stared at the spot he'd disappeared, perched on the edge of her toes, like she might still run after him. But finally, she stuffed her hands into her suit pockets.

After ensuring Marco would keep Mia's temper in check, I moved to Lauren's side. "You knew he was married, didn't you?"

"He made me promise not to tell."

"Sometimes we do stupid things for people we love."

Lauren's shoulders sagged. "I deserve better."

I put my arm around her shoulder and squeezed. "Yes, you do."

"You know what's weird? I'm not sad to see him go. Maybe all these years I've loved the *idea* of Jared more than the man himself. This company has been my whole world for so long . . . Maybe I thought I loved him because I associate him with JD Fitness. The real Jared is—"

"—a dick?"

"Yeah," Lauren said, laughing darkly.

I understood completely. "He's been my celebrity crush for so long, it never occurred to me that if I got to know him, I might not like him." Or maybe I only ever loved him because Daisy did. Perhaps it was time to pick someone entirely for myself.

Lauren raised an eyebrow. "Please tell me you're over him."

Glancing back at Marco, a warm glow bubbled up inside me. I'd never felt that from Jared. Not once.

"Definitely over him."

She pulled a taffy from her pocket and popped the candy in her mouth, the white wrapper crinkling as she wadded it up. "This is why you're never supposed to meet your heroes."

"Do we need him to come back though?" I asked. "To finish the show?"

Lauren stiffened. "Yeah, or we're all out of our jobs." She stormed away with her phone pressed to her ear, but I had a feeling Jared wouldn't answer. This was the end of JD Fitness.

When I returned to my family, Marco pulled me straight into a hug. "I'm proud of you," he whispered, his voice husky in my ear. "But I've got to go. I'm going to drive the stretch between here and Tennessee, to see if I can spot Jackson."

"Give me a minute and I'll come with you." He squeezed me tighter.

Daisy was still sitting on the floor, eyes empty, but she reached out one hand to Mia. "I'm so sorry about your dress," she whispered.

But Mia took a step back, like she would catch a disease if Daisy inched too close.

I squatted down, at eye-level. "Everything you touch, you light on fire. You see that, right? I'm tired of getting burned. But your brother's as toxic to you as you are to me."

Her eyes darted to Dominic, then back to me. This time, he didn't laugh.

"All my life, you've kept me isolated from other people. But this week, I finally made real friends. They showed me what it feels like to be loved and accepted, and to have confidence in myself."

Daisy whimpered. "What are you saying?"

"She's saying," Mia said, "that she's done letting you treat her like shit."

My heart erupted. My little girl wasn't so little anymore. Perhaps her sass was just what I needed right now.

"That's exactly what I'm saying." I stood a little taller. "We've done this a hundred times—maybe a thousand—where you apologize, then promise to be better, and I'm foolish enough to believe you. In fact, I genuinely believe you mean it, every time. But I won't dance around this fire with you anymore."

"Bee?" Her voice sounded so small, so lost.

"I'm tired of punishments I don't deserve. I'm tired of living in fear, wondering when you'll hurt me next. But starting right now, I'm not afraid anymore. If you want revenge for this, go ahead. You want to help Dom fight for Mia? I'll wage that war against you until I die. But nothing you could dish out would be worse than staying as we are. So, punish me all

Bailey in the Corner

you want, but when you're done, I have a family here to help me pick up the pieces of my life."

Marco moved to my side and wrapped his strong arm around my shoulder. Stella nodded, and Lyneeka said, "Amen."

But Daisy crumpled like I'd smashed a hammer into her heart. "Please, Bee, don't abandon me."

Lyneeka snorted, loudly.

"You're doing it again," I said. "Acting like I'm the bad guy when you're the one who tore my daughter's dress in half."

The old me would have wavered. Even this morning I might have caved. But with Mia clasping my hand and Marco pressing tightly against my side, plus a room full of real friends—family. At last, I understood what Marco meant when he said I was *choosing* to give Daisy control.

"This time," I said, "I'm not falling for it."

"Bee?" Daisy barely whispered the word.

"I'm letting you go. But tell me truly, do you want to change? Do you want to have real friends?"

Daisy nodded, so I pointed to her brother who stood silently behind her.

"Then send him away for good." Daisy's eyes widened. "But no matter what you choose, neither of you are allowed near my daughter again. *Ever.*"

Dominic scowled. The stage crew stayed close by his side, tense, never taking their eyes off him.

"Don't listen to that bitch," he growled to his sister. But then he turned to me. "And I don't care what Daisy says, I don't want to play daddy to your kid."

"Good," I said. "We don't want you to."

"You're not gonna come after me for child support? Or babysitting?"

"Nope. Never."

Dominic nodded, and I nodded back. An agreement. A contract. I'd send him the paperwork to sign, and we'd never make contact again.

At Lauren's signal, the crew grabbed his arms and pulled him backward, off the stage, then through the exit.

Daisy watched them go, then looked at me, then back at the door.

"This is your chance," I said, as the door clanged closed behind Dominic. "Let him go. End this. Stop begging for approval he's never going to give you."

Daisy held my gaze for a long second.

Then two.

Then three.

On four, she sprinted after her brother, the metal door banging shut behind her.

I stared after her, part of me hoping she'd come back.

She didn't.

Lauren watched me, eyes full of empathy. She didn't need to say anything—I knew exactly what she was thinking.

I deserved better.

Mia stepped in front of me and I put my hands on her cheeks. "Are you okay?"

She nodded, but Lauren drew everyone's attention. Dark circles had appeared beneath her eyes, and her voice was high with panic. "Jared says he's not coming back today, and I'm sure we've lost all our viewers. We can't finish the show."

"Does that mean we're out of business?" Stella asked. A murmur rumbled through the room, like people hadn't realized how dire our situation had become.

"Unfortunately, yes. I'm so sorry, everyone. This is the end of JD Fitness."

The room fell into a tense silence, like no one knew what to say. Lyneeka sank into a chair and Marco squeezed my shoulder, kissing my temple. The silence stretched on—until my phone vibrated on the stage floor. Lauren scooped it up and handed it to me, and I glanced at the half

Bailey in the Corner

of the screen that still worked, expecting to see Jared's name pop up. Or Daisy's. Instead, my nerves switched into high alert.

Jackson was calling.

Chapter 34

Everyone gathered around as I put the phone on speaker. "Jackson, are you there?"

"Bailey?" He sounded distant and staticky. "Can you hear me?"

"I'm here."

"You said I could call if I ever needed help?"

"Always, kiddo." I breathed slowly, so I'd sound calm for Jackson. "We've been trying to find you. Where are you?"

"Almost to Tennessee. I got off the bus to pee, then it left without me. I used my only change to call my dad, but he said he couldn't come get me, so I've been walking for hours. This is the first time I've had reception."

"Are you hurt? Are you safe?"

Jackson paused for a long minute. "I'm cold and hungry, but I'm okay. I just wanted to find my dad. I never meant to ruin Mia's audition; I thought we'd be back in plenty of time." The speaker fuzzed as he started crying. "Please, tell her I'm sorry."

"I'm here," Mia said, scooting closer to the phone. "I'm just glad you're okay. You're way more important than a stupid show."

"No, I'm not. I ruined everything."

"No, you didn't," she said. "Now send Marco your location in case you lose reception again, then don't move. We're on our way to get you."

"Is Marco there too?"

Bailey in the Corner

Marco wrapped his hand around mine and squeezed, tears filling his eyes. "I'm here. Have you been outside all night? Do you have a safe place to wait?"

"I'm at a gas station now. I can survive a few more hours."

"We're leaving right now."

"Thanks, Uncle Marco."

The second I hung up, Marco stomped across the stage and punched the back wall. "I'm so tired of Jackson's asshole dad. How many times will he abandon his son?"

"We won't abandon him," Mia said. "Let's go."

Marco's phone beeped. "I have his location."

Then Mia turned to me, though her eyes darted to Marco. "If Jackson's feeling up to it, could we still audition tonight?"

"Possibly."

"Then let's hurry, we have to get home before six." She stopped in her tracks, her face falling. "Mom, what about my dress?"

Lyneeka scooped the ripped pieces off the floor, plus the unused clothes Daisy had tossed onto the stage. "I sewed this once; I can sew it again—if you don't mind me cutting up more clothes."

There were only two spare outfits left, one bright blue, the other pale yellow.

"There won't be enough," I said. "And the colors won't match."

Lauren raised her hand. "Use Waterfall fabric."

"Jared won't mind?" Lyneeka asked.

"He's not here to say no, is he? Plus, I own half the company." Lauren grinned, like a weight had lifted from her shoulders.

"I'll help sew," Stella said. "But we'll have to move quick."

They bustled toward the door, then stopped abruptly. In fact, everyone stopped as Christian from ZCB left his spot against the pillar for the first time. His eyes found mine and stayed there, appraising, studying.

Shit. I'd forgotten about him entirely.

"You emailed me?" Christian finally said, his voice raspy and low. "About giving JD Fitness a second chance?"

I nodded, barely.

Christian stuck his hands deep into his classy blue slacks. "I won't lie, I came here fully expecting a disaster of a show—and that's exactly what you gave me."

Lauren glared and folded her arms.

"However, I spent yesterday on Michael Kay's set, and his show was equally disastrous. He filmed three episodes, each with a different celebrity, and none of them knew a thing about lifting. It was a safety disaster, the cast burned out before they'd filmed the first episode, and Michael Kay himself was a ridiculous diva, snapping at everyone and making absurd demands."

Christian strolled onto the stage, until he reached the front of the crowd.

"I didn't expect yours to be any better," he continued, pulling one hand out to rub the stubble on his square chin, "so I planned to tell my network to bag the whole fitness segment altogether."

"Do you have a point?" Lauren growled. "Since I'm sure we didn't change your mind."

"Actually, maybe you have."

Everyone perked up.

"Obviously, this was a PR nightmare. Not only did that psycho lady storm on set and cause a scene," his eyes lingered on mine, "but then Jared revealed to the world that he's cheating on his wife."

"There's no way *that* changed your mind," Lauren said, her sarcasm growing drier by the second.

"You're right. It's what came next that impressed me." The corner of Christian's mouth turned up. "ZBC is a family network. Our daytime viewers are almost exclusively stay-at-home-moms, and your performance today fits perfectly with our values. When that lady stormed in here—"

"Her name's Daisy," Mia offered.

Bailey in the Corner

"Ah. When Daisy stormed in here, I watched an entire office family band together to protect a child. Then, I watched her mother choose the welfare of her daughter over a lifelong, but clearly unhealthy, friendship."

Lauren sucked in a breath, and Christian finally grinned.

"Then a second child in trouble called, and the entire company dropped everything to help him. It's like a soap opera!"

"That's a good thing?" Mia asked.

He winked down at her. "Soap operas make a ton of money." When he spoke again, he addressed all of us. "But workout programs make money too, and you guys promote the family values we're looking for. So, let's make a deal. You find a way to finish the show, *without* Jared, and I'll sign the contract before I leave tonight."

"But we've been dark for twenty minutes," Lauren said, "our viewers are long gone."

Christian's eyes twinkled. "Are you sure?"

She scrambled for her phone and pulled up our YouTube feed, which was, in fact, broadcasting a black screen. Then she slowly covered her mouth with her hand. "We have two hundred thousand live viewers?"

"Sure do," Christian said.

"But why? We've never had more than fifty thousand at once."

"Drama stirs up gossip—especially if someone storms on stage, reveals the secret identity of the fitness community's biggest Influencer, announces a scandalous affair, and then the screen goes dark. Everyone's anxiously waiting to see what happens next. Like I said, a soap opera."

"They're just staring at a black screen on YouTube?" I asked.

"Yup, but they won't stay there for long." He turned to Lauren. "Finish the show, and you won't have to close your doors this weekend. I'll even get you an advance to cover your debts."

"You're serious?"

"It's a risk, but I have a good feeling about this place." He pulled a taffy from his pocket and untwisted the blue wrapper. "I appreciate that you're the kind of person who stands up for yourself. We'll work well together."

Lauren's eyes widened. Then her face shot straight to mine, and I nodded. We could do this. Without a doubt, we could pull it off. But we'd need to move quickly before those viewers got bored.

"Everyone get back to your places!" I shouted, and the stage exploded into a flurry of noise and commotion. Lauren came straight to me, depositing a hard, plastic bundle into my hand.

"What's this?" But I already knew. It was Jared's mic pack, the one connected to the live stream. Lauren was giving me the show.

"Do it, Mom," Mia said. "This is your dream." She and Marco were the only stationary people in a room full of movement, standing side-by-side in the center of the stage. "I'll go chase mine and you chase yours. We'll tell each other about it tonight."

I almost laughed, almost cried, then pulled Mia into a tight hug. Had I put Daisy's dreams before Mia's for so long that she wouldn't blink an eye if I abandoned her? Was this my normal behavior?

Not anymore, and never again.

Starting right now, I'd rewrite her expectations of her mother. Sure, I loved the stage, and I loved weightlifting. But were those my biggest dreams? Not at all.

My biggest dream was Mia.

I crossed the stage to Stella, then placed the headset in her hands. "It's your time to shine."

Her eyes leapt out of her skull. "You can't be serious."

I smiled at Mia, the shock on her face confirming that I'd made the right choice. "There's always another fitness class, but I only have one daughter. I can't stay."

"But we need you!"

"No, you don't. You're a great teacher—I've seen you. And Lyneeka and Lauren can handle everything backstage. You've got this."

Bailey in the Corner

She lowered her voice to barely a whisper. "But what if the internet hates me?"

"They won't. Not if you put your heart into it."

"Wait," Marco said, interrupting. "I have something that will help." He sprinted off the stage and grabbed his cane, then dug through the secret compartment. "I always eat these when I'm nervous," he said. "It's like confidence in a pill."

"Are you giving me drugs?" Stella's forehead scrunched up. "The family network won't like that."

"Not exactly." Marco dumped six perfect Hot Tamales into Stella's hand. "There you go. Confidence in a pill."

Stella popped all six candies into her mouth at once. "I always knew I liked you."

"Save all our butts," I told her. "Okay?"

"You got it, boss."

After a quick hug, Stella took Jared's spot at the center of the stage, and I checked on Lyneeka. "You'll keep everything running back here?"

"Don't worry, you've trained us well. And the second we're done, I'll sew that dress. You just get Jackson home safe."

Finally, I found Lauren. She hadn't started pulling her hair, but she was close.

"I can't handle this," she whimpered. "Without you or Jared here . . ."

I lowered her onto the stool that should have been Daisy's. "Forget about me, forget about Jared, forget about what's at stake. For the next twenty minutes, all that exists are the people on that stage, and this." I wrapped her fingers around the cold handle of the microphone.

"Me? We both know I can't correct anyone's form."

"Forget about form, Stella will handle that on stage. Your job is to keep everyone safe. If someone's off their X, tell them to scoot over. If someone leaves a dumbbell out, nudge them to put it away."

"Just keep everyone safe?"

"Don't let anyone embarrass themselves."

"I can do that."

"Of course you can. You've got this."

At last, I grabbed my purse, and everyone waved as we hurried out the door. But Marco stopped, the map of Jackson's location open on his phone. He glanced at his watch, his face falling.

"We have a problem. Jackson made it to the Tennessee state line. That's a three-hour drive *each way*. Mia's audition is in four hours. No matter how fast we drive, we can't make it to St. Louis in time."

Once again, the warehouse fell silent. All eyes turned to Mia as her face fell and her shoulders slumped. I pulled her body against mine, trying to hold her together as her breathing grew ragged. How much stress could one girl handle in a day? She'd reached her limit.

Christian stepped away from his pillar again. "What audition is this?"

"Ballroom dance," I said. "She's auditioning to perform at a breast cancer fundraiser in New York. It'll be broadcasted on . . . live TV."

Christian met my eyes, smiling. "What network?"

"ZBC," Mia said, then she peered up at Christian. "Is that you?"

He grinned wider. "I flew out here with the guy running your audition."

"Can you help her?" Stella asked. "Can you change her audition time?"

Christian raised his hands, defensively. "I'll try, but no promises."

We waited in anxious silence as Christian made the call. Mia squeezed my arm so tightly it cut off my circulation. After a hurried explanation, glossing over every detail, he hung up.

"Well?" Mia gasped.

"He moved you to the end of the list, eight o'clock. But if they finish up and you're not there yet, they're not waiting. It's the best I can do."

Mia turned to Marco, bouncing between her feet. "Is it enough time?"

"It'll be close," he said. "But I'll drive fast."

Bailey in the Corner

He pushed the door open again, but Lauren stopped us, her arms loaded with water bottles and powder packets. "He'll be hungry," she said, "and exhausted. Here's Neon Nutrition for food, Blue Juice for hydration, and Green Fizz for right before the show. He'll need all the energy he can get."

"Lauren, thank you." I pulled her into a hug. She stayed stiff like a tree trunk, but at least she didn't push me away.

"You're coming back, right?" she asked. "On Monday, I mean. We need you around here."

I gazed around the room, at all the people, remembering the drama and darkness I'd experienced between these walls. Years of torment from Daisy, of hiding and cowering. But then I found Stella, Lyneeka, and Lauren, and every other employee.

Most of them I hardly knew.

But I wanted to know them better.

"Yeah," I said. "I'll come back, as soon as I take care of my family."

"We'll be in St. Louis at eight," Lyneeka called, "with the dress!"

With one final wave, Mia, Marco, and I sprinted out the door.

Chapter 35

Marco's black car smelled like his tropical cologne. He kept one foot heavy on the gas, and one hand squeezed tightly around mine. Mia's legs bounced rapidly in the back seat, and she chewed the skin around her nails until her fingertips bled. It said a lot about her stress level that she never once asked to turn on the radio.

"He'll be okay," I said, reassuring myself as much as them. Marco had given me his spare sweatshirt, but I still trembled.

At last, we neared Jackson's location and Marco slowed down, pulling off the freeway to a small one-pump gas station surrounded by nothing but gray, leafless trees. It didn't even have an interior for Jackson to warm up in.

But there he was, sitting on a stump, shivering.

Marco screeched to a halt and jumped out of the car. Jackson plowed into him, wrapping his arms around his uncle like they'd been apart for a lifetime.

"I'm so sorry," Jackson cried. "I shouldn't have run off. It was so stupid." Jackson's black jacket was far too thin for him to be outside all night, and his tan skin had paled dangerously white.

"Don't worry," Marco said. "We're just glad you're okay."

"My dad's only an hour away, and he wouldn't come get me. Why doesn't he care about me? Doesn't he love me?"

Bailey in the Corner

Marco held Jackson tighter and rubbed his back. "I don't know, but I love you. No matter what, I'll always come get you."

Jackson cried harder, burying his face in Marco's shoulder. They stood that way for a long time, until Jackson's sobs finally slowed.

"I'm done running after him," Jackson said. "I never want to see him again."

He wiped his face and gave Mia a tentative wave, nervous, like he wasn't sure how much she hated him. But she dashed forward and threw her arms around his neck.

"I'm so sorry about the show," he said. "I know how important it was to you. I screwed up."

"I'm not mad. But don't do anything stupid like this again."

"I promise." Jackson's body relaxed, barely. "But are you sure you don't hate me?"

"You're more important than a performance. But . . ." she scrunched up her face, like she was choosing her next words carefully. "If we hurry, we might still make it."

Jackson glanced at his watch. "Our audition's in half an hour."

"We pushed it back, but only until eight. Your uncle's going to have to break a lot of laws to get us there."

"Sounds good to me."

Jackson gave me an awkward hug, then we climbed back in the car. Marco pressed the pedal to the floor, and we tore back down the freeway. Mia wrapped Jackson in a blanket, then I handed him a Neon Nutrition shake. Half an hour later, the color returned to his face.

"So," he said, when his body finally stopped trembling, "how'd you get our audition time changed?"

Mia launched into a rundown of our crazy day, but when she reached the end, she cocked her head. "Mom, are you really Fearless Felicity?"

Marco also shot me a curious look.

"Maybe," I said, and Mia squealed with laughter.

Jackson's eyes jumped between us. "Who's Fearless Felicity? Sounds like a YouTuber who posts videos doing stupid stuff."

I laughed. "She's something like that."

A few minutes later, Jackson asked if we could turn on the radio.

"What do you want to listen to?" Marco asked.

"How about Pearl Jam?"

Marco immediately vetoed him. "Matchbox 20's better."

"No matter how many times you say that, it will still never be true."

"Agree to disagree," I interrupted. "What are your second choices?"

"*Nirvana,*" they said in unison, and both men laughed. Marco plugged his phone into the stereo and turned on the music, which happened to be one of Mia's favorite songs. Her mouth dropped open, gaping at them both, like she'd never fully grasped their caliber until that moment. When she pressed her hand against her heart, I knew exactly what she meant.

We'd found our people.

Jackson fell asleep barely a minute after we turned on the music. Two hours later, as we entered St. Louis, I gently shook him awake. He rubbed the sleep out of his eyes and blinked rapidly.

"Drink this." I handed him a half-dose of Green Fizz. "Your body could use the caffeine."

Fifteen minutes later, Marco pulled into the theater parking lot. The clock said five minutes after eight.

"Are we too late?" Mia asked.

"I have no idea."

Stella and Lyneeka pulled in only a minute behind us, and they raced over with the costumes. When Lyneeka held up the new dress, Mia and I both gawked. Without the original black bodice, she'd had to use Waterfall material for the entire thing. Mia's costume shimmered like a multicolored rainstorm.

"We improved it a bit," Lyneeka said, and Mia hugged the dress to her chest.

"Do the layers still work the same?" Jackson asked.

Bailey in the Corner

"Exactly the same. Now go change, quick."

The kids grabbed their dance shoes, and all six of us raced into the theater. Marco took the kids to the bathroom while I peeked in through the stage doors. Someone with a clipboard stopped me from entering.

"Are the auditions still going?"

"The final act is on stage now," the burly man said. He looked more like a security guard than stage crew—he even wore black sunglasses indoors—but hallelujah, we weren't too late.

"I have Amelia Dupree and Jackson Davis with me. They're here to do a ballroom routine."

The man glanced at his clipboard again. "Oh yeah, the kids that were running late, right?"

"They're getting dressed in the bathroom."

"Bring them here as soon as they're ready. Guests can watch from the waiting room down that hall."

Two minutes later, the kids arrived, fully dressed in everything but their shoes.

"Did we make it?" Mia asked.

"You're up next," the security guard said.

She paled, making Jackson laugh. "Don't worry," he said, "I won't let you screw up."

They raced to put their shoes on, tossing the shoe brush frantically back and forth.

"We really need to get them another one," Marco said, but Jackson scowled at his uncle.

"What are you talking about? This one's perfect."

With only two minutes to go, they ran through the most complicated sequences in their routine. With thirty seconds left, Mia pulled me into a hug.

"No matter what happens," I whispered, "I'm so proud of you."

"I love you, Mom."

They scooted behind the security guard and through the door to the stage, while we found the waiting area. It was small, the size of Lauren's conference room, with a crate of room-temperature water bottles and a dozen chairs splayed randomly around the floor. The air smelled stuffy and hot, and a few other families stared lazily at their phones or watched the tiny television with a pixelated view of the stage. The four of us weaved through the chairs to get a closer look, but I could barely make out Mia and Jackson when they arrived on the stage.

"This is stupid," Lyneeka groaned. "We can't see them."

Even when I squinted my eyes, they looked like barely more than blurry stick figures. I sank into the closest chair, hard and metal, with a sticky spot on the edge where someone must have spilled food. But I kept my eyes glued to the TV. How would I know if they fumbled their steps?

"You know what?" Marco said, pulling me right back up. "Screw this. We're watching the real thing."

"How? We can't get past that security guard."

Marco didn't answer, just strolled out of the room with us at his heels. It only took him a minute to find the door labeled stairs. It was locked, of course, but Marco unscrewed his cane and dug through an assortment of pins. He picked the lock in under twenty seconds and it opened with a click.

"Where'd you learn to do that?" I whispered.

"High school. One of my many efforts to annoy my dad."

We sprinted up the stairs, then crept through a thick red curtain onto the mezzanine level of the theater. Marco led us to the front row of the balcony, then pulled me into the purple velvet chair beside his, with Stella on my other side, and Lyneeka puffing after her. Mia and Jackson were on stage, talking to the judges, but we couldn't make out their words.

"How was MaxFit99?" I whispered to Stella.

"I was so nervous," she squeaked.

"She was perfect," Lyneeka said. "Christian and Lauren signed the contract right there."

Bailey in the Corner

I cheered as silently as I could, hugging Stella from the side. "I knew you could do it." Then the kids' music began.

Mia danced her heart out.

With every Cha-Cha step, she stayed focused, determined, energetic. She hit every arm line, and Jackson perfectly supported every lift. When the music shifted to Samba, the drumbeat vibrated up through our chairs, echoing through the enormous speakers. Jackson unsnapped the bodice of her dress, and the judges gasped as it tumbled into a ruffly skirt around her knees.

But Marco was frowning. "Samba is Jackson's worst dance," he whispered. "He needed another day to practice."

Stella pulled a box of Hot Tamales from her purse and passed it silently down the line. All four of us shoved a handful into our mouths. It helped with the stress.

But we shouldn't have worried. Jackson threw himself into the routine. His hips moved in a perfect double-figure-eight, and his arms pumped in unison with Mia's. When it came time for the Samba rolls, they spun across the stage like a top. One of the judges whistled.

Then the music paused, and Jackson ripped her ruffly skirt off completely, leaving nothing but a long, flowing skirt that draped behind Mia like a waterfall. He pulled her close against his body and the Rhumba began, their movements flowing in and out like the ebb and flow of the tide. Never once did they break eye contact, and the judges ate it up.

Marco and I exchanged a look.

"They're just dancing," I whispered, "right?"

"Of course."

But I remembered when we danced this exact same routine for our own crowd of people. "Maybe next time you choreograph them a dance . . ."

"Less intimate. Got it."

Jackson lowered Mia into the routine's final dip, then he flung her to the side and she spun into four, five, six rapid turns. As soon as she stopped, they bent over into unison bows. As promised, Jackson hadn't let Mia screw up. And as expected, she'd performed beautifully.

All six judges rose to their feet, their applause reverberating through the large auditorium. We clapped too. In fact, we didn't pretend to be quiet—we jumped and screamed until the kids laughed and waved. When they finally left the stage, we hurried out of the balcony to meet them. But as Lyneeka and Stella raced down the stairs, Marco pulled me to a stop, leading me behind the red curtain where no one could see us.

"Thank you," he whispered.

My heart lurched. Every barrier keeping us apart had crumbled, but the question still lingered in his eyes.

"For what?"

"For helping me connect with Jackson. And for sacrificing your job to drive across the state. Without you . . ." He exhaled slowly, his cinnamon breath breezing against my cheeks. "I couldn't have done it."

"Don't worry," I gave him my most mischievous grin, "I couldn't let you disappear when you still owe me a debt."

He raised an eyebrow. "I do?"

I lifted one arm to study the date on my pink watch. "You were supposed to take me out forty-eight hours ago. You owe me a date."

Marco's face split into such a grin that my heart stopped. Then he took my cheeks in his hands and pressed his lips against mine. I wrapped my arms around his neck as he sighed, our bodies melting together.

"You owe me dinner tomorrow night too," I whispered against his lips.

"For what?"

"Not showing up last night. And dinner on Sunday, to pay me back for all those supplements Jackson drank."

His chest shook against mine as he laughed. "The ones you get for free?"

"Yup."

"Anything else?"

Bailey in the Corner

"You owe me dozens of dinners." My voice came out breathless. "More than I can count. I'll come up with reasons later."

"How long will it take to pay you back?"

"Months. Years, even."

"Then it sounds like . . ." He brushed his lips against mine. "I'll be sticking around . . ." He kissed me again. "For a long, long time."

Epilogue

Three Months Later

Lauren Cross raced between the cubicles of JD Fitness, searching frantically for Bailey with an unsigned contract in her hand.

If she left already, I'll kill her.

Panic bubbled inside until her lungs wanted to explode, so she grabbed a handful of her hair and pulled hard, grinding her teeth. A few strands came out in her fingers, and Lauren shrieked. At this rate, she'd be bald by the time she turned forty. But it did take the edge off her anxiety.

She checked Bailey's office first, then the fabrication room and the cafeteria. She wasn't in the gym, either, where a dozen employees were lifting weights and the air stank of sweaty bodies and rubber dumbbells. Why was everyone so obsessed with fitness around here?

With growing panic, she checked the mailroom as a last resort. But only Daisy was in there, dutifully cutting open envelopes and scanning them into the system. She didn't say anything as Lauren charged in, but that wasn't a surprise—Daisy rarely said anything to anyone anymore, not since they'd stuck her with Stella's old job. No one could figure out why she hadn't quit.

Frustrated, Lauren trudged to the conference room for an executive meeting with the contract still unsigned. Four people sat around the table,

Bailey in the Corner

including Jared, Stella, and Lyneeka. Five neat stacks of papers were at its center, along with a bottle of champagne and five fluted glasses.

Bailey was already seated.

"Have you been in here the whole time?"

"What whole time?" Bailey asked. "And can we hurry? My plane leaves soon."

Lauren shook her head to clear it—she'd give anything for even a fraction of Bailey's endlessly calm demeanor—and started the meeting.

"We're here to officially restructure the organization of JD Fitness," Lauren said. "As you all know, I'm stepping down as President and Jared is stepping down as CEO. Both of those titles will be officially passed to our new leader, Bailey Dupree."

Everyone applauded as Lauren slid the first contract to Bailey and handed her a pen. With a rustle of paper, Bailey signed each page on the lines marked with yellow tabs, then passed the contract back.

"Thanks," Lauren said, breathing easier. "You're saving us all."

"Amen," Lyneeka muttered, and Stella raised her water bottle.

"Next, Jared is becoming the face of the company full-time as our Chief Fitness Officer." She slid him a contract, doing everything in her power to avoid his eyes. Or his face. Or the muscles showing through his tight-fitting shirt. Had they grown even bigger since Bailey started doing his office work? She closed her eyes altogether. If she couldn't see him, she could pretend she didn't still love him, right? "He'll film regular fitness programs, pre-recorded—not live-streamed—for both our YouTube channel and ZBC television. We're also working on deals with Netflix and Apple TV. By stepping down as CEO, he can focus on fitness while Bailey handles the logistics."

When Lauren opened her eyes, she zeroed in on Bailey, who hopefully heard the gratitude in her words. Bailey nodded.

"Next up is Stella." Lauren squared her shoulders and sat taller. This part was easier. Stella sat on the opposite side of the table as Jared, which meant she could look at her without even seeing him out of the corner of her eye. "Your new employment contract gives you the green light to develop your own exercise program as JD Fitness's new official trainer. This puts you, along with Jared, as one of the public faces of the company. Congratulations."

Stella's face flushed red. Ridiculously red, like the awkward house Lauren grew up in, in the most run-down corner of Burien, Washington.

"It also takes you officially out of the mailroom and makes you our in-house fitness expert. When you're not working on your own show, you'll work with Jared as he develops his. But more importantly, you'll work with his casts to ensure they're lifting safely."

As Stella signed her contract, Lauren turned to Lyneeka. "You're next. As the resident 'mom' of the office, you are now our desperately-needed head of HR."

"Thank goodness," Stella mumbled, shooting a scowl at Jared.

Lauren pressed on, grateful to hand this job over to the most intimidating person in the building. "You'll be pulling double-duty until we find someone to replace you in fabrication, but that shouldn't take long. Thanks for taking this off my plate."

Lyneeka's new braids hung over her broad shoulder as she leaned onto the table to sign her contract.

Only two stacks of paper remained.

"Next is me," she said, pulling one in front of her. "I'm finally stepping down to do what I set out to do all those years ago."

Lauren's hands shook as she held the contract between her fingers, savoring the job that seemed too good to be true. Marketing. Promoting. Jared's agent—and nothing else. Bailey nudged her encouragingly, and it finally felt real.

"This contract officially terminates my employment with JD Fitness, so Jared can hire me as a PR Contractor. I'll become the independent agent for Jared, Stella and any other on-staff trainers we hire. I already have conventions and tours and new TV deals in the works for you guys, so you'd better get busy putting together new programs."

Bailey in the Corner

Everyone cheered as Lauren signed her name, ending her old life and stepping into a new one. Bailey popped open the champagne, the bubbly smell filling the air. She handed Lauren the first glass, then poured the rest. Lyneeka gave a toast and they all clinked them together.

"What's that?" Bailey asked, pointing to the final contract, the one Lauren had run through the office with. It remained, alone, in the center of the table. But before Lauren had a chance to explain, Marco stuck his head through the door.

"Hey, everyone."

"Come have some champagne!" Stella called.

His eyes found Bailey and stayed there, leaving Lauren with a trickle of envy. She couldn't help glancing at Jared. She'd thought she was over him—her rational brain knew he was nothing but trouble. But that hole remained, growing wider every time she looked at him. Hopefully this new job would help fill that emptiness.

But she still wished Jared would gaze at her the way Marco gazed at Bailey.

"Thanks, Stella," Marco said, "But I've gotta go. Bailey, you ready? We can't miss our flight—the kids are anxious to do some New York sightseeing before their performance."

Bailey grinned at him, then turned back to Lauren. "Was there anything else?"

"Yes . . ." Lauren slid the final contract across the table. "This one's for you."

Bailey's eyes scanned the paper, her mouth moving as she silently read the words. "An agent contract? For you to represent me?"

"I want to represent Fearless Felicity. My phone never stops ringing with people wanting to hire you. You could pick and choose jobs, only taking the ones that fit your life. And I'd manage it all."

Bailey angled her head toward Marco, then back at Lauren. They'd all danced around this idea for months, but Bailey had always wavered, never making a real commitment. She worried it would encroach too much on Mia's life.

"I don't know," Bailey said. "Will Mia hate it if my life gets busier?"

"Of course not, Mom!" Mia's voice rang in from the hall. "Just sign the contract and let's go. New York City is calling our names!"

Lauren chewed feverishly on the back of her pen. So much of their future depended on Bailey signing that document. Bailey stood, eyes lingering on the contract, and swung her purse over her shoulder. Then she leaned over . . .

And signed her name.

Lauren could have done a backflip right there. But instead, she waved goodbye as Bailey dashed away with her family.

Then she started counting the days until Bailey returned.

Lauren couldn't wait to begin.

The End

Acknowledgements

An essential part of my book-writing process is my soundtrack! When I begin a new manuscript, I search out an album that fits the mood of my story, then it's all I listen to until I've finished the whole book. I wrote this particular story when nobody was talking about Bruno, which meant I listened to the Encanto soundtrack non-stop. I'd like to give an enormous shout out to Lin-Manuel Miranda. Your lyrics are brilliant and inspiring. Thank you for sharing your craft with the world—but mostly with me!

That being said, it takes a giant village to create a book, and I'm so grateful to every person who took the time to contribute to this one.

First and foremost, I owe everything to my family. Jake, my entrepreneur husband, you get as excited about my book business as I do. I can't tell you what that means to me! I'm so glad to walk through this crazy life by your side. And my kids, Abby, Gabe, Izzy, Griffin, Scarlett, and Gage, you guys rarely complain when I disappear for a few months to write new books. You're my inspiration. My books are my gift to you. I love you!

To my Mom, I couldn't do this without you. You're both my first reader and my last, and you've seen every draft of this book, yet you still believe in me! I can't tell you how grateful I am. To my Dad, I hope you know that I write books to impress you. Your opinion means everything. I love you! And thank you to my mother-in-law Sally, who has always encouraged me and loved my books. I'm so glad we're family.

To my Monday Night Writing Group: writing friends make the best friends. If we didn't get together every single week, I don't know how I'd stay motivated. Breanna Trost, Brenda Lower, Bruce Jacobs, Jayden Meyer, Kate Anderson, Katrina McPheters, KayLynn Flanders, Kelly Wilson, Michelle Henrie, and every other person who has ever joined us for a writing session, you guys are my heroes. Thanks for diving into my story and making it better!

My Third Thursday Writing Group: never in a million years could I dream up better cheerleaders. Every time imposter syndrome knocks me down, you guys pick me back up. Alli, you're my lifeline. I couldn't survive this industry without you! Bonnie Pierson, Heidi Boyd, Kayla Tillotson, Kelsey Larson, Marci Richards, Natalie Kraus, Sally O'Keef, and Tarry Perry, I love every one of you. You inspire me every day!

Melinda Fredrickson and Marlene Willis, you deserve an enormous thank you. You were my very first writing group, and you've stayed with me all these years! It wouldn't be the same without you.

Dustin Hansen. How can I possibly give you enough thanks? First, you provided my beautiful cover art. I drew a ridiculous sketch, and you turned it into something perfect! But even more importantly, you've talked me off the ledge every time I've second-guessed myself. That means everything to me. You're an essential part of my team and I'm so glad we're in this together!

Thank you to my wonderful editor, Andrea Robinson. You seriously went above and beyond. I'm so glad I found you!

Thank you Sally O'Keef, for being an amazing proofreader. You caught so many things I never would have.

And most importantly, thank you to my Heavenly Father. Without you, I'm nothing.

About the Author

Lindsay Hiller grew up near Seattle, Washington, and still believes it's the most beautiful place on earth. She met her husband Jake while living an adventurous year in New York City, and they eventually settled down near Salt Lake City, Utah. After studying child development at the University of Utah, they had six delightful kiddos. When she isn't writing, Lindsay loves Disneyland, watching movies, and going on long drives in her husband's fun cars. She loves chatting with fans so please reach out to her via social media!

Made in the USA
Middletown, DE
08 November 2023

42062759R00179